Also

Fourteen Days Later

The Fashion Police

Be Careful What You Wish For

About the author

Sibel Hodge has dual British/Turkish Cypriot nationality and divides her time between Hertfordshire and North Cyprus. Her first romantic-comedy novel, *Fourteen Days Later*, was shortlisted for the Harry Bowling Prize 2008 and received a Highly Commended by the Yeovil Literary Prize 2009. *My Perfect Wedding* is the sequel to *Fourteen Days Later*.

Her second novel, *The Fashion Police*, was a runner up in the Chapter One Promotions Novel Competition 2010. It is a hilarious comedy-mystery novel, the first in the series featuring feisty, larger-than-life, Amber Fox. *Be Careful What You Wish For* is the second Amber Fox Murder Mystery.

For more information, please visit www.sibelhodge.com

My Perfect Wedding
Sibel Hodge
Third Edition

Copyright © Sibel Hodge 2011

The moral right of the author has been asserted.

Praise for *My Perfect Wedding*

"I loved this book. It is funny, witty and intriguing. If you are a fan of Sophie Kinsella I am positive you will love My Perfect Wedding by Hodge" - Geeky Girl Books

"I uploaded this book on my Kindle this morning and was so engrossed, I let everything go for the day. A must read, you will enjoy" - I'm just Sayin...Book reviews by KK

"In this laugh-out loud, real to the bone, commentary on what being married is like, I felt like I got to the know the two main characters very well and learn a thing or two about relationships. I recommend this to anyone!" - Hot Gossip Hot Reviews

"My Perfect Wedding was entertaining and funny. The dialogue is sharp and witty, which had me laughing out loud at times. If you enjoy chick lit, this book is for you." - Inky Impressions

My Perfect Wedding

Sibel Hodge

"Love one another and you will be happy. It's as simple

and as difficult as that"

MICHAEL LEUNIG

Chapter 1

The customs officer flipped open Kalem's passport and scrutinized the photo.

I tapped my foot. *Come on, come on, don't you know we've got a wedding to get to? My perfect wedding, nonetheless.* And on top of that, the duty-free shops were seriously calling my name. We'd already been shuffling along in the security queue for forty-five minutes like a couple of tortoises, and I could almost smell the teasing waft of bargain perfumes, designer lipsticks that stay on for three days, and bumper packs of chocolate sending out silent *buy me* signals in the shopping area beyond.

Luckily, we'd got to the Airport in plenty of time. Kalem wanted to check in early to try and get a seat with extra legroom. Not that it bothered me, really. At five foot nothing, I never had a problem with being crammed in like a stuffed sausage, but Kalem's legs were long and toned and...well, pretty damn sexy.

Kalem ran a hand through his cropped dark hair and nodded towards the passport. 'I probably had more hair then,' he said to the customs officer.

I giggled, remembering the frizzy out-of-control footballer's perm he'd had when the photo was taken, which resembled my unruly curls on a good hair day.

'I *don't* think so,' the customs officer muttered, narrowing his eyes at Kalem.

I stepped out from behind Kalem and leaned on the counter. A wave of loud tutting broke out from the queue behind me.

'It's a serious offence to tamper with a passport, sir,' the customs officer said in a deadly tone, glaring at Kalem.

'Pardon?' Kalem's eyes widened with surprise. 'I can assure you that my passport hasn't been out of my sight. And it definitely hasn't been tampered with. If you'll just let me show you –' Kalem reached out his hand.

The customs officer shot his hand in the air, passport held up high, so Kalem couldn't get anywhere near it.

'Sorry...' my eyes shot to his name badge, 'Officer Head.

1

What seems to be the problem?' I asked, thinking he was obviously some sort of jobsworth with nothing better to do than annoy innocent travellers.

Officer Head tried the same suspicious glare on me and shot his other hand up for silence. Then he picked up a phone on the counter and whispered something into it. I heard the words 'possible' and 'terrorist' but the rest of it was inaudible.

I gulped. What was going on? This was ridiculous.

'Right. You two will have to come with me.' Officer Head climbed out from behind the passport control booth and marched off along the airport floor.

Another loud tutting session erupted from the group of people behind us.

I glanced at Kalem with a questioning look. 'What's happening?'

He shrugged. 'I don't know. It's probably just some kind of simple misunderstanding. The quicker we get this over with, the quicker we can get on with our pre-honeymoon.' He lowered his voice to a whisper. 'And don't say anything.'

'What do you mean, don't say anything? If he asks me a question, I'll have to say something, won't I?'

'You know what I mean – don't say anything ridiculous.'

Me? Ridiculous? As if.

We fell into step behind the crazy customs guy. '*I* know.' I smirked at Kalem. 'This is the surprise you said you'd organized, isn't it? I bet we're really going to be escorted to a VIP lounge, where we can drink champagne and eat those little canapé things. Ooh, great. I love those. I wonder if they've got those little smoked salmon rolls with the cream cheese fillings. Yum.'

'This isn't the surprise.' Kalem's forehead scrunched up into frown lines.

'Oh, yeah, good one. I bet you're just saying that so I'll be even more surprised when we get there.' I paused. 'Well done. Good surprise.' I giggled. Wow, this was going to be such a great start to our brand new, exciting life together.

'It's *not,*' he hissed at me.

My jaw dropped open. 'What do you mean, it's not? What is it then?' A sudden blanket of fear swept over me.

Kalem was saved from answering as we reached a door

marked *Customs – Private.*

Officer Head punched in a security code on the keypad lock and led us into a massive rectangular interrogation room with a desk at the far end, separated by two chairs on one side and two on the other. The desk seemed miles away from the entrance, like I'd suddenly been transported into a freaky Alice in Wonderland world, where everything was out of proportion. I felt like Kalem and I had turned into tiny little munchkin-type people, but everyone and everything else was ginormous.

'Sit,' Officer Head barked so loud that my ear almost imploded.

We dropped down onto the hard plastic chairs. This was not good. Not good at all.

'Another officer will be joining us shortly,' Officer Head began, 'but until then, I'm going to ask you some questions.' He opened Kalem's passport again. 'Right. Let's start with you.' He looked at Kalem. 'What is your name?'

I gazed at Officer Head, who actually looked like Mr. Potato Head – only his nose was a little less red – and panicked. My brain flickered away like a dodgy light bulb. There had to be some completely rational and normal explanation for this mix-up. I mean, yes, normal and rational weren't words that I could usually associate with my life. I would probably describe myself more as accidentally challenged. But still, this was just a simple mix-up, surely.

'Kalem Mustafa,' Kalem replied.

'Ha-ha.' I let out a nervous laugh.

Officer Head gave me a narrow-eyed stare, then turned back to Kalem. 'Is that your real name?'

'Er...excuse me. Is that a trick question? It's obvious what his name is. It's in his passport,' I said, not wanting to state the obvious, but someone had to do it.

Oh, I get it now. It must be a dream. Yes, that was it. Recently, I'd been having a few of those pre-wedding jittery dreams – well, more like nightmares, actually – where I turned up at the venue in front of all our guests, and my wedding dress had suddenly turned see-through. And, even worse, I'd somehow decided to have my bikini area waxed into the shape of a dartboard, complete with bullseye. This was just one of those nightmares, that was all.

I leaped off the chair. 'Come on Kalem, let's go.'

'You can't go until I say you can go,' Officer Head insisted.

'I can do whatever I want. It's *my* dream,' I said to him with a haughty gleam in my eye.

'SIT DOWN,' he shouted back at me.

I heard a loud ringing in my ear. Surely you didn't hear ear-ringing in a dream? I pinched myself. Ow! Shit. I was still awake. I slumped back in the chair. Uh-oh. This was for real.

The door swung open and another customs official with a toilet brush crew cut walked in.

'Richard,' the second officer acknowledged his colleague with a tilt of his head and then turned to us. 'I'm officer Goodbody.' He sat down, and I heard a noise like a whoopee cushion exploding. I couldn't tell if it was him or the chair, though.

'Let's start again, shall we?' Officer Head leaned forward. 'Is that your real name?'

Kalem swallowed. 'Of course it's my real name.'

I looked between the customs men with suspicion. Richard Head? Was this for real? The light bulb was back on full power now. 'Ha! I know what's going on.'

They both raised an intrigued eyebrow and waited for me to enlighten them.

'No one could be called Dick Head and Officer Goodbody. It sounds like something out of a bad Seventies porn movie. This is one of those TV shows, isn't it?' My eyes darted around the room like a maniac, looking for any signs of hidden cameras and cabling. 'It's like Candid Camera, or You've Been Punk'd, or something. Or...I know.' I squinted at them. 'Are you Ant and Dec in disguise? Are we going to be on their Saturday Night Takeaway show where they're always playing practical jokes on people?' I leaped up and leaned over the desk, so I was inches away from their faces, examining them for signs of false noses and excessive, disguising make-up.

Kalem shot me a horrified look.

'Give me your passport.' Goodbody ignored my outburst and held his hand out to me.

OK then, maybe not.

I reached into my bag and handed it to him.

'Now, where were we?' Dick Head shuffled in his chair. 'Ah, yes. Kalem Mustafa. I will ask you again. Is that your real

4

name?' He glowered at Kalem.

'Yes.' Kalem shot me a silencing side glance.

'And what's your name, hmm?' Goodbody asked me.

'You know what my name is; it's on my p–'

Kalem stared at me, jerking his head towards Dick Head and Goodbody, silently willing me to just answer their questions.

I sighed. 'Helen Mustafa.'

'Ah ha!' Goodbody waved my passport around. 'It says Helen Grey here. Is this a fake passport?'

'No! Sorry, I meant to say that my name's *going* to be Helen Mustafa in six days time. We're getting married. At the moment, I'm Helen Grey. You know how it is when a girl's getting married: she gets a bit over-excited and starts signing her new married name for months in advance and repeating "Mrs. Mustafa" over and over again.' I could tell by the look on his face that he didn't have a clue what I was on about. 'In fact...' I glanced at my watch. 'We're supposed to be catching our plane in about forty-five minutes. We're *supposed* to be having a few days of relaxing pre-wedding sand, sea and s... '

'Sharap,' Kalem interjected.

'Did you just tell me to shut up?' Dick Head frowned at Kalem.

'No, he said sharap. It's Turkish for wine,' I informed him. Since I'd found out that Kalem and I were going to be moving to North Cyprus, I'd desperately been trying to learn some Turkish words. So far, I'd mastered the important things like: "More wine please" and "Where are the toilets?" I could also say: "cat", "thanks", "very much", "I'm full", "cucumber", "large", and "melon". It wasn't a lot, I know, but it could make for an interesting sentence.

'Why have you got a single plane ticket? Why aren't you returning to the UK?' Dick Head peered at us as if this were highly suspicious.

'We're moving abroad. We're going to live the dream.' I gave him a wistful smile as I thought about how perfect our new life was going to be.

'What dream?' Goodybody said.

'You know, we're escaping the dreary British weather and the rat race to experience life in the sunny and relaxing Mediterranean.' Daydreams rapidly filled my head: walking hand in hand with Kalem on a sandy beach after a leisurely swim in the warm sea; sitting on our orange blossom scented, sun-baked villa terrace with a chilled glass of rosé as we watched the blazing sun set over the sea; sipping tiny cups of strong coffee in a chic waterfront café; eating succulent, freshly caught sea bass or juicy king prawns, cooked to perfection on a barbeque.

'Your name sounds like a Muslim name. Are you a Muslim?' Officer Head's voice broke into my daydreams, sending me spiralling back to the reality of being stuck in a tiny, lifeless room with overpowering lights and a sweaty, stale smell. 'Well?' He peered at Kalem, waiting for his answer.

Kalem folded his arms casually across his chest. 'Not really.'

'Hmm. Not really. That's a strange answer. What does "not really" mean?'

'Well, my parents are Turkish Cypriot. The religion of Turkish Cypriots is Muslim, but we don't exactly practice it or anything. Most Turkish Cypriots are relaxed in their religious practices and very tolerant of other people's religions.' Kalem shrugged.

I jigged my leg up and down. We were going to miss our flight. My wonderful pre-honeymoon would be ruined.

'Is that what *they* told you to say?' Goodbody leaned in closer, resting his elbows on the desk.

'Who?' Kalem asked.

'Are you a member of Al-Qaeda?' Officer Head looked deadly serious. 'We have to be extremely vigilant these days, you know.'

'*What?*' Kalem blustered. 'Of course not!'

'Where are you travelling to?' Goodbody wanted to know.

'North Cyprus,' I said, jigging harder. 'We'll miss our flight if you keep us here any longer. What's going on?' I whined, feeling my heart bouncing around in my chest. I was going to have a panic attack in a minute. Maybe if I fainted, they would let us go. I slouched down further in my chair, so I wouldn't have as far to fall if I hit the ground.

'Are you a suicide bomber?' Dick Head growled at Kalem.

'He's a teacher!' I cried.

'And who do you teach? Terrorist cells?' Dick Head beamed with excitement at Officer Goodbody. 'I think we've got one of the Al-Qaeda's main men here.'

6

Kalem shook his head in amazement. 'I teach woodcarving and sculpture!'

'Is that a code name of some sort?' Goodbody asked Dick Head. 'I seem to recall one of the Bin Laden breakaway groups had a code name like that. What was it now?' He scratched his toilet brush head, deep in concentration. 'Ah yes! The Splinter Group.'

'I haven't heard of that one before.' Dick Head frowned. 'But it's possible. Woodcarving... splinter...yes, it sounds possible to me.'

'Why are we here?' I furrowed my brow and gazed at both of them, interrupting what seemed like the most surreal conversation I'd ever heard in my life.

Dick Head ignored my question and stood up. 'Hand over your bags, please. I want to take a look inside.'

I gave him mine. Kalem lifted his rucksack and put it on the table in front of us.

Goodbody rummaged around in my bag with interest and then pulled out my camera. 'Why do you need such a big camera? Are you going to be taking surveillance photos?'

'I'm a photographer,' I said.

'Hmm. A likely story.' Goodbody's eyebrow shot up.

Dick Head started on Kalem's rucksack, pulling out a book, a couple of apples, and a tub of edible chocolate body paint. He held up the body paint to Kalem. 'What's this?' He unscrewed the lid and glared at it as if it were packed full of Semtex.

Kalem shrugged. 'Well, it *is* going to be our pre-honeymoon.'

I felt my insides turn to goo. He still had that effect on me. *Oh, yes, bring on the chocolate body paint!*

'Was *that* the surprise you were talking about?' I said to Kalem, turning my head away from the customs men who were busy scouring our bags for hidden compartments.

Satisfied there was no Semtex, suspicious looking shoes, or packets of nails in our hand luggage, they returned their attention to us.

'We're going to miss our flight.' I looked at my watch again, desperately hoping they'd hurry up.

'Why has your passport been tampered with?' Dick Head asked Kalem again.

'It hasn't,' Kalem insisted.

'Well what do you call *that* then?' Dick Head turned the passport around to face Kalem.

I gulped and my brain did a silent mental shriek. 'Oops,' I squeaked, suddenly feeling nauseous.

Kalem stared at the photo section on his passport. The picture of a footballer-permed Kalem had been replaced with a picture of an old, fat, bald man with huge black square glasses.

'I think I'm going to pass out,' I muttered. If I caused a distraction, maybe we could just make a run for it.

'What's *that?*' Kalem gasped, turning his head slowly to me with dread.

Dick Head and Goodbody gave me an icy glare.

'Ah,' I croaked. It was all my fault. How was I going to explain this one?

'Well?' they said in unison.

'Erm...well...what happened was...Kalem is always playing practical jokes on me,' I paused, thinking how this was going to sound. 'Anyway, about four months ago I bought this hair dye...'

Goodbody snorted.

'What does hair dye have to do with this?' Dick Head growled.

'It's very relevant, actually,' I started again, running a shaky hand through my hair. 'So, I bought this hair dye, and when I got it home, I realized I didn't like the colour.' My eyes darted to Kalem, who gawped at me. 'A few days later, I took it back to the shop and asked the woman at the counter if I could return it. But when she took the box back off me, she stared at it for a while with a puzzled look and then turned it around to show me.'

Dick Head and Goodbody had deadly straight faces.

'Do go on. This is thoroughly enlightening,' Goodbody said in a voice that clearly meant it wasn't at all.

'Well, that was when I noticed that someone had drawn a moustache and beard on the picture of the woman on the front of the box.' I narrowed my eyes at Kalem, who chuckled under his breath, remembering.

'Anyway, I was really embarrassed and had to pretend that it must have been like that in the shop when I'd bought it.'

'Is there a point to this?' Goodbody asked, glancing at his watch.

8

'I wanted to get Kalem back, and I knew he was going to the building society a few days later to get some money out, and he needed to take some ID. He can never find his driving licence, so he always takes his passport,' I paused. 'Because I'm a photographer, obviously I've got loads of old photos lying around, so I thought it would be really funny to pay him back for all the practical jokes he plays on me. I found this photo, cut it out, then stuck it over his passport photo with removable adhesive and put it back in the drawer. Then, of course, I forgot all about it.' I tried to swallow, but my throat felt like I'd swallowed a Brillo Pad. 'Until now.' I tucked my hair behind my ears with shaky hands.

Kalem coughed. 'Actually, I managed to find my driving licence and took that to the building society instead.'

I cast him a sheepish look. 'Yes, I realize that now.'

'You see! This is all perfectly innocent,' Kalem said to Dick Head and Goodbody. 'Can we go now?'

'Not yet. Are you a Muslim too?' Goodbody asked me.

'No, I'm not a Muslim,' I said.

A confused glance passed between Dick Head and Goodbody. 'Well you certainly look like one. Can you please explain why you're wearing a burka if you're not Muslim,' Goodbody asked me.

I glanced down at the floor length, head-to-toe black burka that I'd almost forgotten I was wearing. Even if the rest of the stuff sounded slightly odd, there was at least a perfectly reasonable explanation for this.

'Well, there's an ancient tradition with Turkish Cypriot families. When a new bride-to-be arrives in North Cyprus to get married, it's good luck for her to be wearing a burka, isn't it?' I glanced at Kalem, willing him to explain this peculiar custom further. Instead, he kind of gave me a small shake of his head, and his jaw dropped.

Oh, God. I recognized that look. There was no such custom. This was another one of his wind-Helen-up practical jokes. If they could've seen my face, which of course they couldn't because I only had a two inch rectangular slit for my eyes, they would've seen it completely drain of colour. Luckily, they accepted this explanation, and neither of the customs officers seemed to notice that my eyelids had just pinged open in surprise or that Kalem's face had turned a scorching-hot shade of pink.

Dick Head picked at the adhesive on Kalem's passport photo and pulled it off, examining the official picture of Kalem underneath. 'What do you think?' He handed the passport to Goodbody.

'Mmm.' Goodbody scrutinized it. 'It looks legitimate.' He sounded disappointed.

'That's a shame,' Dick Head huffed and turned to Officer Goodbody, frowning. 'Seems like we'll miss out on our CAT bonus.'

'What's that?' Kalem asked.

'Catch-a-terrorist bonus,' Dick Head grumbled at us. It was clear from the look on his face that he'd already worked out what he was going to spend it on.

'Can we go now?' I pleaded.

'OK,' Goodbody said with much reluctance. 'But don't let this happen again.'

'Thanks, Dick.' I yanked Kalem's arm and hurried him away to catch our plane before they changed their minds.

We arrived at the gate with minutes to spare, just as a rather harassed looking baggage handler was about to search for our luggage to offload.

OK, maybe this wasn't exactly the kind of start to our perfect life together that I had in mind, and one day I was actually going to laugh about this, but I couldn't allow myself to relax until we were sitting in our allocated seats and the plane was taxiing down the runway. We were on our way to an exciting destination, full of possibilities. Living a life abroad that most people just dreamed about but never got to experience. An amazing adventure that nothing was going to spoil.

Nothing will spoil my wedding. Nothing will spoil my wedding. Nothing will spoil my wedding.

Or so I thought.

Chapter 2

'Look on the bright side.' I smiled at Kalem as we boarded the packed plane and pulled out my boarding pass.

'And what's that? We've just saved hundreds of pounds by not missing our flight?'

'You started it all,' I said.

'I hardly think that defacing a box of hair dye is on a par with defacing a passport.'

'Actually, I was going to say, at least we managed to get the seats with the extra legroom.' My eyes darted between the seat number on my boarding pass and the corresponding seat row, realizing that an elderly couple were sitting in our seats.

The couple stared at me in my burka and melted back into the leather upholstery.

'Suicide bomber,' the elderly man whispered to his blue-rinsed wife, grabbing her arm in a death-grip.

I seriously hoped she didn't have osteoporosis. He'd pull it off at this rate.

'It's OK, madam. These passengers have been through the same security checks as everyone else. There's absolutely nothing to worry about,' the air stewardess whispered to the couple

Bloody cheek! Thinking that I'm a suicide bomber, just because I'm wearing a burka! And anyway, I didn't think it was politically correct to refer to them as suicide bombers these days. I thought the new terminology was Death Enforcement Technician.

The elderly woman made a sign of the cross.

The stewardess turned to us. 'I'm afraid we've had a little medical emergency. As you were late boarding, we've had to move some passengers into your seats at the front.' She leaned in closer. 'Nearer to the toilets,' she whispered.

'There goes the extra leg room,' Kalem whispered in my ear.

'Follow me. There are a couple of seats in the middle.' She shot off down the aisle as the engines roared to life.

We ignored the suspicious looks from the fellow passengers as we got settled in our seats. I could've sworn I heard a little boy

11

in the seat behind me ask his parents why I was dressed as a letter box.

Kalem reached for my hand, gazed into my eyes, and smiled. 'OK, we're finally onboard.' He let out a sigh of relief. 'We can relax now.'

My heart did a loop-the-loop as I reached over and tried to kiss him, then realized that was probably one of the many things you couldn't actually do wearing a burka.

'You can take the burka off now if you want.'

I gave him a playful punch on the arm. 'I can't. I haven't got anything on underneath it.'

He gave me a seductive grin. 'What, nothing?'

'It is actually a bit hot under here.' I wafted the material around. 'I can't believe I fell for it. Why didn't Ayshe or your parents tell me it was a joke that brides-to-be have to wear burkas when they arrive in North Cyprus?'

'They thought I'd tell you at the last minute that it wasn't for real.' The grin got wider.

'Anyway, you really did start all this. You've been playing practical jokes on me since I was a kid. You deserve some payback.'

'Well, I've known you were the girl for me since I was about four years old. I had to get you to notice me in that way somehow. And just think of all the fun we have! Wouldn't life be boring if we didn't have a laugh together?'

'I am *so* going to get you back for this!' I chuckled.

'Well, it looks like the practical jokes paid off in the end. I've finally got you now.' He squeezed my hand. 'So I don't want anything to get in the way of the wedding.' He slid an arm around my shoulder and the momentum of the plane taking off pushed me towards him.

Ouch! The arm of the seat between us dug into my ribs. Not exactly designed for romance. Oh well, we'd have plenty of time for that when we landed.

I glanced out of the window as the green fields disappeared into tiny little distorted blobs below, and I almost couldn't believe this was really happening. When Kalem had been offered a new job at a university in North Cyprus, I admit I was a little worried. For a start, I'd miss his mum and dad, Yasmin and Deniz. They'd pretty much been my surrogate parents after my own parents died when I was just a kid, and I'd gone to live with my nan. His sister, Ayshe, was my best friend and someone I saw almost every day. In fact, she was more like my own sister than Kalem's. And it was her fourteen-day life-changing challenge that had actually got Kalem and me together – but that's a whole different story! I just didn't want to think about what was going to happen after the wedding, when she would be going back to the UK with her husband, Atila, and giving birth to her baby girl. No more talking or texting each other several times a day. No more shopping trips. No more girly chats about everything and nothing. No more having someone who was just so close and so much on the same wavelength that it really felt like we had some kind of telepathic link. Sometimes we could just look at each other and know what the other was thinking, and we'd often finish off each other's sentences. And I wouldn't be there to see her little bump be born or be a big part of bump's life like a doting Aunty should. These were the things I'd desperately miss.

But at the same time, I could feel an excitement burning in my depths. Or maybe it was indigestion – one of the two. Actually, maybe it was neither. Maybe it was dread. Most people told me it was really brave to move to another country and start again. After all, there was a lot to do. After the wedding and honeymoon period, we had to get Yasmin and Deniz's house habitable for us to live in until we got a place of our own. No doubt Kalem would have ups and downs with his new dream job, and I would have to try and build up my photographic business again from scratch. We had to make new friends. We had to get used to living in a foreign country where everything would be so different. Maybe we'd both die of malnutrition or dysentery or something, because I could only ask for wine, toilets, melons, and cucumbers.

And Kalem liked the simple things in life and getting back to basics. I could picture my new life as sipping foamy ice coffee or strong espresso from those teeny cups in a sun-drenched harbour buzzing with life, while the tall palm trees filtered out the scorching sun on my back. I had visions of white sandy beaches with the calm roll of the glistening waves lulling me gently to sleep, and a modern country with cosmopolitan and designer shops, sophisticated people, and sunshine twenty-four-seven. I mean, he'd said North Cyprus was unspoiled and undiscovered. But I was a tad worried about exactly how unspoiled. If Kalem's idea of being basic was reaching out of the kitchen window to pull a lemon off our tree for an early evening gin and tonic, then hey, I was all for basics. But somehow I didn't think that was exactly what he meant. His vision was probably more like me as Felicity Kendall in *The Good Life*, living off the land, picking olives, mucking out chickens, and herding goats. And how was I supposed to do that in my favourite spikey-heeled boots?

Since Kalem popped the question and told me about his new job offer in North Cyprus six months ago, everything had been a kind of whirlwind of activity and planning. It was only now, on the plane, as I finally stopped to think about it, that it did actually seem a bit scary.

Oh, shut up, Helen. Stop worrying. What's the worst that can happen? The most important thing is that you and Kalem are together. And you're getting to do something that most people dream about but never get the chance to do. It will be a fantastic opportunity.

'Ah, here comes the real surprise.' Kalem glanced at another stewardess prancing down the aisle with a tray of something and a couple of bottles of red wine.

'Oh, how sweet of you.' I grinned at him.

'Sorry, but there was a mix-up with your pre-ordered bottle of champagne and canapé selection.' The stewardess waved a bottle of wine at me and glared accusingly.

I could read her mind: *The burka-clad woman is going to drink alcohol. Bad burka-clad woman.*

'We've only got bottles of red wine left,' she said. Translation: *May she rot in hypocritical burka hell!* 'And we have no canapés.' Translation: *She will have to starve the temptation of alcohol from within.* 'The only spare meal available onboard is the Ramadan menu from last September.' Translation: *Let me remind you, burka-clad woman, of your religious roots. You will be cast out as an infidel. No alcohol for you, ha-ha!*

'That sounds exciting.' I smiled at her, thinking that I might as well start getting into the Turkish Cypriot culture as soon as possible. 'What's on the Ramadan menu?' It sounded quite interesting, whatever it was.

'This.' She thrust a packet containing two shrink-wrapped olives and one date in my direction. Translation: *Don't you know that burka-clad women fast during Ramadan? You are a disgrace!*

It was a good job she didn't know what I'd just been thinking about the chocolate body paint. I'd really be in trouble then.

'Miss,' the little boy behind us asked the stewardess as she was about to walk away. 'Can I see the Captain's cockpit?'

Her lips pursed with annoyance. 'Sorry, his cockpit is currently out of bounds, due to all the *suicide bomber* alerts lately.' She glared at me when she said this.

'What about his armpit, then?' The boy sniggered behind me and promptly got told off by his parents.

She ignored him and stomped back down the aisle.

'Well, we won't exactly get full up on that lot.' I pulled a face at the minuscule offering. 'But I made some sandwiches, so at least we won't starve. Or I've got a packet of custard creams in here if you want some.'

'No, a sandwich will be fine.'

I delved into my bag and grabbed a now squashed and sweaty packet of cheese sandwiches and a packet of bacon, lettuce, and tomato ones as Kalem poured two glasses of wine.

'Oh, no!' I gasped as I tried to close the zipper on my bag again, and it broke. I peered at the now gaping open bag with disgust.

Kalem handed me a plastic glass of wine. 'Here you go. To a perfect wedding and a fantastic new life together.' He kept his gaze firmly locked on mine and brought the glass slowly to his scrumptiously kissable lips.

'To us.' I had the glass midway to my lips when I realized that there are some things you just can't do in a burka:

1) Drink – Grumpy Stewardess would be pleased with this.
2) Eat – Damn, I was pretty peckish by now.
3) Snog – Well, it was our pre-honeymoon.

But, ah ha! I had a cunning plan. Nothing was going to get in the way of me and my wine. I'd just ask Grumpy Stewardess for a straw.

****

A bottle of wine later – I'd worked out how to manoeuvre the straw through the eye hole in the burka to my mouth without giving myself an eye-ectomy; difficult, but not impossible – I was feeling slightly tipsy.

Kalem was flicking lazily through the in-flight magazine when he suddenly sucked in a breath.

'What?' I asked, gazing over his shoulder.

He pointed to an article. It showed a big, posh hotel with lots of flamboyant purple and silver furnishings. Next to it was a picture of a middle-aged, dark-skinned man about fifty years old, wearing a friendly grin, and a picture of what looked like an old Egyptian sculpture of a queen's head and shoulders. The Queen had oval eyes, a beaky nose, and a double chin. It looked like she had a bit of a moustache, as well. Maybe they weren't into waxing in those days. On the side of the bust, a small picture of a regal looking cat had been carved.

'That's an Ancient Egyptian sculpture of Cleopatra made of solid gold.' Kalem's voice rose with excitement. 'It's the only one that was ever discovered in Cyprus. Wow, I can't believe it. Listen to this: "The plush, seven-star Plaza Hotel will be hosting its extravaganza opening night on Friday."'

'Hey, that's two days before our wedding day!' I butted in.

He carried on reading aloud. '"The multi-million pound, five-hundred roomed hotel includes a luxurious spa, a casino, and even a port for hotel guests to moor their yachts. The hotel will host a special opening concert, featuring international award-winning superstar singer Jayde, and the famous Queen Cleopatra sculpture will form part of an exclusive art exhibition on display for the occasion. The priceless sculpture is thought to be the only one in existence that was commissioned to celebrate Cleopatra's wedding to Mark Antony in 37 BC."'

'Ooh, maybe it's a sign that we're going to have a fabtastic wedding day.' I leaned forward to examine the picture of the sculpture more closely.

Kalem carried on. '"Turkish Cypriot entrepreneur, Ibrahim Kaya, is the brains behind the Plaza Hotel. Kaya, best known for his international chain of twenty successful hotels and his property development businesses, also has international export companies that specialize in meat, fruit, and clothing. His rags-to-riches lifestyle has prompted many accusations of ruthless business practices and allegations of underworld connections, but Kaya maintains that he is a professional entrepreneur. Kaya is a self-confessed fitness fanatic who follows a strict diet and daily exercise regime. He credits his healthy mind and body with his business success and believes the disciplines of physical training prepared him for the business world. Known for his love of art, Kaya has one of the biggest private collections in the world. The Cleopatra statue was originally discovered by Kaya's father, a renowned archaeologist, during an excavation at the ancient Greek city of Salamis, Cyprus, in 1952. The statue will be revealed in public for the first time to an audience of carefully selected politicians, stars, and high-rollers before the concerts begins."'

'What was Cleopatra doing in Cyprus?' I asked.

'Mark Antony gave the rule of Cyprus over to Cleopatra after their wedding. Then after that you had the Romans, the Byzantines, the Ottomans. Even the Knights Templar controlled Cyprus at one point.' He carried on staring at the statue in awe. 'I can't believe this.' He shook his head softly to himself. 'I did my thesis on this sculpture for my art degree. I've actually used it as one of the main examples in my Egyptology sculpture course. I always wanted to see it in real life.' He had a wistful look on his face.

'Why is there a cat on it?'

'Well, cats were supposed to be lucky in Egyptian society.' Kalem went back to the article, his eyes nearly popping out, like he couldn't bear to turn his head away from the picture of the sculpture. 'Wow! This is fascinating.' He looked like he'd gone into a trance.

Maybe the sculpture had one of those funny curses that I'd heard about before, where if you stared at it for too long, it made your brain explode or something. Yes, I'm sure I'd read about other weird curses where people had uncovered ancient Egyptian artefacts, and they'd all ended up dead.

Agh! Don't look at the picture. Don't look at the picture! I pulled the magazine away, just to be on the safe side.

'Hey, what are you doing?'

'Well, you're acting all funny.'

'No, I'm not.' He grabbed the magazine back.

Don't look at the picture!

'It might have a curse,' I said. 'I don't want a curse. I have enough weird things happen to me as it is without having a curse on top of it.'

Kalem laughed. 'It's not cursed! I really have to see this up close. It's such a rare piece. You know, this sculpture is probably worth around five million pounds. Amazing, huh?'

I could think of better things to spend five million on, like a luxury yacht or a hundred bedroomed mansion in the Bahamas, but there you go.

I snatched the magazine back off him and thrust my *OK! Magazine* in his hand instead.

'There, read about Angelina and Brad's love life instead of cursed sculptures.'

Kalem stared into space, all glassy-eyed. 'Mmm, five-million. What would you do with five-million pounds?'

He was definitely going a bit funny. Kalem liked the simple things in life. He had a battered old Land Rover and a habit of wearing clothes until they had more holes than a bumper pack of donuts. Not that he was stingy or anything. He just wasn't really into material things. So it was très bizarre now that he kept mumbling on about money.

'Well, we're hardly going to get an invite to the opening party, so maybe you should just forget about the statue.' *Yes, forget about it before if fries your brain and jinxes us!* I tried to slowly prise the magazine away from his vice-like grip on it as the plane started descending.

We stood with the rest of the horde of new arrivals, waiting for my luggage to emerge and go round the conveyor belt. Kalem had already got his suitcase, but mine was taking forever. It was honestly amazing the things that actually appeared. I felt like I was on one of those game shows, trying to memorize objects: A set of skis, a giant cuddly teddy bear wearing an *I Love You* T-shirt – oops, its arm just got caught in the ramp and ripped off – a plunger, a half open hold-all stuffed full of a black paint, and a bike with no wheels. Well, someone was in for a strange holiday, that was for sure. I watched the skis go round, wondering if there was someone out there in some freezy-ass country watching a surfboard going around and around on an endless, unclaimed loop.

I was sandwiched in between Kalem and an impatient ferrety looking man with field-mouse coloured hair and beard and a pointy nose and chin. I kept getting a whiff of lemon cologne and cigarettes, making me feel slightly nauseous under the stifling warmth of the burka.

From out of nowhere a fluffy looking German Shepherd with a white harness jumped on the conveyor belt and trampled over all the luggage.

'Oh, look! A poor blind person's lost their guide dog.' I pointed at it, looking around for someone with a white stick, so I could reunite them.

The dog was in a little world of its own as it pranced around the luggage conveyor, dribbling and wagging its tail. Then it jumped off the conveyor, ran around the room sniffing people's crutches – particularly women, for some reason, I might add.

Kalem chuckled. 'It's a drug sniffer dog, not a guide dog.'

'Well, where's its handler then?' I glanced around.

Kalem shrugged.

Ferret Face's eye started twitching as he reached to pull his case off the conveyor. Maybe he was allergic to dogs.

'Ah, here's my case.' I was nearer to it than Kalem, so I pulled it towards me.

And that's when the cute little doggy jumped on me, sending me slamming right into Ferret Face.

'Agh!' I fell on top of Ferret Face, squashing him and knocking over both of our suitcases in the process. Not a nice experience, really. I mean, what if he had conjunctivitis?

The dog's nose dived into my handbag, grabbed my uneaten packets of sandwiches, and then it ran off. Can you believe it? I was going to eat those when I got to the hotel!

'Are you OK?' Kalem helped me struggle to my feet.

I dusted myself off, avoiding the stares of the other people. 'I don't know. Am I? Did I just imagine that?' My arm throbbed from where I'd banged it on the suitcase. I gave it a tentative rub.

Oh, God. The curse of Queen Cleopatra had begun.

'No, I think I'll live. Come on. Let's go before it comes back.' I looked at Ferret Face who was grabbing his suitcase again. 'Are you OK?' I asked him. He looked a bit flustered, but he nodded he was all right.

I grabbed the handle of my suitcase and wheeled it towards the customs office and the exit beyond with Kalem swiftly following.

Ferret Face mumbled something, hurrying after us. He smiled, as if he wanted to apologize. Then he seemed to think better of it as the customs officer called us over to his desk, and he rushed past us and out into the crowded Arrivals area.

I groaned. What now? I'd had enough of customs men to last a lifetime.

'What sandwiches did you have?' The customs officer peered at me.

Well, I didn't want to say bacon, just in case I upset him. Even though Kalem and Ayshe ate bacon, I knew that most Muslims still didn't eat pork, and I couldn't do with any more upsets today. 'Er...cheese.' I frowned, confused. What did that have to do with anything?

'Hmm.' He thought about this for a while. 'I think that's the problem. The dog just loves cheese.' He waved us on. 'It's OK, you can go.'

Chapter 3

We stepped outside and the warm night air seeped into our skin.

I sniffed. It was heady holiday air that made your skin prickle with the excitement of arriving in a foreign country for the first time: a mixture of jet fuel, heat, and some kind of plant that I couldn't distinguish. I took a big gulp of it and glanced up at the stars. Wow! There was hardly any light pollution so it was like looking up at my own personal planetarium.

'Aren't your mum and dad or Charlie picking us up?' I asked.

There were plenty of people milling around, but I couldn't see Yasmin or Deniz, or, for that matter, our own personal wedding planner, Charlie. I could, however, see a man who looked suspiciously like a Mexican bandit, waving at us so hard I thought his arm might pop out of its socket. He was about fifty years old with a bandit moustache, bushy black eyebrows, and moist dark eyes, a bit like a spaniel's.

'Who's that?' I asked Kalem.

Kalem squinted at the man, trying to place him. 'I think it's Dad's cousin, Osman.' Kalem waved back. 'I haven't actually ever met him before, but I recognize him from some photos that Dad showed me.'

Osman rushed towards us and kissed Kalem on both cheeks, Turkish style. 'Kalem! We finally meet!' He then gave me a bear hug. 'So, this must be Helen. Why are you wearing a burka?' He pulled back, examining me with interest before settling on a puzzled look.

Kalem rattled off something to Osman in Turkish. Osman raised his eyebrows, which seemed to have a life of their own, and chuckled.

'Your dad said you were always a practical joker – even when you were a little boy.' Osman smiled. 'Come, come. I've got the car waiting with my mother in it. She's dying to meet you too. Yasmin and Deniz wanted to come as well, but there's not enough room in the car with the sheep.' He herded us towards an ancient Renault – probably the same era as the Cleopatra statue – that looked like it was about to fall to pieces. I think it used to be grey, but it was quite hard to tell underneath all the rust patches.

It had a roof rack made out of bits of old scaffolding held together with some dodgy looking frayed rope. A threadbare armchair was tied precariously to the top.

'Er...did he say there's a sheep in the car?' I whispered to Kalem.

Oh, my God. What have I let myself in for? Is this what Kalem meant about the simple life? I didn't want to be rude or anything, but...no, he had to be joking about the sheep. A big, smelly, hairy sheep. In the car?

Osman's mum, a wrinkly woman with bright, shiny eyes, opened the car door and repeated the kissing, talking quickly in Turkish to us.

'She can't speak English,' Osman said, shoe-horning the suitcases in the boot of the car.

So I nodded and said 'yes' a lot to her. I hoped she wasn't asking me if I was a suicide bomber.

Osman motioned for us to get in the car, and that's when I saw the sheep, curled up on the backseat.

Right. So maybe not a joke, then.

I slid in next to the sheep. It made a bleating noise and suckled the arm of my burka.

'Agh! It's so sweet,' I cooed.

'She's called Kuzu.' Osman beamed at me.

'Nice name. And what does that mean in Turkish?' I asked.

He shrugged. 'It means lamb. I'm training her to be a sniffer sheep.'

'A what?' What the hell was that?

'Well, have you seen the state of the sniffer dogs here? They can't do a thing right. No, this is going to be the way of the future. Sniffer sheep.'

'Er...and what can Kuzu sniff so far?' I frowned, scratching her behind the ears, which had just pricked up, like she knew we were talking about her.

'She can sniff out olives. If the wind's in the right direction, she can sniff out wild sage.' Osman sounded so proud, as if he were talking about his own child. 'She can sniff me out when I'm hiding in the garden. She's a quick learner, though. I've been training her for a year since she was a little lamb. Soon she will be fully trained.'

What had I let myself in for? Osman had to be nuts, surely. I tried to disguise my look of unbelieving terror as polite interest. I'm not sure if it worked, but Osman didn't seem to notice.

'Yasmin and Deniz have been having trouble with the rental car. It keeps breaking down. Not like this reliable beauty.' Osman patted the dashboard lovingly.

Maybe loving old heaps of cars was hereditary. Now I knew where Kalem got it from with his wreck of a Land Rover back in the UK.

'What car did they hire?' I asked Kalem.

'I booked a Land Rover for us all. I wanted to take you off-roading up in the mountains. The scenery is absolutely amazing – views for miles over the sea and the Kyrenia mountain range. I thought we could have a romantic picnic up there this week before the wedding, just the two of us.' Kalem hugged me towards him.

'It broke down again on their way to pick you up, so I volunteered instead,' Osman said.

'I had a Land Rover in the UK for fifteen years. It never broke down.' Kalem shook his head to himself.

Osman tried to drive off, when suddenly his mum yelled something at him, and he did an emergency stop, the ancient Renault creaking and shuddering like something was about to snap.

She ambled slowly out of the car, then proceeded to break a hardboiled egg on the bumper and peel off the shell. Next, she climbed back in the car and handed it to me with a nightmarish cackle.

I shook my head manically and gave her my best I-don't-really-think-you-are-a-nutcase smile, but really I was thinking three words: Crazy. Crazy. Crazy.

OK, now I was building a mental list of bad things about moving here. First up was:

1) Crazy extended family.

The car made a scraping sound as it pulled away, like a bit of bumper was hanging off, or, even worse, our suitcases were falling out the back. Luckily, it distracted me from my anxiety attack.

I turned around to check that our clothes weren't billowing out in a stream behind us and saw Ferret Face following in a black Mercedes. Actually, if he were any closer, he'd be on our laps. His eye had stopped twitching, but he was giving me a funny look. Glaring at me almost. Strange.

'They're all waiting for you at the hotel,' Osman said. 'It's been so good catching up with Yasmin and Deniz since they arrived.'

'Do you think you should turn the headlights on?' I asked Osman as we drove up to the exit barrier of the car park with Ferret Face following close behind.

Osman shook his head. 'I always forget that.' He flipped on the lights and pulled a coin out of his pocket, licked it, then shoved it in the money slot. The barrier lifted and we slowly drove off.

Ferret Face jerked to a halt at the barrier and slammed his money in the slot, but the barrier wouldn't open. The last thing I saw out the rear window was Ferret Face kicking the barrier machine and waving his fist at us. How bizarre. Maybe my elbow had crushed the ferret food in his suitcase when I fell on top of him and he wanted to sue me. Whatever it was, I wasn't going to stop to find out. He looked a bit upset to me.

We turned onto a dual carriageway. Well, that was a good sign anyway. At least it wasn't a narrow little dirt track that was only suitable for donkeys. Not that I'd ever actually analyzed the finer points of a dual carriageway before. But the place couldn't be that basic and unspoiled if it had one, surely?

As we got nearer to Kyrenia, which was one of the main tourist resorts, we came over the mountains and saw the twinkly lights of the town below. To our left, a large section of the mountain was lit up like a giant Christmas tree; a dazzling display of white neon. It looked amazing in the dark, but someone must have had a hefty electric bill.

'What's that?' I pointed out the window.

'St Hilarion Castle,' Osman said. 'You should visit it when you get the chance. It's a spectacular sight. Perched high up in the Kyrenia mountain range, the views of the Mediterranean are like nothing you've seen before. You can see for miles up there.'

'It looks amazing.' I gazed at it.

'The castle was named after a monk who fled from

persecution in Palestine in the seventh century,' Kalem said. 'There's a legend that he was deaf, so he was able to resist the tempting cries of pagan demons who lived on the mountain. I'll have to take you up there after the wedding when we have more time.'

'What happened to the demons?' I asked, feeling a tad worried. It was bad enough with a cursed statue on the island, never mind demons as well.

'Well,' Osman went on, 'because the monk couldn't hear them, they finally left the mountain in peace, and a monastery later sprang up around his tomb. After a while, a fort was added as well. It was built into the mountains, and it's got a kind of fairytale look about it. All towers and walls. In fact, there's a rumour that Walt Disney based the Snow White Castle on it. Richard the Lionheart captured the castle on his way to the Third Crusade, and some people still think that the Holy Grail was actually hidden somewhere inside.'

Demons, Disney castles, and Holy Grails? Sounded a bit *Da Vinci Code* to me. Still, if Indiana Jones and Walt Disney were inspired by North Cyprus, it had to be a good sign. I started an opposing mental list of things I was going to like about being here, and thought I was doing pretty well. So far, I had:

1) Kalem
2) Sunshine
3) Beaches
4) A Disney Castle
5) Indiana Jones searched for Holy Grail here (not sure if that was technically correct, I couldn't remember the actual plot of the film)
6) A dual carriageway.

'It's even more impressive during the day.' Kalem stroked the inside of my palm with his thumb.

A bolt of electricity zapped up my spine. *Ooh, just you wait until I get you to the hotel, Kalem Mustafa, and try that chocolate body paint out.* Who said a girl couldn't have chocolate and an orgasm?

'Have you ever climbed it?' I asked, nuzzling into his shoulder.

'Yes, Mum and Dad made us climb it the last time we all came here on a family holiday when I was about ten.'

We finally pulled up outside our hotel – not quite the plush Plaza, but still pretty damn nice – to a welcome party of Yasmin and Deniz, Ayshe and her husband, Atila, and Charlie. Yasmin's hands flapped around when she saw us. Deniz looked pretty plastered with a glass of whisky in his hand (a regular occurrence). Atila rubbed Ayshe's back as she shuffled her glowing pregnant body from one foot to the other with a beaming smile. And Charlie…well, he was in a tight, pink jumpsuit, bouncing up and down. Need I say more? It left little to the imagination, and I'm pretty sure he had been stuffing socks down there again, if you know what I mean.

Hugs and kisses galore from everyone before they all admonished Kalem for carrying on the burka joke too far.

'I'll leave you all to catch up then.' Osman gave a puzzled look at Charlie's attire and clambered into the Renault.

We all waved goodbye as it popped and groaned back down the driveway.

'I've missed you all already, and you've only been out here for two days.' I could feel my eyes welling up. 'God, what am I going to be like when you all go back to the UK after the wedding?' I swallowed to stop my eyes watering.

Ayshe started crying then as well. 'This is supposed to be a happy occasion. Look at the pair of us.' She smudged her eyeliner as she dabbed at her eye.

'Now, now. No tears.' Yasmin hugged me into her warm, cuddly body.

'I know, let's have a drink.' Deniz's eyes lit up at the thought.

Yasmin slapped him on the head. 'I think you've had enough already. You don't need a reason to celebrate.'

Deniz yelped. 'Get off me, woman.' He slunk backwards, out of slapping distance. 'We need to celebrate their coming niptuals.'

I giggled. 'I think you mean nuptials.'

Charlie jumped up and down again, clapping his hands together. 'And talking of nuptials, the wedding plans are going to perfection! I've confirmed and reconfirmed all the arrangements. I'll get my clipboard in a minute and go through the details with you so far.'

26

Deniz looked surreptitiously around the hotel entrance before leaning in closer. 'Wait until you see what's in the mini-bar,' he whispered.

'Oh, I know. They've got those fabby honey-roasted nuts in there.' Charlie licked his lips. 'Yummy.'

'No, not the nuts. They've got condoms in there.' Deniz nodded at us all.

Yasmin rolled her eyes. 'He's obsessed with the condoms now.'

'Yes, but these aren't any old condoms. They're curry flavour!' Deniz's eyes lit up like he'd just discovered some really complicated mathematical theory. 'We've only got mild flavour in ours, though.' He looked disappointed at this. 'I'm trying to find spicy ones. If you've got any spicy ones in your mini-bar, I'll swap you for the mild ones,' he said to me.

'Ssh!' Yasmin said to Deniz. 'I think we'll say goodnight now and let you youngsters have some fun. It's about time Whisky Face here gave his drinking arm a rest.' Yasmin jerked her head towards Deniz and then gave us all a kiss. 'We'll see you tomorrow for breakfast.' She grabbed Deniz's arm, pulling him into the entrance of the hotel and steering him – quite reluctantly – away from the bar area.

'Right, let me just grab a bottle of champagne.' Charlie disappeared.

Atila picked up my suitcase and led the way to our room after we'd checked into the honeymoon suite.

Honeymoon suite! God, I still couldn't believe this was really happening. I was getting married and I was so excited I was about to pop something. I'd finally be a grown up. Not that not being married didn't make you a grown up, of course, it's just that I would finally have everything I'd dreamed about. I was actually going to be married to the perfect man at my perfect wedding, and it kind of felt like a fairytale for grownups. I just wished my parents and my nan were alive to see it.

'Oh, this is fantastic.' I glanced at the huge super king size bed, draped with gold and burgundy cushions of varying shapes and sizes. Antique looking Turkish carpets adorned the marble floor, and the walls were covered with expensive looking wall paper, embossed in a matching colour scheme. But the best bit was a circular Jacuzzi in the middle of the room, overlooking the floor to ceiling glass windows that gave us a fantastic view of the lights below. I couldn't wait to give that a go.

'This room is fabby-dabby.' Charlie appeared behind us with a clipboard in one hand and a bottle of champagne in the other. He set the bubbly down next to a tray of glasses on top of the mini-bar and ran a finger over the wallpaper. 'I thought my room was nice, but this is amazing.'

I dumped my handbag on the floor. 'I have to get out of this burka.' The room was hot, and I was beginning to feel a little claustrophobic in it. I clawed at the eye hole and heard a ripping sound as the material gave way, leaving me with a gaping hole at the front, which now left my whole face exposed. Well, at least I could have a drink easily now.

Atila put my suitcase on a gold chair near the bed. 'Right. Let's get the champagne out.' He grinned.

Kalem did the honours, pouring out a toast for everyone, including Ayshe, who had a thimbleful. He slid an arm around my waist and drew me towards him. 'To my wonderful bride-to-be and our exciting new life in Cyprus.'

I grinned up at him to the sound of chinking glasses, and my anxiety about the move slipped into oblivion.

Charlie cleared his throat. 'Now, if I can have your attention, everyone. I want to go through the finer details of the wedding with you all.' He perched some reading glasses on the end of his nose and concentrated on his clipboard. 'OK, we have six days until the wedding. Not a lot of time, people, I know, and most of the arrangements are finalized, so we shouldn't have to do much. But everyone needs to be on hand, just in case any last minute crisis pops up. Agreed?' He peered up at us.

We all agreed.

'Now, there should be plenty of time for the pre-wedding relaxation that Helen and Kalem need before the big day. I'm envisioning sunbathing, cocktails by the pool, and a bit of exploring thrown in. Sound good to everyone?'

Everyone agreed.

'But we do have a bit of work to do.' He held a finger up to emphasize the point. 'The container that's shipping Helen and Kalem's personal stuff from the UK will arrive on Thursday, and you both have to be there to sign for it and have it inspected. So I expect you'll both be a bit busy sorting out the boxes and

28

furniture when it arrives.' Charlie glanced at Kalem and me. 'The wedding venue is confirmed, double confirmed, and re-confirmed.' He peered at us all again to make sure we were taking it in. 'I've already been to Bellapais Abbey several times to check the seating plan, table décor, menu etc. So we should have no problems there. Beautiful place, by the way. What could be more perfect than a wedding set in the ruins of a historic abbey, backlit by exotic lighting, and dotted with jasmine? Superb.'

Since I'd never actually been to North Cyprus before, I'd had to choose a venue based on photos and the testimonials of other brides. It sounded like that choice was going to be a perfect one, too.

'Ooh, I can't wait to see the Abbey,' I said to Kalem. 'We have to go and have a look at it tomorrow.'

'Your wedding dress needs to be hung properly and aired,' Charlie went on. 'If there are any creases from the suitcase, I've sourced a dry cleaner to steam them out. The same goes for your suit, Kalem. If you give them to me tomorrow, I'll arrange everything.' He paused for a slight breath. Only slight, mind you. 'Dresses and suits of other parties attending have already been inspected and found to be crease-free and in excellent condition.'

I giggled. Charlie sounded like he was in the army, arranging warfare manoeuvres with extreme precision. I didn't think I'd ever seen him be so serious about anything. 'Other parties? You mean, Ayshe, Atila, Deniz, Yasmin, and you?' I asked.

Charlie raised an eyebrow at my giggling. 'You may mock, but planning a wedding is a very difficult task, you know. And when you asked me to be your official wedding planner, I swore to uphold my duty and give you a perfect wedding.'

I stopped giggling abruptly. 'Sorry, Charlie,' I said, not pointing out that, actually, we hadn't asked him. He'd kind of volunteered for the job. And as he was a best friend of all of ours, and he'd been so excited about being involved, I couldn't exactly refuse. And I was really grateful, of course. It would be so nice to be able to sit back and let him take care of the finer details, saving me from spontaneously combusting with nerves. I just hoped to God that he'd followed my colour scheme. If Charlie had anything to do with it, everything at the wedding would be pink, pink, and more pink.

He released his grip on the clipboard and placed it carefully on the writing desk as if it were a fragile work of art. 'Finally, I've had a slight issue with the wedding song.' His cheeks turned the same shade as his jumpsuit.

'What sort of issue?' I took a sip of wine and gazed at Charlie over the rim of the glass.

'Well, you wanted *Love Me Tender* by Elvis, and I could've sworn that I double-checked that the CD I brought with me was actually the one with *Love Me Tender* on it. But…erm…unfortunately, there's been a mix-up.'

'Spit it out, Charlie. What sort of mix-up?' Kalem looked amused at how serious Charlie was taking his duties.

Charlie let out an embarrassed cough. 'Paul is always putting the wrong CDs back in the case. It drives me mad, you know–'

'Yes, get to the point, Charlie,' I interrupted.

'The thing is, he was doing a stripping gig at the London Gay Pride festival recently, and he made up a CD for his routine. And…well, that's the one in the CD case I've got.' He glanced down at his shoes. 'If you want to change your mind and have Barbara Streisand or Gloria Gaynor as your wedding song, then this CD is perfect, but…well, I'm afraid there's no Elvis on it.'

I shrugged. 'That's not much of a problem. You must be able to buy another CD of Elvis here.'

'Mmm, that's the problem, you see. I've been looking and I haven't found one yet. But don't worry about it. I'm sure I can source that song soon. It's absolutely nothing to worry about.' Charlie waved a dismissive hand through the air.

I smiled to myself. I didn't even really like Elvis, but it was my nan's favourite song. Sadly, she'd passed away three months ago so she couldn't be at the wedding with me, and I thought the next best thing was to have one of her favourite songs playing to remind me of her. That, and the lucky charm she'd given me before she'd died would mean that she really would be with me in spirit, looking down on me for the most important day of my life.

'So, any questions, hmm?' Charlie asked.

I gave him a kiss on the cheek. 'No, I don't think so. I know you'll do a fabulous job. Nothing is going to spoil my perfect wedding.'

'Maybe we should let these love birds get to bed.' Ayshe collected everyone's glasses and put them on the ornate desk. 'They must be tired from all that travelling.' She kissed Kalem and me goodnight on both cheeks. 'We'll see you in the morning for a bit of relaxation and de-stressing.' She gave me a knowing smile. 'Oh, it's so exciting!'

She hugged me tight, her long, almost black hair sweeping over my shoulder. She could read my mind. We were so close that she knew how anxious I was feeling about the wedding and the move here. Yes, what I needed to do tomorrow was just relax with my friends and look forward to a glorious day. Especially the cocktail part.

Everyone milled out, and I turned to Kalem in the now silent room. Slowly, he traced my cheek with one finger, sending a shockwave of pulses shooting in all directions.

He leaned forward, brushing my ear with his lips.

Oooh, goosebump alert!

'So, do you fancy some chocolate?' He dropped his voice to a whisper.

Well, if the tingling sensation down below was anything to go on, then HELL, YEAH!

I yanked the burka over my head, revealing some new *Victoria's Secret* red, lacy underwear, which, according to the description, were the number one bestseller in their *Minx* range. *Grrrrrr, baby. Here I come!*

I quickly fumbled with the buttons on his pert-arse-hugging jeans and pulled his black T-shirt over his head.

'Stay right there.' Kalem gave me a sexy, lopsided grin and strode to his hand luggage, rummaging around with purpose. 'No!' His eyelids flew open. 'The chocolate body paint has leaked out of the tub. The inside of my rucksack is covered with brown goo. I bet that customs guy didn't put the lid back on properly.'

I rolled my eyes. 'That bloody Dick Head! Ruining my *Minx* moment!' I huffed.

Kalem's eyes suddenly lit up. 'OK, plan B.' He held a finger in the air, then hurried towards my suitcase. 'I planted a tub of tutti fruiti body paint at the bottom of your suitcase without you noticing. Kind of an extra wedding pressie for you.'

'Oh, goody.' I sashayed to the bed, beckoning him towards

31

me. 'You've been a very bad boy. You haven't been getting your five fruit and veg a day.' I winked at him and struck a pose on the bed. Think coy with a hint of raunchy, and you'd get the picture. 'I'll give you some tutti fruiti, and you can give me some veg,' I drawled, giggling.

Kalem's brown eyes darted between me and the suitcase, as he fumbled impatiently to get the key in the lock.

'You need to have a complete body exam by Nurse Fruity.' I slowly undid my bra, getting into my minxy role-play.

Kalem roughly tried to thrust the key into the lock. 'I can't get it in!'

'Nurse Fruity wants you to get it in!' I cried, swinging my bra around, à la sexy stripper.

With a final shove, the lock popped open.

Kalem opened the case and all the blood drained from his face. 'What the…' He stared at the inside of the case and gulped.

'What's wrong?' I frowned.

'This isn't your case.'

I shot off the bed. 'It has to be. It looks exactly the same,' I wailed, clipping my bra back on and pulling out men's trousers, toiletries, and shoes from the half-empty case. 'No, no, no!' I kind of freaked at that point and words came out in an explosion. 'Shit. Where's my wedding dress. Fuck. What am I going to do? Bollocks. Whose case is this? Double fuck. My perfect wedding will be ruined.'

Kalem stood there, thinking. 'It must've happened when you got jumped by the dog.'

I tried to engage my rational-thinking brain from my freaking-out brain, so I could picture the events that had happened in my head like an action replay. I'd been standing next to Ferret Face. We both grabbed our suitcases at around the same time. The dog jumped me and I fell on the floor on top of Ferret Face. The dog stole my sandwiches and ran off. Ferret Face and I dusted ourselves off. We both grabbed our cases and walked to the exit. Ferret Face tried to say something. Kalem and I were stopped by the customs man. Ferret Face scurried away. Ferret Face followed us. Ferret Face got stuck behind the car park barrier.

'Aghhhhhhhhhhhhhhhhhhhh!' I flopped my head forward, tugging at my roots.

'Maybe that guy took your case back to the airport when he

32

realized he had the wrong one.' Kalem stroked my hair. 'I'll give them a ring and see if it's there.'

I sat on the edge of the bed in slow motion and stared at a pair of tartan Speedos in the case until my eyes watered.

'Helen, say something.'

'Nothing is going to ruin my perfect wedding. Nothing is going to ruin my perfect wedding,' I squeaked out my mantra.

'It will be OK in the end. Your case is probably already in lost luggage waiting for you.' He snatched up the phone by the bed, his forefinger jabbing at the buttons. He fired out rapid Turkish to the receptionist. 'She's putting me through to the airport.' He grabbed hold of my hand, giving it a quick squeeze.

More rapid Turkish and a few heated hand gestures.

'What did they say?' I said before he'd even replaced the receiver.

'The lost luggage department is closed for the night. I have to ring back in the morning.'

I lifted my head, tears bouncing down my cheeks. I needed my wedding dress to have my perfect wedding. Not only because it was the absolutely perfect dress, but because it had my nan's lucky gold heart charm stitched inside the hem. It had been in the family a long time – passed down from her grandmother to her, she'd pressed it in my hand and made me promise to have it with me on my wedding day to let me know she would be thinking of me from up in that old retirement home in the sky. It was the *something old* I needed for my wedding day. Maybe it was stupid superstitious nonsense, but if I didn't get the dress and the charm back, I knew, I just knew, that our marriage would be cursed with bad luck.

I had to get that dress back if it was the last thing I did.

Chapter 4

I tossed and turned that night, bouncing around on the bed like a Li-lo lost at sea.

I barely slept, and when I did, I had really freaky dreams. At one point, I was walking up the aisle dressed in a woolly sheep suit, complete with hooves and everything. And I had a diamante tiara resting between my furry ears. I couldn't quite get the hooves to fit in my strappy cream high heels, so they kept falling off. All the guests were trying to shout something to me, but I couldn't work out what they were saying. Their mouths opened and closed in slow motion, like goldfish. Anyway, when I got to the altar, Kalem wasn't there. The groom turned around to face me, and it was a giant ferret.

When the Mediterranean sunlight filtered through the curtains at 5.30 the next morning I woke up in a cold sweat with a feeling that something wasn't quite right.

I lay in bed, on top of the gold satin sheets with my head resting on Kalem's chest, still staring at the bloody suitcase, my mind going over and over what happened at the airport.

Because now I had a really horrible feeling.

'You can't ring the airport.' My voice came out a hoarse crackle.

'What? Why not?' Kalem opened a sleepy eye and looked at me like I'd completely lost any marbles that I actually had left in the first place.

'Because Ferret Face knew I had his case.'

'Huh?'

'Yes, he knew I had it. That's why he tried to chase after us, but I just didn't realize that's what he was doing at the time. Don't you remember? When the customs guy stopped us, he ran away. Then later, when we were driving out of the airport, Ferret Face was following us. I think he wanted to find out where we were going so he could get his case back without drawing attention to it. And also, when I picked up that case, it felt like the same weight as mine, and I packed enough clothes and toiletries to stock a small department store. But the weird thing is that it looks like there's hardly anything inside it.'

And then I had two horrific thoughts: 1) This was going to ruin my perfect wedding; and 2) Apart from some very unflattering tartan Speedos, what the hell was in that case?

I slid from the bed and towered over the suitcase. It looked fairly normal and suitcaseyish.

I sat on the floor and pulled out the contents until everything was lying around me. Black trainers – slightly scuffed. Three pairs of black trousers. A selection of Speedos in tartan, purple, white – does anyone actually wear white Speedos? What about when they got wet? It didn't bear thinking about. A black baseball cap. Five pairs of new, black boxer shorts, still in their packets – at least I didn't have to finger any used ones. A weird, black thing that looked like some sort of money belt, but wasn't. It had a soft pad in the centre, with an adjustable strap either side. A small toiletry bag, containing shaving gel, a razor, a pair of scissors, deodorant, and a toothbrush. Six black T-shirts. And that was it.

So why was it really heavy?

Kalem swung his legs over the bed and sat up as I picked through everything again, inspecting them for hidden items. The inside of the baseball cap had a zip in it. I undid it and looked inside.

'What's this?' I probed my finger in and pulled out a piece of soft, lightweight black cotton material. Then my jaw dropped as I unravelled it. 'It's a balaclava! Why would someone need a balaclava in ninety degree heat?'

Kalem fiddled with the money belt thingy. 'This is a shoulder pad.'

'Weird looking shoulder pad. It doesn't look anything like the ones they used to have in the Eighties.'

'No, it's not a shoulder pad for clothes. It's a shoulder pad to use when you're shooting a gun.' Kalem tried it on, fixing it over his shoulder and strapping it around his chest to show me.

There could be only one reason why someone wanted a shoulder pad for a gun. They were intending to shoot something. Or someone.

We stared at each other, wide-eyed.

Kalem picked up the now empty case. 'It's still heavy. There must be some kind of secret compartment in it.' He set it down on the floor and knelt down, feeling along the sides and the

35

bottom of the case.

I sat forward and peered over his shoulder. Then I heard a click, and the bottom of the suitcase unclipped from a section underneath it.

Kalem threw the false bottom panel to the side to reveal what was hidden there.

A sheet of what looked like some sort of carbon paper hid whatever was below it.

'What's that for?' I asked as Kalem lifted off the paper.

'Probably so the X-ray machine at the airport couldn't detect what was hidden inside it.'

And that's when I knew we were really in trouble.

We stared at wads and wads of cash, packed into tight bundles.

I pulled one out and examined it. 'They're all one hundred dollar notes. What the hell is going on?' I pulled out more bundles until they were all on the floor around us. 'And what's this?' I reached into the case. Under the wads was a large, folded up piece of paper covered in scribbly writing.

I unfolded it and spread it across the floor, the paper crackling in my fingertips. Folded inside was a bigger piece of paper with lots of writing and diagrams on it.

Kalem examined the bigger piece while I tried to decipher the writing on the other one.

'This is a building engineer's floor plan of the Plaza Hotel,' Kalem said.

'Well this is an itinerary of events that will happen on the day of the official opening of the hotel on Friday.' I turned it over and read the back. 'It's also got details of the Cleopatra sculpture and directions to an art dealer across the border in South Cyprus.' I sat back on my heels and fanned at my flushed face, feeling light headed.

Kalem reached into the case again and pulled out the only remaining item. A black and white picture of Ibrahim Kaya.

'How much money is here? Count them,' I said, flicking through the wads.

We did. All five hundred thousand dollars of them.

We looked at each other. Kalem's face mirrored my own panic.

My brain was having a hard time trying to take it all in. This

36

couldn't be real. It had to be a joke. Maybe Ayshe and Charlie were trying to play a pre-wedding trick on us. Instead of filling our bed with Cornflakes or whatever, they'd planted fake money in my suitcase and replaced all my clothes and my wedding dress with men's clothes. I bet they were having a good old laugh in their rooms right about now. But hang on…they weren't with us at the airport. They couldn't have known I would accidentally pick up Ferret Face's case. OK, so if it wasn't a joke, maybe I was dehydrated and starting to have a heat stroke induced delirium. Yes, that was it. Or maybe I had a serious illness. Maybe I was feverish and hallucinating. That would explain a lot, wouldn't it?

I wiped a bead of sweat from my upper lip and stared at the contents of the case, hoping they'd vanish into thin air. Nope, they were still there. I wasn't hallucinating.

We fell silent for a few minutes, trying to absorb the extent of the situation. Based on everything we'd found, a horrifying conclusion was floating around in my head. A shoulder pad for a gun; the money; the floor plans, and the details of the sculpture and art dealer. It could only add up to one thing.

'It looks like Ferret Face is going to steal the sculpture on the opening night. But why is there a picture of Ibrahim Kaya?' I asked the question, but I didn't really want to hear the answer. I could already guess why.

'I think he's going to assassinate Ibrahim Kaya at the same time.' Kalem's eyebrows rose half an inch. 'Trying to kill someone is bad enough, but stealing the sculpture as well!'

'I told you it had a curse. And now it's cursed us.' I exhaled a slow breath. 'OK, we'll just take it all to the police and let them deal with it.'

'Yes.'

I gave him a vigorous nod. 'And then we have to get them to find my suitcase and, more importantly, my wedding dress.' I sighed. 'But I love my wedding dress! What if I never see it again?'

'You will. Don't worry. The police will find your case and get your wedding dress back.' He kissed my eyelids, his lips brushing gently against that soft spot – yes, right there – that made my insides turn squishy.

Ooh, hello! No, I couldn't be thinking about sex at a time like this. After we'd sorted this mess out today, then I could think about it. Quite a lot.

'Right,' I said. 'We'll just take everything to the police, and they can sort it out. That's their job. And as long as we never bump into Ferret Face again, we'll be OK.' I paused, having a sudden mental brain shriek. 'Although...it's a pretty small island. What if we do bump into him somewhere?'

'Well, you'll be OK. You were wearing a Burka, so he doesn't even know what you look like. But he'd probably recognize me again.'

I gripped Kalem's hand. 'You won't be able to leave the house for years! You'll have to hibernate.' I pondered this. 'Or we could just move back to the UK. You know, not even live here like we planned.' This option was becoming more and more appealing to me at that very second.

My mental list of bad things about moving here was rapidly increasing:

1) Crazy extended family.
2) Involved in assassination and art heist. (Note to self: could possibly end up killed ourselves by psychopathic killers.)
3) We were now cursed by Queen Cleopatra.

I thought the bad things were seriously outweighing the good at this point.

Kalem thought about this for a while. 'No, hang on a minute. We can't take it to the police.'

'What do you mean? Why not?' I whined, struggling to digest what he was saying. I didn't want to get caught up in this. Well, I wouldn't mind keeping the money. I was only human after all, but no...I definitely didn't want to get caught up in anything that involved blowing people's brains out or stealing a priceless and annoyingly cursed sculpture. 'Of course we have to.'

'This is obviously a professional job. You don't travel with five hundred grand in your suitcase, unless you're trying to launder money.'

Well, yes, I got his point. You could hardly just pop into the bank and pay it in or transfer it electronically if you were into criminal dealings. They asked all sorts of questions these days. I could just imagine it...

Bank Manager: Where did you get this five hundred thousand dollars from, Miss Grey?

Me: Er…I sold my house.

Bank Manager: Really? You don't own a house. (Narrowing his eyes at me)

Me: Well, my friend sold her house and gave me the money.

Bank Manager: Hmm. Why did she do that?

Me: Because… (Thinking of some distraction quickly)

Bank Manager: Are you money laundering?

Me: Oh, look at that plane up there with no wings. (Pointing to sky outside the window and running away)

'If someone wants to assassinate the country's most famous businessman and steal a five million pound sculpture, then they're probably going to need a bit of help,' Kalem said. 'You don't know who's involved in it all. North Cyprus has a small population, and therefore a small police force. It's possible that a bad apple in the police force could be involved in all of this somehow. If we pick the wrong apple, we could be in trouble.'

I tried to swallow, but my throat felt like I had a porcupine lodged in it. I silently debated this. 'So, you're saying that we need to go higher up than the police?'

Kalem nodded. 'I'd prefer to go straight to the top. I think we need to go to the President, just to be on the safe side. Now we know about this, it involves our safety as well.' He leaped out of bed. 'Although I doubt if we can just barge into his office. I'll ring and try to get an appointment or something.' He reached for the phone.

Kalem was passed from one government department to another and left hanging in a telephonic abyss for what seemed like an hour. When he finally got through to the President's Office, I'd paced up and down the room at high speed enough to wear a groove in the floor.

'We've got an appointment to see the President's Secretary at two o'clock this afternoon.'

'Thank God.' I stopped pacing. 'And that will be the end of it.' I breathed a huge sigh of relief. 'We can't tell your mum and dad what's going on. I don't want to give them a heart attack or something.'

'I agree. Shall we tell the others?'

I shook my head. 'I don't want to worry Ayshe, either. She doesn't need the stress at six and a half months pregnant. We'll just act normal.'

Kalem chuckled. 'You? Act normal? That'll be the day.'

I grinned back as someone knocked on the door.

'Just a minute,' I called out as we quickly shoved the money, building plans, and note back in the case and zipped it up.

Wrapping a towel around me, I swung the door open. Ayshe, Atila, and Charlie spilled into the room. Well, Ayshe waddled.

'Er…we have a slight situation,' Charlie said.

I groaned. What else could possibly happen?

'Mum and Dad have got a virus, or it could be food poisoning,' Ayshe said to me. 'I bet it was that fish they insisted on eating last night. I told them it smelled funny.'

'Ha-ha! Very funny,' I said. 'They can't have food poisoning. Deniz is always eating out of date things, and he never gets ill. In fact, he must consume enough whisky for the entire Turkish Army, and he never even gets a hangover.'

'It's true,' Atila said.

My mouth flew open involuntarily.

'Mmm. I had swordfish once and it tasted like wee.' Charlie pulled a disgusted face.

I couldn't comment on that, never having tasted wee myself.

'I was ill for days after.' Charlie wrinkled up his nose.

Ayshe carefully positioned herself on the edge of the bed. Charlie plonked himself down next to her and crossed his legs.

A look of concern clouded Kalem's face. 'Will they be OK? Do we need to get them to the hospital or anything?'

Ayshe shook her head. 'No, they've seen the hotel doctor. He's taken some samples from them and given them some medication. He's pretty sure that it's food poisoning, but just to be on the safe side, they have to stay in their room in case it's something catching. Hopefully they should be fine in a few days.'

'Well, I don't suppose they can do much else with the projectile vomiting and squits,' Charlie added, as if he were being helpful, but now I had a really horrible image in my mind that I didn't particularly want. 'We can pass notes under their door. But I don't want either of you going to see them.' He wagged a finger at Kalem and me. 'We can't have the bride and groom out of action on the wedding day.'

'It's probably just food poisoning,' I said. 'We're not likely to catch that, are we?'

'Well I'd better not see them in case I get something that affects the baby,' Ayshe said 'Neither can Atila. We can talk to them through the door.'

'God, I hope they'll be OK by Sunday. What are we going to do without them at the wedding if they're still ill?' I asked.

'Who's the man in that picture?' Charlie noticed the picture of Ibrahim Kaya, pushed half under the bed that we'd inadvertently left out of the case.

'What man?' Ayshe leaned over to try and get a better look.

Atila picked up the picture. 'I recognize him. There was an article about him in the in-flight magazine. That's Ibrahim Kaya – the mega-rich hotel owner. Why have you got a picture of him?'

I looked at Kalem. Kalem looked at me. Damn. We would have to tell them now. I knew that if we made up some quick excuse they'd see through it in an instant.

Charlie waved the picture around. 'Well?' He noticed the look passing between us. 'Uh-oh. Helen, what have you got yourself into now?'

Oh, that's nice! Blame me! I mean, yes, I did get myself into a few incey wincey peculiar situations now and then, but come on, this wasn't exactly my fault.

We all sat in the bustling hotel restaurant, eating breakfast. As Ayshe was so skinny – even at six and a half months pregnant – I'd had a choice of wearing Kalem's clothes or Charlie's. Not much of a choice at all, really, since Kalem was so tall and Charlie's clothes were loud with a capital L.

So there we all were, with me dressed in Charlie's cerise pink trousers that hung round my waist, showing off the top of my lacy *Minx* knickers, and a cropped top with the words *I Love Men* on the front. I'd consumed about five iced coffees and nothing else. I didn't know what the standard amount of caffeine required after a shock this big was, but it was safe to say that my brain was reaching buzzing overload.

'It will be fine,' I said, with more confidence than I actually felt. 'We'll just give everything to the President's Secretary, and that will be it. Over and done with. Finito. The End.'

'Yes,' Ayshe, Atila, Charlie, and Kalem agreed in unison.

'So what do you want to do before you go there?' Ayshe asked.

I glanced down at my clothes. 'Well, I suppose I need to go shopping first. I haven't got any clothes or shoes or toiletries. I need to get a few things to tide me over until I get my suitcase back.'

Charlie clasped his hands together. 'Oh, goody. I'll come too.'

'I think I'll stay at the hotel in case Mum or Dad needs me,' Ayshe said.

'I'll stay with you.' Atila draped an arm around Ayshe's shoulder.

We walked the short distance into Kyrenia town with people staring at my rather unique attire. One woman actually had the gall to stop and point at me, agog. I desperately needed something to distract me, so I'd started trying to count the cosmopolitan and designer shops. So far, I was up to a big fat zero. The main high street was tiny with even tinier shops. I was used to popping up to Oxford Street or a huge shopping mall. This was like the opposite of a busy London shopping street times a squillion. Could I actually live here without shops? Could I be a fully functioning woman? Would I get bored?

Oh, stop it, Helen. You're being ridiculous. And materialistic. Of course you can live without shops. It's not like it's a medical necessity or anything. Maybe they are here, but you just haven't found them yet. Anyway, you've got Kalem. And your new life will be an exciting adventure. And he wants this new job so badly. You can't just let him down and say you want to leave. Can you?

We scoured the few miniscule boutiques. I bought some black flip-flops, a turquoise bikini, a couple of plain summer dresses, and some underwear – not quite as sexy as the vast array of new honeymoon ones I'd packed, but they were quite pretty. Charlie bought a pink kilt.

Since we were in town, I decided to window shop in a couple of wedding dress shops. I had to try and be practical, and it was good to be prepared, wasn't it? What if I didn't get my dress back? It was unbearable and unthinkable, and I'd be doomed to bad luck if I couldn't get married with Nan's lucky charm. But I had a horrible, niggling feeling in the back of my mind that Ferret Face wouldn't be giving my suitcase back any time soon.

The first wedding shop we went in was home to a vast array of flouncy meringue dresses, which was great if you liked that sort of thing. I wanted something more sleek and sexy. They were big puffy things that would make me look like I was wearing a giant French Fancy cake. It was the same in the next. And the next. And the next. Uh-oh.

'Don't worry.' Kalem wrapped his arms around me. 'You'll definitely get your suitcase back. Probably today. And even if you don't, we've still got time to find another wedding dress.'

I scowled at the nearby French Fancy shop and nestled into him, having a hard time trying to stop the tears pricking behind my eyelids.

'Group hug.' Charlie launched himself around both of us. 'This heat is making me thirsty. Let's get a drink.'

We wandered down through some old cobbled streets and ended up above a horseshoe shaped harbour, lined with a mixture of historic buildings and chic pavement cafes and restaurants. People ambled along, tourists and Cypriots alike, as if they had no place in particular to go, and were in no rush to get there anyway.

'This is fantastic!' I lifted up my sunglasses to get a better look, taking in an ancient castle to the right and the flotillas, fishing boats, and luxury yachts in front, bobbing on the surface of the deep blue sea.

Kalem pointed at the castle. 'That's Kyrenia Castle, another of the Crusader Castles in Cyprus. I'll take you around there when we have more time.'

I peered at it. 'It looks very gothic.'

'Inside they've got a Shipwreck Museum with the oldest shipwreck in the world in it,' Kalem said.

'What, the oldest shipwreck in a museum, or the oldest shipwreck in the sea?' I asked, fascinated.

Kalem smiled. 'It's one of the most remarkable marine finds in the world. It was a cargo ship, probably coming from one of the Greek islands, laden with large amphoras of wine. They discovered around four hundred amphoras still inside it.'

'Amazing. What's an amphora?' I asked.

'They are a type of ceramic vase with two handles that were used in ancient times to store liquids,' Kalem said.

'Was there still any wine left inside?' Charlie asked. 'Probably a bit off by now, though.'

Well, this was certainly cosmopolitan. A perfect blend of old and new. The historic hulk of a castle framed the surrounding trendy bars and renovated harbour-side buildings. With the backdrop of mountains and the calm sea in front, it was, in fact, the prettiest harbour I'd ever seen.

We lounged in some comfy chairs in one of the cafes, sipping iced coffee, as I surveyed my surroundings.

Apart from being quaint, another thing I noticed was the lack of commercial worldwide franchises. No McDonalds or Burger Kings here. No Debenhams or John Lewis. And it was weird, but no one was rushing about. In the UK, everyone was always in a rush. Rush to work, rush home from work, rush to the gym, rush to the supermarket. Everyone worked so hard to pay the bills that life became one long stressful race to get things done. But here, it was like time had stopped. Tourists people-watched and chatted with waiters; old Cypriot men drank Turkish coffee and played backgammon, arguing over the finer points of the game or politics, as if they didn't have a care in the world. The place had a whole vibe of relaxation about it that felt strangely hypnotizing.

I quickly added that to my list of things to like.

Chapter 5

Heat invaded every pore as we arrived at the President's Office in the capital, Nicosia.

My heart danced to an irregular beat in my chest. I wiped my moist hands on my new dress.

Everything will be OK. Everything will be OK, I repeated. That was going to be my new mantra of the day. And I had to believe it, because otherwise...well, otherwise the possibilities were just too scary.

At the entrance to the white Seventies style building, there were security checks. We showed our passports and were asked to put the suitcase through an X-ray machine. Since we'd replaced the carbon sheet of paper over the money, I expected that they wouldn't be able to detect anything, other than some very unsexy swimwear.

Even so, I still held my breath as we both watched, fascinated, when they didn't bat an eyelid at the X-ray image. After that, we were escorted upstairs to a large office.

As offices go, it was pretty functional with the usual officey type of equipment. A large, official picture of the President hung on one wall, like an eerie presence, surveying his kingdom. I wondered briefly if some surveillance security officers were hiding behind it, staring out at us, like one of the two-way mirrors they have at police stations. Maybe it was a two-way President. Freaky.

A smartly dressed woman in her early thirties sat behind the desk directly in front of us, filing her nails. She didn't bother to look up when we entered.

Miss Nail File's mobile phone rang as we approached the desk. With a quick flick of her hand, she picked up the phone, nestling it in the crook of her neck, and carried on filing in the manner of someone who's performed this task a million times before.

We stood there waiting: me, hopping from one foot to the other, and Kalem, looking equally nervous, unsure what the usual etiquette was. I mean, it wasn't like I popped into a president's office every day. Did you bow? Courtesy? Do some kind of ritualistic hand shake

Even though the air conditioning streamed out full blast, sweat pricked the hairline at the base of my neck.

She gabbled down the phone in Turkish.

I coughed loudly, trying to catch her attention.

Kalem glared at me.

Miss Nail File gave me an impatient look and held her finger up for silence. Then she went back to her phone call and started giggling girlishly.

Oh, for God's sake. Stop bloody arranging a night out with your boyfriend and let's get down to business so I can get on with my wedding!

I tapped my foot as we waited for her to finish. I thought about grabbing her phone, throwing it on the floor and jumping up and down on it, but I didn't think that would go down too well. It might have made me feel slightly better, though.

Finally, she put the phone and nail file down. 'Yes?' she asked in a bored voice.

Before she could be distracted by anymore telephonic interruptions, I blurted out, 'We're here to see–'

She cut me off. 'Sorry, the President is *very* busy at the moment. Running the country and things like that,' she said in a tone that implied we were complete idiots. 'You need to make an appointment with his Secretary.

'We already did.' My voice jumped a couple of octaves in panic.

She gave me a disbelieving look.

Kalem gave her one of his best heart-stopping smiles. 'Can you check the appointment book, please? I only made it this morning.'

The smile didn't seem to work on her, though. She made a big show of pulling out an appointment book from her desk draw and flicking through it with a pointy red talon at a pace that even a snail would have been proud of.

She tapped the book. 'No, sorry. There isn't any appointment listed.'

'But I only made it this morning,' Kalem insisted.

Oh, God. Oh, Goddy God. We had to see him. I felt like screaming at her. Instead, I ran a shaky hand through my hair.

She gave us a tight smile. 'Well, that's the problem, you see.

I'm just filling in for a colleague who's off sick today, so it's a bit disorganized at the moment.'

Disorganized? How about you stop filing your nails and get organized.

'I can make another appointment for you. How about...' Pointy talon out again, she flicked a few pages in the diary. Pause. More flicking. 'The twenty-fifth of November?'

'But today's the first of June!' I wailed. 'We need to see him urgently. It's a matter of life and death!'

She tilted her head slightly. 'Life and death?'

Quick! I had her attention now. I went for the kill before she slid back into bored, zombie nail-filing mode.

'Yes, life and death. We have to see him or the President immediately. Otherwise I'll...I'll,' well, I didn't know what I'd do, but I was sure I'd so something. *Think! Think!* 'I'll...I'll run around the building naked!' I said with an angry gleam in my eye. 'That will get his attention, surely. And if not, I'm sure the press would love it.'

She looked me up and down. I didn't know which she was more worried about, the threat of the press turning up and catching her filing, or the sight of me naked, but it seemed to have the desired effect anyway.

She picked up the phone on her desk and whispered into it.

'Have a seat.' She pointed at a dark green leather sofa, situated opposite the two-way President.

Great. Now the secret security police would have a chance to study us in all our full frontal glory.

I sat down and smiled at the President. Nothing happened. No one came rushing out from behind it. I gave him a small wave. He didn't wave back.

Kalem pulled my hand down and shot me a what-the-hell-are-you-doing? look.

I was just reaching the point of nervous, bubbly bowels when a door flew open behind Miss Nail File and a man walked in. He locked eyes with Kalem. Kalem locked eyes with him. And I almost threw up on the spot.

The man who now stood in front of us, decked out in an Armani suite and smelling of expensive aftershave, was Erol Hussein, someone who Kalem and I had gone to school with in the UK. Someone who hated Kalem's guts with a vengeance.

Uh-oh. Just when I thought things couldn't get any worse.

'Well, well, well. Kalem Mustafa. What brings you here? To the President's office, of all places?' Erol inclined his head and raised a slight, amused smile. Then he turned to me. Same smile, same arrogant tone. 'Helen Grey, isn't it? I must say that you've changed a lot from the chubby, freckly tomboy at school.'

Well, I hoped he'd changed a lot too. He was the school bully. Someone who'd do anything to get what he wanted. He was manipulative, cold, and determined. He had hooded dark eyes that were creepy in an axe murderer kind of way, and slicked-back black hair that was creepy in a Dracula kind of way.

I racked my brain, trying to remember if I'd heard what happened to him after he'd left school. There was some kind of rumour...what was it? No, my brain wouldn't work. I was too shocked. I was going into shock overload. Oh, wait a minute...something about him being the owner of a successful security business in the UK. Yes, it was coming back to me now. He'd had a business partner, but the contract they drew up between them in the early days was a bit vague. Then Erol sold it from under his partner's nose and didn't split the money. As Erol was Turkish Cypriot, he'd then disappeared to North Cyprus before any official enquiries could take place. And now he was here. In the President's Office. And I was definitely going to faint. A whooshing noise pounded in my ears. Things started swimming in and out of focus.

Erol folded his arms, waiting for an answer.

I steadied myself on the edge of Miss Nail File's desk, blinking to clear my eyesight.

'We need to speak to you about something of national security.' Thankfully, Kalem took over.

'Well, come into my office,' Erol said.

I closed by gaping mouth sharpish. I think I might've been dribbling a bit as well, so I surreptitiously wiped the corner of my lips as I followed Kalem into the elegant room.

'Tea or coffee?' he asked after we all sat down.

At least he was being polite. Maybe he'd turned over a new leaf. Yes, that was it. Everything would be fine. Perfectly fine.

'Just water for me, please,' I croaked.

'No, thanks,' Kalem said.

Erol pressed an intercom on his desk and ordered a glass of

water, then lounged back in his leather chair, steepling his fingers. 'So, a matter of national security? That certainly sounds intriguing. Well, in my role as Secretary for the President, I also deal with all security matters so you've come to the right place.' He eyed the suitcase that Kalem set down on the floor. 'You're not planning on moving in, are you?' He chuckled at his own joke. Kalem and I didn't share his amusement, so he carried on. 'But what could you possibly know about national security?'

'We've discovered a plot to assassinate Ibrahim Kaya and steal his Queen Cleopatra sculpture at the opening night of the Plaza hotel,' I reeled off in a garbled rush.

Erol cut his eyes from Kalem to me. He stayed silent for a while, and then: 'Really?' He examined me like I'd suddenly sprouted two heads. 'Funny, you always were a drama queen at school, weren't you? A plot, you say. Sounds very far-fetched.'

'Yes, a plot to steal the sculpture and murder Ibrahim Kaya,' Kalem repeated it in a more forceful voice so it might sink in. I could tell he was getting a bit annoyed now. Hell, so was I.

Erol threw his head back and laughed. Well, it was more like a cackle, actually. 'OK, let me just humour this ridiculous suggestion for a moment.' He waved a dismissive hand like he was swatting a fly. 'I've personally been in charge of all the security arrangements for the opening night. There is absolutely no possibility whatsoever that what you are trying to suggest can happen. For a start, the sculpture will be displayed in a reinforced glass case. The outside of the glass case will be covered in a shell of censored laser beams, unseen to the naked eye. If even one ray is breached by someone trying to tamper with the casing, an alarm will sound, triggering an impenetrable steel case to enclose the sculpture. But there will be no opportunity to tamper with it, anyway, because it will be surrounded by four armed and highly trained guards. 'No. There is no way it can happen. No one can access the electronic security system that controls the case except Ibrahim Kaya and myself.'

'What about the assassination?' Kalem asked.

Erol glared back at him. 'Why would anyone want to assassinate Ibrahim Kaya? He is a respected businessman who employs millions of people and gives to numerous charities.'

'But there were rumours about him being involved in the

underworld. Maybe he's upset a few people?' Kalem suggested.

'There are rumours about all sorts of people,' Erol said. 'There were rumours about me, if you remember.'

Yes, but personally, I could believe the rumours about Erol.

'And look where I am today.' Erol smiled, but it didn't quite reach his eyes. 'Anyway, Kaya will have his own personal security guards nearby. He is very security conscious. He will not make himself any kind of target.'

I sat forward in my chair. 'But what about the safety of the other people there? What about all the guests?'

'The opening night will be full of international celebrities, politicians, and high-rollers, most of whom will probably have their own personal bodyguards. You would be a fool, Helen, if you thought any of them could be targeted.'

Miss Nail File entered the room with a glass of water. She practically threw it at me as she rushed to get back out. Probably more urgent filing to attend to.

Erol sat upright and began shuffling papers on his desk. 'Now, if you'll excuse me, I have very important work to do.'

'Wait! We have evidence.' I unzipped the suitcase and handed Erol the photo of Ibrahim Kaya, the building plans of the Plaza, the scribbled notes about the art dealer, and the itinerary. 'When we arrived at the airport last night, there was a mix-up with my suitcase. I accidentally picked up this suitcase, and the owner of this case picked up mine. We've found some disturbing things inside.'

Erol snatched them from me, studied each item briefly, then discarded them on his desk. 'This probably belongs to one of the many journalists who will be arriving here for the press coverage. Mere background information for their story,' he scoffed, like we should really know better.

'But there are details about the sculpture on there and directions to an art dealer over the border in South Cyprus. Why would a journalist need those?' I asked.

Erol shrugged. 'Maybe they're getting some further background information on the statue. Research into its value and so forth. Nothing seems amiss to me.' He tapped the side of his head and looked at me. 'I think it's that overactive imagination of yours running wild again.'

And then a thought struck me. Had Kalem and I jumped to

some irrational conclusion about the suitcase, when really it was just a simple matter of background information gathered by a journalist? Had we been overreacting?

'There's something else in the suitcase as well that you should know about.' Kalem's voice interrupted my doubtful thoughts, pulling out the shoulder pad and balaclava and putting them on Erol's desk.

Erol picked up the shoulder pad, turning it over in his hand. Then he turned his attention to the balaclava. 'A money belt and a balaclava? Hardly evidence of an assassination.'

'It's not a money belt. It's a shoulder pad. For a gun,' I said, sipping the icy water that burned my parched throat.

No, when you put it all together, our conclusion didn't seem irrational at all. When you considered all the evidence, the only conclusion could be the one we'd come up with. So why couldn't Erol see it as well?

Erol shrugged. 'It will be hunting season in North Cyprus in a few months. Some people prefer using a shoulder pad for comfort when they're hunting.'

'But what about the balaclava? Surely, this all seems suspicious to you?' Kalem insisted.

'Not really. Hunters sometimes use balaclavas as well.'

'Yes, but–' I started, feeling my back stiffen.

Erol's hand shot up, silencing me. 'Enough! I don't want to hear any more about ridiculous death threats and robberies. The matter is under complete control.' He paused and did the steepling thing with his fingers again, which was getting a bit annoying. 'Actually, I'm more interested in what you two are doing in North Cyprus.' Erol glanced between the two of us. 'The last thing I heard, you were teaching some peculiar art subject,' he shot narrow eyes to Kalem, 'and you were the tea lady in a photo shop.' He turned his attention to me.

I took a deep breath. Right, he was really pissing me off now. Mr. Bloody High-and-Mighty President's Secretary, who was a complete arsehole at school – and a nasty arsehole to boot – and still seemed to be a complete arsehole. This was my wedding day we were talking about. I had to get this mess sorted out before I got married on Sunday so I could get my lucky wedding dress back. And if I didn't get it sorted out, and a crime really did happen, then it would all be my fault for not trying my hardest to warn people.

And they had to find Ferret Face and catch him. What if he was still roaming the streets looking for us? Knowing that we knew that he knew that we knew that he knew? Regardless of the mental for and against lists I was building about whether moving here was the right thing to do, how could we even think about staying here to start a new life in paradise if Ferret Face was out there? Watching. Planning an ambush on us. Waiting to do ferrety things.

'*Actually*, I'm a wedding photographer. And Kalem's a very sought-after sculpture and woodcarving teacher. In fact, his own works of art have been exhibited in many national exhibitions.' OK, that last bit was a little white lie, but he wasn't to know that. I gave Kalem a beaming smile. Kalem gave me a small shake of his head, as if to tell me to shut up. '*And*, I might add, he's now been head-hunted by a university here in North Cyprus to teach and found a new research department on historical sculpture.' I sat back in the chair with a smug smile on my face. *Take that, Mr. High and Mighty!*

Erol tapped his forefinger on the desk. 'Interesting. Which university?'

'The Cyprus University of Architecture and Ancient Art,' Kalem said.

'Sounds a bit of a prestigious position for a sculpture and woodcarving teacher,' Erol said.

'Well, my specialist subjects are actually rare and ancient artworks and sculptures. But there's not much call for that in the UK.'

Erol considered this for a while. 'Well, enough of this nonsense.'

'There's something else in the case, as well, that you should be aware about,' Kalem said.

Erol sighed impatiently. 'Really? And what's that? Suntan lotion? Sunglasses? Speedos?' He raised his hands in mock horror. 'A plot to enjoy a holiday!' He shook his head.

Ooh. I was this close to boiling point now. 'Right.' I dumped all the clothes on the floor and opened the false bottom of the case. Removing the carbon paper, I pointed to the wads of hundred dollar notes underneath. 'What about this, then? You don't think this is in the least bit suspicious?'

That got his attention rather quickly.

Erol's eyes nearly pinged out of his head. He stood up, walked around the desk and waste paper bin next to it, and bent down in front of the case. He stared at the money, then picked up a bundle and sniffed it. He examined it carefully. Then another one. Then another.

'There's half a million dollars inside,' Kalem said.

'Well, this puts a slightly different slant on things,' Erol said, unable to take his eyes off the money.

'So we can leave it all with you, and you'll investigate it?' I asked hopefully.

'Hmm?' Erol sniffed another bundle, seemingly oblivious to our presence.

'You'll investigate it? The plot to steal the sculpture and kill Ibrahim Kaya,' Kalem said, slightly louder.

'Yes. Yes of course I'll investigate it.' Erol slammed the lid of the case shut and zipped it up. 'Leave everything to me.' He walked back around to his side of the desk and sat down. 'You don't have to worry about a thing.'

'Well, there was actually something else. You see, we're getting married on Sunday, and my wedding dress was in the suitcase that this other man picked up. I need to get my dress back. When you investigate, can you make sure you get my wedding dress back? It's very important.'

'Of course! Of course. No problem at all,' he said, suddenly all helpful and polite. 'Where are you staying?'

'At the Ottoman Hotel,' Kalem said.

Erol stood up and nodded towards the door, indicating we were dismissed. 'Don't worry about a thing. I'll look into everything straight away.'

'Great.' I stood up too. 'Thanks very much.'

As Kalem and I strode towards the door, I sneaked a glance over my shoulder just before I pulled it closed behind me and saw Erol depositing the building plans, itinerary, photo, and note into the waste paper bin.

'What are we going to do now?' I flopped down onto a bench outside the building. 'If it was someone else, maybe they might've listened to us.' I leaped from the bench and paced up and down. 'Erol bloody Hussein, of all people. He's thrown all the evidence in the bin. Well, all the evidence apart from the money. He's not even going to bother investigating this, is he? I should've known he couldn't change.'

'Arrogant bastard. I don't understand why he's still carrying on this grudge thing he's got against me.' It was Kalem's turn to start pacing now.

'It's been going on for years,' I said. 'He should have grown out of it by now. We're not exactly kids in the playground anymore, are we?'

'It goes back further than that. His dad and my dad did their military service together when they were about sixteen, and they were best friends. I don't know what happened; Dad would never talk about it, but he had some kind of fall out with Erol's dad. I guess that's when it all began. And Erol has just carried on some kind of grudge because of it.'

'So what are we going to do?' I glanced up at the building behind, suddenly having a creepy feeling that Erol was watching us from his office window.

Maybe he'd even bugged us somehow. Since I wasn't exactly experienced in murder and art theft, I didn't know how these things worked. Maybe Miss Nail File had put a bug in my water, and it was floating around in my stomach. Although I suspected the only thing they'd be hearing at the moment was a nervous, churning sound.

'You're right,' Kalem said. 'If he's thrown everything in the bin, he's not going to bother to investigate things. I know what he's like. I bet he'll just keep the money instead.' He ran a hand over his closely cropped hair.

'Come on. I don't want to sit here.' I grabbed Kalem's arm and pulled him towards the car. 'I think we've got no choice but to go to the police and report it to them after all. We'll just tell them we've handed all the evidence over to Erol. Then we can get on with our lives. They can't just ignore us as well if we're reporting a crime, can they?'

Yes, that was it. The police would investigate. They'd find Ferret Face and stop any crime happening. Then they'd find my wedding dress, and I could concentrate on enjoying the rest of my new life here. Simple.

An oppressive weight suddenly lifted from my shoulders as Kalem started the engine.

Five traffic lights, four roundabouts, and another dual-carriage way later – a good sign for cosmopolitan, modern countryishness; would add to list – we pulled up outside the police station.

I was out of the car and almost at the entrance before Kalem even locked it. I wanted to get this horrible task over with as soon as possible.

'Wait,' Kalem called to me as I stepped into the entrance. 'I left my mobile phone in the Land Rover. I'll just grab it in case someone needs to get hold of us.' He walked back towards the vehicle.

But I couldn't wait. I was just about to walk up to the front desk on my right, staffed by two middle-aged policemen drinking Turkish coffee, when something down a hallway in the distance caught my eye.

No. It couldn't be. Was it? I squinted, trying to get a better look. Yes! It was!

My eyelids flipped wide open, and I stood, rooted to the spot like someone had just used industrial strength Superglue on my feet.

The air was hot, but I felt icy cold.

It was him – Ferret Face – in the distance, having a very cosy chat with a tall policeman wearing glasses. Actually, judging by the amount of gold stars on his epaulettes and shirt sleeves, it looked like he was a pretty high-up policeman.

I watched as they leaned in close to each other, murmuring something. Ferret Face had an intense look of concentration on his face. He nodded a few times, whispered something back, then did a furtive glance around the hall to see if anyone was nearby. That's when he caught my eye.

Agh! Quick! Move!

My heart danced around in my chest. *Act normal! Act normal!*

I waved at the policeman behind the front desk, as if I knew him. 'Goodbye, thanks for your help,' I said to the policeman, who gave me a peculiar look.

Then I managed to place one foot in front of the other, ambling calmly out of the station like I didn't have a care in the world. Like I hadn't just stared evil in the face.

I nearly bumped into Kalem coming in the door. 'Quick! We've got to go,' I hissed at him.

'What? Why? We just got here.'

'Quick! Ferret Face is in there.' I yanked his arm in the direction of the car before Ferret Face spotted Kalem.

Chapter 6

'I need a coffee – no, I need something stronger. A glass of wine. Or even a bottle. Maybe five bottles,' I said to Kalem when we arrived back at our hotel room.

I shrugged off my handbag and stepped onto the balcony, staring out into the endless deep blue Mediterranean. It was completely still, resembling a sheet of navy coloured ice, and looked so inviting. So pure and natural and uncomplicated. All I wanted to do was dive in and swim away to anywhere but here. It was about forty miles from here to the tip of Turkey. How long would it take me to swim there and disappear, far out of reach from Ferret Face? Would my arms fall off from too much front crawl, or would I get eaten by sharks and end up as fish food?

'I'll order some room service.' Kalem's voice dragged me out of my escapist thoughts and brought me charging back to reality.

'I need a cigar as well.'

'You don't smoke!'

'Well, occasionally I do, when I'm really stressed.' I gave him a sheepish look. 'And I know it's weird, but I'm feeling REALLY FUCKING STRESSED! Oh, God. I'm sorry. Didn't mean to shout, but it feels like our whole world is falling apart.'

'O...K. I see your point. I'll order some.' Kalem managed a grim smile and ordered the supplies.

I stared out to sea, contemplating the disastrous couple of days so far. What the hell were we going to do now? How were we supposed to save the sculpture, Ibrahim Kaya, *and* have the perfect wedding and live happily ever after? At the moment, it didn't seem possible.

A chill of fear clutched at my heart. How could we ever survive this?

Someone knocked at the door with a loud bang.

I jumped. My heartbeat clanged around like an orchestra. I was definitely going to have a heart attack at this rate.

'Only me!' Charlie barged in as Kalem opened the door. 'How did it go?' He sat next to me. 'I want to hear all about it. Ayshe and Atila are on their way.' After observing my pained look,

Charlie gave my hand a quick squeeze.

Ayshe and Atila arrived at the same time as the room service.

'Hi, everyone.' Ayshe rushed over to me. 'Well, what happened? What did they say?'

'Here you go.' Kalem kissed the top of my head and handed me a glass of red wine, then proceeded to pile up a plate of chicken shish kebab, salad, and moist bulgur wheat with tomatoes, fresh chillies, and olive oil in it.

I downed the wine in one go as the others looked on expectantly.

Charlie eyed my now empty glass. 'That bad?'

'Worse.' I slowly filled them in on the day's events as I picked at my food.

'I know why Dad and Erol Hussein's dad don't get on any more,' Ayshe said.

'Why?' Charlie's ears pricked up at the whiff of a bit of gossip.

'Erol's dad was in love with Mum,' Ayshe said. 'They all used to hang around together when they were younger. Apparently, he never got over it when Mum fell in love with Dad instead of him. That's why they fell out.'

'Ooh! So your mum was a sought after woman.' Charlie's eyes widened with excitement.

'Look, guys, I think we need some kind of a plan,' I said, trying to steer them back to the problem at hand.

'I'd say that was an understatement,' Atila said.

I pushed away my half-eaten plate, willing my brain to go into overdrive plan-thinking mode. I wasn't very good at planning. I'd tried to plan the perfect wedding and look what had happened so far.

Kalem stared out to sea, a pensive look clouding his gorgeous face.

Ayshe rubbed her stomach distractedly.

I gave a defeated shrug. 'Well, if someone in the police is involved and Erol Bloody Hussein doesn't want to know. What else can we do?' I asked to no one in particular. 'Storm the President's office and demand to see the big man himself?'

Kalem shook his head. 'We'd just get arrested.'

'Take out a newspaper ad?' I said.

'They probably wouldn't even print it,' Ayshe said. 'They'd

think you were a nutcase.'

'She is a nutcase,' Charlie said. 'But in a nice way,' he added with a grin.

'Well, what then?' I got up to fill my glass, weaving around everybody. 'Anyone else want one?' I wiggled my glass in the air.

Everyone agreed except Ayshe.

I filled a couple of glasses that were left over from the champagne the night before, and just after I'd refilled mine, I noticed a newspaper on the room service trolley, sandwiched in between the empty plates. The headline read: *President to Open Apricot Festival.*

I grabbed the paper and read it, my eyes devouring the information with heightened interest. The article mentioned various apricot facts – they've been around for four thousand years; astronauts ate them on the Apollo moon mission; they're related to peaches – and ended with details of the annual three-day festival to celebrate the abundant Cypriot fruit.

'Hey,' I cried out to the others. 'The President is opening the annual apricot festival tomorrow night at six. Why don't we try and talk to him there?'

'What's an apricot festival?' Charlie shrieked. 'Is it anything like the Gay Pride festivals but people have to be smeared in soggy apricots?' His eyes lit up at the thought of that. 'Kinky!'

'They have lots of festivals here – apricots, olives, sheep. It's just a celebration, really,' Ayshe explained.

'There will be stalls selling local produce and wares, traditional dancing and singing, little restaurants set up – that kind of thing,' Kalem added.

'Oh, so not quite Gay Pride then.' Charlie looked a tad disappointed. 'Still, I think it's a fab idea trying to speak to him there. What have you got to lose?'

'I don't know if we can get close enough to have a conversation with him. But I suppose it's worth a try,' Kalem said.

Ayshe nodded. 'I agree. It sounds like a good plan.'

'I can't think of anything else you can do,' Atila said.

'Right. So we can't do anything until tomorrow evening. It's only five days until the wedding, and I'm not confident that I'm ever going to get my wedding dress back in time at this rate. I still need to look for a replacement one, just in case. And that means I need to get back out there and go shopping.'

'No,' Charlie said. 'I'm the wedding planner. Leave it to me. I'll go out and do some research. I know the kind of things you like. If I find any possible dresses, I'll let you know, and you can come and have a look. You need to try and relax before the big day.' He smiled at me. 'Capiche or not capiche?'

I managed to raise a slight smile. 'Capiche.'

'Anything else you need me to do?' Charlie asked.

'Have you managed to find a CD with *Love Me Tender* on it yet?' I said.

Charlie nodded. 'Yes. Well, it's not actually a CD. It's on tape.'

'Tape?' Atila looked shocked. 'Do people actually still use tapes?'

'I was talking to the really helpful lady on reception, and she said she's got a copy of some of Elvis's greatest hits on tape and *Love Me Tender* is on there. So, no need to panic anymore. Anything else you want me to do?'

'No, thanks,' I said.

'Right. In that case, I'll scoot off and get started on the wedding dresses. No French Fancies and no meringues.' Charlie ticked off the list on his finger. 'Check.'

'Do you want to relax by the pool or go and look at Mum and Dad's house?' Kalem asked.

Hmm. Difficult question. On the one hand, I wanted to laze around, drinking cocktails in the swim-up bar, pretending that I was having a normal, pampering pre-wedding couple of days. On the other hand, I was excited to see the house that we'd be living in after the wedding until we found our own place. Yasmin had actually been born in the house, so it had been in her family a long time, although in recent years they hadn't used it much as a holiday home.

'Ayshe and I haven't actually been out to stay there since we were about ten,' Kalem said. 'And the last time Mum and Dad stayed there was a couple of years ago. So it might need quite a bit of cleaning and tidying up.'

I suspected it would need more than a bit after all that time of being uninhabited. 'Maybe it would be a good idea to see the house – ooh! And I want to go and have a look at Bellapais

Abbey as well. It looks a fantastic wedding venue from the pictures, but I want to make sure it's as nice in real life. And let's do some exploring. I want to check out the amenities here.'

'You mean more shops?' Kalem shot me a knowing look.

'Well...not just the shops. What about supermarkets? I need to know where to get food. Food is important, isn't it?'

'We don't need supermarkets. We'll be living off the land. We can plant lots of fruit trees to sustain us. We could even have a couple of chickens and stuff.' Kalem's eyes lit up at the thought of getting back to nature.

I had a vision of *The Good Life* again. Me in wellies, with one arm up a cow's backside – like I'd recently watched on a vet documentary – and not a spikey-heeled boot in sight. Yuck. Horrible thought. 'Er...maybe we should check them out anyway. I mean, do they have a *Finest Range* here? And what about custard creams? I need to know where to find them if I'm going to survive.'

'OK, let's explore and check out the local custard cream spots.' Kalem gave me an amused smile.

'Atila and I had better stay here in case Mum and Dad need anything, or they take a turn for the worse,' Ayshe said.

'OK, we'll just go and say hi to them and find out how they're doing before we go.' Kalem pushed the food trolley into the hallway.

I grabbed my handbag and herded Atila and Ayshe out.

A red *Do not disturb* sign hung on the outside of Deniz and Yasmin's door, and a note had been left on the floor in front.

Ayshe picked it up. 'This is Dad's handwriting. It's addressed to the maid.' She read through it, her eyebrows furrowing.

'What does it say?' I said. 'Are they asking for a doctor or something?'.

'It says, "Dear Maid, I am experiencing a problem with the mini-bar selection. You have placed mild curry flavour condoms in there, and I really wanted spicy flavour. I will use the mild flavour condoms under duress, but can you please supply ten spicy flavour packets. If you have no spicy flavour, do you have any cheese and pickle? Thank you."' Ayshe glanced up at us, her own look of horror mirroring ours. 'What the hell are they up to in there? They're supposed to be ill.'

Kalem pulled a lemon-sucking face and banged on the door. 'I don't know. But *I'm* not asking them.'

'Me neither,' Atila said. 'Gross.'

'I'll just stay out here in case it's catching.' Ayshe hovered outside the door.

'Dad? Mum? How are you?' Kalem banged on the door.

'Hang on a minute,' Deniz's voice said from the other side.

I heard a shuffling sound, and Deniz swung the door open, wearing a dressing gown. He looked rough. His normally olive skin had turned clammy and pasty.

'How are you feeling?' I asked.

Deniz wandered back inside the room and climbed into bed. 'Well, I've had eight bowel movements and three projectile vomits today.'

Ew, too much information, thanks.

'Where's Mum?' Ayshe asked from outside the door.

'In the loo. Again. The good news, I suppose, is that the doctor has confirmed that it's food poisoning and not something catching. So you can all come in if you want,' Deniz shouted.

'Oh, OK.' I took small steps inside as Kalem, Ayshe, and Atila followed, hovering at the bottom of the beds.

'I'll kill whoever gave me that fish. Unless I die first.' Deniz sank his head back on the pillow. 'And if the fish doesn't finish me off, I'm going to die of boredom, stuck in here. Have you got any girly magazines?'

I was swallowing at the time, and I nearly choked. Let's just say that Deniz had always been unconventional and very un-PC. I didn't think he could actually say anything that shocked me anymore, but that did. 'Erm...girly magazines?'

Kalem shook his head to himself.

'Dad, I think you're getting a bit old for that!' Ayshe reprimanded him. 'And anyway, you should be taking it easy if you've got food poisoning.'

'I *am* taking it easy, but I'm bored. I've been stuck in here, and all I've had to read are your mother's girly magazines, but I've finished those now. They're actually quite enlightening.' He raised an eyebrow. 'I'm discovering lots of interesting things in these magazines that I never knew before. So, come on, then, have you got any? What are they called? Neopolitan? Mary Cary?'

And then the penny dropped. 'Oh, you mean *Cosmopolitan*

and *Marie Claire?*'

'Yes.' He held up a finger in acknowledgement. 'Any of those. I need something to stop the boredom and get my mind off toilets.'

'I've got an *OK! Magazine* you can have,' I said.

'I've got *Cosmo*, and Charlie's got a couple of women's mags you can have,' Ayshe said.

'Have you got any condoms?' Deniz asked us. 'I've run out.'

Kalem put his hands over his ears so he wouldn't have to listen.

'Do you think it's wise, you know...doing...when you're ill?' Atila said, looking simultaneously horrified and uncomfortable.

Yasmin emerged from the bathroom. Her hair was sticking out in all directions, as if she'd been tossing and turning all night, and her cheeks had a bit of a greenish tinge.

'How are you feeling, Mum?' Ayshe asked.

She climbed into bed. 'Your father is annoying me.' Yasmin sighed, sounding tired. 'And I don't even have the energy to slap him.'

Deniz pulled an over-innocent face. 'What? All I said was could I have an intravenous drip of whisky to help me recover. What's wrong with that?'

Kalem and I drove out of Kyrenia (single carriageway road) passing lots of five-star hotels, shops, and villas along the main road. There was a mixture of traditional Cypriot styled flat-roofed houses and sparkly new whitewashed villas with pools. No large superstore supermarkets so far, but plenty of individual little butchers, furniture shops, off-licences, petrol stations, roadside stalls selling colourful and ripe-looking fruit and veg, and odd assorted little shops. I particularly liked the off-licences. It meant I could buy lots of wine. God, did I need it at the moment.

Nestled up in the mountains, about four miles out of town, lay the quaint village of Bellapais. The Land Rover climbed a hill with some ginormous luxury villas set in acres of abundant gardens on either side.

I let out a slow whistle.

'This is the new part of Bellapais. It's supposed to be the Beverly Hills of North Cyprus,' Kalem said.

'Beverlypais. Ooh, I like that.' Well, this looked pretty chic and cosmopolitan to me. Maybe I could handle this simple life after all.

We rounded a corner and were granted spectacular views of the old colonial style village to our left. The Abbey, surrounded by palm and fir trees, rose up from its mountain ledge like some kind of gothic apparition.

We followed the narrow, winding road into the village until it forked. To the left, I could see the village square and the amazingly well-preserved ruins of the Abbey in all its splendour. The right led to some even narrower streets that didn't even look big enough to fit a car through. It looked like the village that time had forgotten. In front of the fork was an ancient-looking mulberry tree and some lovely open-air bistros.

'That's the famous Tree of Idleness.' Kalem pointed at the mulberry tree as we drove towards the car park. 'Ancient folklore says that if you sit under the tree you'll become lazy and won't want to work anymore. The folklore goes on to say that because of the tree, the villagers of Bellapais live for so long that even the gravedigger was put out of a job.'

I got out of the car, surveying the scenery.

Oh, my God! I thought I was going to faint. I couldn't believe how amazing it was. Charlie was right.

The magical twelfth century abbey, with its masterpiece in architecture and panoramic views over the glistening Mediterranean, was saturated with a sense of peace and tranquillity so powerful I could almost taste it. Nestled in between lush velvety grass, fragrant jasmine and greenery, it was the perfect place for a wedding.

'Close your mouth.' Kalem grinned at me.

I finally regained working control of my jaw. 'It's fantastic!' I wrapped my arms around his waist and gazed at the views. 'Why haven't you brought me here before?' I rested my head on his chest.

'Because we only arrived yesterday, and we've been a bit busy trying to sort out suitcases and crooks.'

'No. I mean before that.'

'Because we've only officially been a couple for the last six months?'

'Well, yes, but that's just a technicality.'

'Mum and Dad asked you loads of times if you'd come on summer holidays here with us when you were little, but you never wanted to.'

'OK, another technicality.'

He slipped his hand in mine. 'Come on. Let's get a ticket for the Abbey.'

After touring the arched corridors, refectory, common rooms, and chapter house of the Abbey, I left with a sense of serenity like nothing I'd ever experienced before. We headed back past Beverlypais and carried on along the main road, heading towards Deniz and Yasmin's house.

'There!' I pointed to a tiny supermarket that looked like it wouldn't even cover a tenth of the floor space in our old supermarket back home. 'Let's see what kind of supplies they've got.'

We parked up in the minuscule car park, and I approached the supermarket like a secret shopper from a consumer magazine, making mental notes in my head...

North Cyprus Supermarket:

Car park for about twenty cars.

Fresh and organic fruit and veg. Appearance: Lovely looking, ripe, colourful, natural. Some specimens are a bit odd shaped – a potato shaped like a heart (how cute), giant tomatoes, knobbly bent carrots, weird things that look like white willies (just been told they are a Turkish sweet potato).

Sells basic food and drink. The essentials, I suppose. No *Finest Range*, but nice wine, though. Small, but basic deli counter with fresh, delicious looking hot and cold Turkish mezes.

No custard creams!

No clothes!

No household items!

Estimated time to navigate around the store without stopping: two minutes.

Estimated time to navigate around the store with stopping: twenty minutes.

UK Supermarket:

Car park for about three hundred cars.

Limp, under ripe fruit and veg. All perfectly coloured (possibly painted with something to look nicer). Perfectly shaped as you'd expect – pointy carrots with no knobbles, round tomatoes and potatoes matching the potato and tomato circumference tests, etc.

Sells everything: food and drink, clothes, household and gardening goods, stationery, electrical equipment, cards. Huge deli counter (you'd never have to cook a meal again if you didn't want to).

Biscuit heaven.

Huge range of clothes.

Estimated time to navigate around the store without stopping: thirty-five minutes.

Estimate time to navigate around the store with stopping: three days.

Well, not quite what I was expecting. Maybe it would mean that I just couldn't get everything under one roof like I was used to. Maybe I'd just have to stop at three of four supermarkets to do my weekly shop. And how long would that take? I knew I'd have to sacrifice a bit of convenience for living in the sun, but honestly, a weekly shop could now take me a whole week to complete, like a kind of shopping Krypton Factor Challenge. And by then the week would be over, and I'd have to do it all again as soon as I set foot back in the house with my bags.

'Well, that's got everything we need.' Kalem smiled at me as we headed back to the car.

'Mmm.' I forced a smile back.

After about fifteen minutes we took a left turn off the main road, heading towards the coast. I was used to the busy Motorways of the UK, but this was like we were the last few remaining people on earth, with hardly any traffic at all.

I gazed out the window at the sea to my left and the rolling, scorched fields to my right, covered in olive and carob trees. Further on, the Kyrenia mountain range was more visible. A range that swept from West to East, smothered with pine and fir trees.

'That's Five Finger Mountain.' Kalem pointed to a section of the mountain, towering into the distance, as we sped by.

'It looks more like Five Stubby Knuckle Mountain.'

'There are a couple of legends about the name of the mountain. One of them says that a Byzantine hero called Dighenis jumped on the island of Cyprus to escape from the Arabs. As he grabbed hold of the mountain, he left the mark of his fingers there. Another legend said it was a giant who grabbed hold of it.

'You're not far from history and legends anywhere on this island, are you?' I said, beginning to appreciate the allure of the place. Would definitely add to my list.

'All of this mountain range is fantastic for hiking. Just wait till I get you up in those hills.' He gave me a seductive grin.

The open window blasted me with hot air, warm rays, and a gorgeous pungent aroma of orange and lemon blossom from the orchards we passed. As we got further away from Kyrenia, we passed a golf course (must also add to my list as modern and sophisticated things) and several new beachside apartment complexes, interspersed with a vast expanse of undeveloped land. The whole journey gave me a feeling of space and light that I'd forgotten actually existed. After living in the UK all my life, where the sky is normally grey, black-grey, and a kind of bluish-grey, with houses crammed into every possible piece of land, it made such a refreshing change. It was like drinking in sunshine, giving me a buzz of energy. I seriously needed that at the moment to counteract the buzz of pure terror that I'd been feeling.

'I think we turn right here.' I re-read the map and directions that Deniz had scribbled on the back of *Cosmo* magazine for us.

'I don't recognize any of this. It's changed so much since the last time I was here. I can't even remember what the house looks like.' Kalem turned off the main road and onto a more windy one that snaked uphill.

Half way up the hill we had to stop the car to let a procession of goats and sheep cross the road, like a countryside version of a traffic jam. They stared at us like they'd never seen a car before. The weird thing was that the goats actually looked the same as

67

the sheep. The facial features were identical, and the only real difference was that the sheep looked like they'd just had a perm, whereas the goats were more into hair straighteners.

I watched them meander from one side of the road to the other, bells jangling around their necks, baaing and bleating away. Did they speak the same language? And if so, was it Geep or Shoat dialect?

'Wow. It's so...' I struggled for a word.

'Simple?' He winked at me. 'Now you know what I mean about wanting the simple things in life. This is what getting back to basics is all about. It's like the UK was fifty years ago, before we became obsessed with convenience – everything's on a much smaller scale here.' He paused, grinning at me. 'You know, if you think about it, the shops in the UK are saturated with lots of stuff that you just don't need. Life here is much more straightforward with individual little shops selling essentials. Because of the inter-communal problems between Greek Cypriots and Turkish Cypriots and the division of the island, North Cyprus has a remoteness and unspoiled quality with more of a culture about using what you already have and living off the land, instead of buying everything new.'

Yes, that was all very well, but I liked *stuff*. I know, I know, call me shallow and materialistic, but it was what I was used to. OK, maybe having fifty-six pairs of shoes and twenty-three handbags was going a tad overboard, but a girl had to be prepared for all possible eventualities. It made sense, didn't it?

'Here they have a slower pace of life so everyone has more time for each other,' Kalem carried on. 'We'll have less stress. It's cheaper, and you've got sunshine most of the year. Just the simple life. With less crime as well.'

Yes, unless you counted assassinating a businessman and stealing a priceless sculpture.

'How about that for organic then?' Kalem nodded towards the animals.

I gazed at them as they wandered around, nibbling the ground here and there as the fancy took them. Either some of them had missed out on their daily milking sessions or there was a Pamela Anderson fan club amongst the sheep and goat world of North Cyprus, because their udders were huge! Poor things. Some of their udders were nearly dragging on the ground and looked severely painful. Ouch.

'What's happening?' I pointed to one of the goats who looked like she'd overstuffed herself on the olives. 'Why's she making so much noise?'

The goat collapsed onto her side, making funny noises. 'Oh! Is she going to die? Maybe her udders are about to explode with milk, or she's eaten too much. Goats do that, don't they? I read about one who ate so much it popped.' I grabbed the door handle. 'We have to help her. I don't want any exploding, popping goats on my watch.'

Kalem chuckled. 'She's not going to explode. She's just pregnant. And if we stay really quiet, you might just see her kid being born.'

In ten minutes, I witnessed the goat give birth to a tiny, wrinkly little baby, covered in blood and goo. As soon as it was born, mummy goat licked it clean and gently nudged it with her nose, encouraging it to stand up. About another fifteen minutes later, the baby attempted to stand on wobbly legs.

'You see, you wouldn't get this in the UK, would you?' Kalem said.

If I was honest with myself, it really was a truly amazing sight. And simple. Maybe Kalem was actually right about getting back to basics. But could I sacrifice my love of *stuff* for all things au naturel?

He shifted the Land Rover into gear, leaving mummy and baby to enjoy each other as we drove up the windy hill with houses dotted here and there.

I glanced at the handwritten directions that Deniz had scrawled for us on the back of *Cosmo*. 'Well, the house number is fifteen, so we're nearly there. There's fourteen. And,' I sat up in my seat, craning my neck for the first glimpse of what would be our new home in paradise. 'Oh,' I let out an involuntary sigh, because coming into view was a dilapidated, ancient looking square building. It wasn't anything like the modern style villas I'd seen on the journey here, with a pool, whitewashed walls, wooden shutters, and sandstone arches. It was...well, the only way I could describe it was a wreck.

On the upside, it had four walls and a roof. On the downside, it didn't have much else going for it. The house stood on an overgrown piece of land, littered with what looked like years' worth of weeds. There was even the skeleton of a dead goat near the front of the building. I didn't know if it had died of natural causes or the shock of seeing such a scary house.

The open shutters hung precariously from the windows, peeling paint curling up from their surfaces. The windows were covered in grime and dust, giving the whole place a spooky, haunted house feel. A porch of sorts had been strung together out of rusty iron, and the only thing with any life in it, a brilliant pink bougainvillea bush, climbed out of control over the top of it.

'How long did you say it's been since your mum and dad stayed here?' I asked, stepping out of the car.

I cupped my hands around my eyes to shield them from the glaring sunshine. Maybe it was a peculiar mirage. Or a trick of the light, even. I squeezed my eyes shut. Slowly, I opened one. Then the other. Damn. Not a mirage. It was still there, in all its state of disrepair.

'Two years.' Kalem stared at the house, looking confused. 'But it looks more like twenty.'

I gnawed on my quivering lip. It would take more than a clean to make it OK. It needed one of those TV shows to come along with a bus full of people and do a complete makeover. Or failing that, a bulldozer.

'Well, this is certainly simple,' I said, trying to hide the disappointment in my voice and failing miserably.

Kalem hugged me into his toned chest. 'It probably looks worse than it is. Maybe the inside is a lot better.'

'Mmm,' I agreed, although, judging by the outside, I wasn't quite convinced.

Kalem dug a key out of his pocket and slipped his fingers through mine, leading me towards the front door. At one time, it would've been a traditional Cypriot wooden door, etched with carvings on the outside, with a small opening in the front to let the air ventilate through whilst keeping the door closed. Now, it was just a rotten chunk of wood.

He slid the key in the lock, and the lock fell out, landing on the other side of the door with a loud thud. I heard something inside squeak and the patter of tiny claws scurry away.

Great. It was probably infested with rats and cockroaches and lots of other nibbly, squeaky creatures as well.

Kalem pushed the door open but met with some resistance on the other side. He barged his shoulder into it, and it gave way, sending him hurtling into the house at twenty miles an hour.

He managed to put the brakes on, and we surveyed the large hallway and derelict kitchen in front of us.

'OK, so probably not better inside,' I murmured, wandering around. One room was worse than the last.

'I don't remember it being like this.' Kalem shook his head.

'Yes, but you were only ten when you last came here.' I flipped the light switch on, but nothing happened.

I tried again another couple of times really fast to see if that helped. Maybe there was a knack to it. No. Still nothing happened. No electric? How was I supposed to live with no electric? What about hair straighteners and epilators? Not to mention essentials like a fridge, cooker, washing machine, and air conditioning.

Agh!

I forced down the lump in my throat.

Things were just going from bad to worse. All I wanted was the perfect wedding and a happy new start to our life in an exotic country abroad. Was that too much to ask? It was that bloody curse of Queen Cleopatra that had jinxed everything. Bitch! How dare she jinx me. I hadn't done anything to her. I was just a normal person with normal dreams. What had I done to deserve a dose of jinxing?

This was all getting too much now. We'd only left the UK twenty-four hours before, and it had been the worst day of my life. How could our lives go so badly wrong in such a short amount of time? Should I tell Kalem that I couldn't take any more? That we should just go back to the UK after we'd got married. I know he'd have to give up his dream job and ideas about the simple life. But I didn't think I could stand it here.

I thought about my list and added this house onto it. Now I had some overwhelming reasons not to stay here:

1) Crazy extended family.
2) Involved in assassination and art heist.
3) Cursed by Queen Cleopatra's statue.
4) Spooky demons and giants running around mountains scaring the shit out of people.

5) Haunted, derelict house full of yucky things (well, didn't know if it was haunted, but it probably was, if the goat was anything to go by).

6) No convenient superstores or big shopping malls.

7) French Fancy wedding dresses.

8) Erol Hussein.

9) No custard creams.

Compared with the reasons to actually stay here:

1) Kalem and his dream job.

2) Sunshine.

3) Beaches.

4) A Disney Castle.

5) The Holy Grail and Indiana Jones (who might visit again, and I quite fancied him).

6) A dual carriageway.

7) Picturesque harbour.

8) Steeped in history and ancient buildings.

9) Golf course (didn't actually play but never say never).

10) Relaxing, unstressy pace of life.

11) Undeveloped countryside.

12) Space and light.

13) Sheepy goats roaming countryside willy-nilly, giving birth (was very sweet).

14) Organic food.

15) Cheaper.

OK, so my second list was longer, but my first list was a lot scarier.

Kalem's voice cut into my thoughts of doubt. 'No, I'm sure the house wasn't even this shape. It had more windows, and it was more of a rectangle.' He rushed out through the kitchen door to the back of the house. 'And it had a swimming pool.'

I had a hard time seeing anything through the two metre weeds towering over the garden, but Kalem grabbed an old plank of wood lying on the ground, beating the weeds down.

I could hear an electric pylon humming loudly nearby. Great. On top of everything, we'd be living next to a loud, and probably dangerous, electric pylon!

'Why haven't we got electric when I can hear that bloody pylon so loud?' I asked as Kalem worked his way around the garden.

'It's not a pylon. It's the cicadas.'

'What are they?' I poked a finger in my ear to try and lessen the deafening hum.

'They're little bugs that come out in the summer. They click their wings together to make that noise. Don't worry, you'll get used to it. It's probably so loud because it's in the garden somewhere.' He finished beating down the weeds to reveal a garden with no swimming pool at all. He held his hand out to me. 'Let me see that magazine with the directions.'

I handed it to him.

He studied it for a while. 'I don't think this says fifteen. I think it says sixteen. Dad's got such messy handwriting.'

I grabbed the paper off him, scrutinizing it for dear life. *Please say sixteen. Please say sixteen. Oh, no, hang on a minute. What if sixteen is even worse?*

'I don't know. It's hard to tell.' I scratched my head.

'It's definitely sixteen. Let's go and find it.' Kalem's long legs were halfway to the Land Rover.

Please don't be worse than fifteen!

We crawled further up the hill until number sixteen came into view.

I exhaled with relief. Finally, something seemed to be going right. From the outside, the house looked old, but it had obviously been lovingly renovated in the last ten years or so. It was a one storey whitewashed bungalow, with masses of huge windows and dark wooden shutters. A cobbled path led from the gate to the solid wood door. And the flourishing garden...well, even Alan Titchmarsh would've been proud of it. It was positively blooming. I spied pink and white oleander bushes, deep red bougainvillea trailing around archways and walls, and tall palm trees, rustling their leaves in the gentle breeze in front of a shaded terrace area that wrapped around the entire building.

I sniffed the air, my nose tingling with the intoxicating scent of Cyprus jasmine, frangipani, and lemon trees. Ooh, I would get my early evening G and T after all.

'Wow!' I grinned.

Oh, yes. This was *much, much* better.

'Ah, yes. This is definitely the place. I remember it now. All my boyhood memories of holidays here are coming back to me.'

We wandered around the garden. It had a small swimming pool, surrounded by more plants in various stages of bloom. And the view!

I rushed to the garden wall to the right of the plot, staring into a ravine on the other side of the wall that dipped low and then climbed up again in the distance. It was dotted with pine and old olive trees with gnarled trunks. A couple of straggling sheep (or goats) grazed in the bottom of it. From the front of the garden, I could see the sea. Imagine! I'd lived in a claustrophobic city all my life, miles away from the sea, where the air was heavy with traffic smells. Yes, there was countryside nearby, but at that moment, I didn't think anything could compare to the unspoiled beauty before my eyes.

To the rear of the house were uninterrupted views of the mountain range, ripe with green trees and bushes.

Wow. This was going to be so fantastic. I didn't think I could ever get tired of this view. I could sit on the terrace in the morning with my cup of coffee, staring at it forever.

Unless we got whacked by Ferret Face, of course.

No, I couldn't think about that now. I wanted to enjoy this spectacular moment. Even if it wouldn't last.

'Look, fresh olives.' I pointed to an olive tree at the bottom of the garden with a collection of black olives on the ground underneath that had fallen from its branches. I'd never actually tasted fresh ones before. Normally, I bought some off the deli counter from my local supermarket. How cool would it be to have your own olives to slip into a martini? I reached down to pick one up as Kalem busied himself staring at the rest of the garden. The olive looked a bit dry. Maybe they were better if you picked them straight off the tree. Oh, well, I'd have a try anyway. Maybe it was a good idea to start embracing the *living off the land* thing. I was just about to pop it in my mouth when Kalem yelled, 'No!' with a horrified look on his face.

'What?' I asked. Were they poisonous if you ate them fresh rather than deli'd to death?

'That's not an olive. It's sheep's plop!'

'Ew!' I threw the plop on the ground and went in search of a sink to wash my hands.

Inside was home to lots of cream Turkish marble floors, black wrought iron, hand-carved wooden furniture, and curtains made of muslin. I found functional ceiling fans in every room for the scorching summer heat, and a kitchen decked out in wooden units and worktops. It was all fresh and clean and bright.

'This is lovely.' I clapped my hands together.

'I preferred the first house. It was much simpler.' Kalem grinned at me.

'Oh, I'd better check the electric.' I flipped on a switch as dusk descended outside. 'Hurrah! Electric as well. Never thought I'd get excited about something I normally take for granted.'

'They do get a few power cuts here, though, so we'll need to make sure we've got lots of candles in the house.'

'How many power cuts?'

'Well, a few. You have to sacrifice a few things for the simple life.' He kissed me softly on the lips. 'Mmm. Just think of the plus side. No electric, just ambient candle light and a bottle of wine, staring at the stars with the woman I love. In fact, they'll be doing us a favour. Think of all those romantic nights.'

'Oh, yes. Now you look at it that way. Bring on the power cuts! Hey, what's this?' I noticed a bottle of wine on the worktop, a card propped against it with our names on. 'Is this in preparation for the power cuts?'

Kalem read the card. 'It's a welcome present from Mum and Dad. It says the whole family spent the last couple of days cleaning it up for us before we got here, as a surprise.'

'How sweet of them.' I smiled.

He rummaged around in a draw, trying to find a bottle opener. 'How about a nice glass of wine on the terrace, watching the sunset?'

I raised an eyebrow at his suggestion. 'Now that's more like it.'

Chapter 7

In my daydreams, this was exactly how I'd pictured an idyllic new life abroad (and I'd had quite a few, believe me).

Sitting on the edge of the terrace, leisurely drinking wine, and watching the colour of the sun turn from lemon to citrus to orangey red with my future husband. For a moment, I could pretend that I didn't have any worries at all. I could forget that we were mixed up in some crazy plot that would probably affect our lives in an irreparable way.

And I wanted to forget.

So when Kalem set down his empty glass on the patio and gazed at me with his intense dark eyes, flecked with green, I couldn't think of anything more perfect than to make love outside under the flickering stars, with the crickets singing in the distance, and the warm air stroking my naked skin.

He cupped my chin and drew my lips towards his.

Oh, God, yes. Just like that. Mmm. Fantastic. Nice and slow.

He gently pushed me down onto the warm terracotta tiles.

Ooh, hello, nipples springing to attention. Down a bit, down a bit. Bit lower. There! Right there. Wow! Yes, yes...

I sat bolt upright. 'Agh!'

Kalem leaped up. 'What? Have you been stung by something?'

'Oh, my God!'

'What? Bitten by a snake?'

'I've just had an idea.' I grabbed my clothes and started pulling them on.

Kalem rubbed his forehead. 'What?'

I kissed him hard on the lips. 'I'm sorry. I'm sorry. I can't concentrate until we get this thing sorted out. I thought I could, but I can't. And I've had another idea we can try.'

Kalem pulled on his shorts, trying to manoeuvre them over his own one-eyed trouser snake. 'Ouch!'

'We can go to the Plaza and warn Ibrahim Kaya ourselves. Now. Tonight.'

'OK,' he drawled. 'Good idea. And then that will be the end of it, and we can get back to this.'

'Yes. Then we won't have anything else to worry about. We can *definitely* get back to this. Right, come on. Start the Land Rover,' I said as we jumped in.

'I'm trying.' Kalem turned the key in the ignition.

Once. Twice. Three times.

Nothing but a clicking sound.

Kalem frowned. 'Strange. Land Rovers are usually so reliable.'

'Yes, your rusty old heap of junk never had a problem starting, and this one's a lot newer than yours. Come on, come on.' I jigged up and down in the seat.

Fourth time and hey presto! We were off and rolling down the hill.

We sped up the long, palm tree lined driveway to the Plaza and parked at a slightly wonky angle. A humongous gold lion statue and an even more humongous shiny black horse greeted us at the entrance. I said hello to the horse (the lion looked a bit scary) and raced to reception.

Ooh – very plush! Purple and silver everywhere. Lots of soft velvet cushions, sofas, and thick curtains. Exotic potted palms that looked so glossy they must have been polished every day, marble pillars galore, a silver piano, fountains, sparkly lights, galleried silver ceiling with shiny diamondy thingies hanging down; lots of chrome, a couple more horses, and something that looked like a silver shark, but couldn't possibly have been (only got a quick look, was in big hurry). You name it, they had it. And this was just the reception area. Even the white marble floor had glittery silver flecks in it. This was the height of plushness.

'We need to see Ibrahim Kaya,' I said breathlessly to the receptionist.

'Do you have an appointment?' She smiled a genuinely sweet smile at me.

Oh, no. Not this again!

'No. But it's very urgent,' Kalem said.

'*Very.*' I nodded vigorously.

'Are you guests here?' she asked.

'YES!' I said, which came out slightly higher pitched than I intended.

'And which room number are you?'

Quick! Pick a number! 'Two hundred and thirteen.' I gave another vigorous nod, just to get the point across. Ouch. Neck ache. I hoped I hadn't given myself whiplash on top of everything else.

'I'm sorry, madam, but you must be mistaken. We don't have any number thirteens here. Some guests think it's very bad luck.'

'No! I meant two hundred and fourteen,' I gushed, turning to Kalem. 'It's two hundred and fourteen, isn't it, darling?'

'Absolutely,' he agreed.

'And what exactly is the problem, sir, madam?'

I thought about telling her the truth, but it would probably end up in some totally bizarre mix-up, knowing my luck, and we'd get thrown out. Or even worse, arrested.

'I want to make a complaint.' I leaned in closer to her over the reception desk.

'Can you tell me what the complaint is regarding? I'm sure someone other than Mr. Kaya can help you with that.' She smiled at me again.

Stop smiling and just go and get him!

She didn't. She just waited patiently with that annoyingly helpful smile.

I glanced round the lobby area, hoping for a sudden flash of inspiration, and spied a bar to the left. 'Er…it's about the mini-bar in our room.'

'Yes, madam, and what's wrong with the mini-bar?'

Uh-oh. What could I say? It was too mini, too bar-ish? She'd probably think we were a couple of complete nutcases on day release from the nearest mental home.

That's it! 'It's the nuts,' I blurted out.

'The nuts?' Her eyebrows flickered up in surprise. 'What's wrong with the nuts?'

Oh, stop being so picky and just get him!

'They're too nutty,' I said.

'So if you could just go and get him, we'll be able to put in our complaint. Thank you very much,' Kalem said.

'Too nutty?' She furrowed her brow and made a note on a piece of paper. 'Anything else?' She looked up again, smile plastered all over her face.

'Yes, they contain nuts,' I said.

'But they're supposed to contain nuts.' She paused, pondering this for a minute. 'You know, I think our Housekeeping Department can help you with this simple problem, madam. I'll just give them a ring.'

'It's not simple at all!' I said. 'It's a *very* serious problem.'

She looked at us both with bewildered eyes. 'Because the nuts are too nutty?'

'Yes! I'm allergic to nuts.' I gave her my best shocked look, like she should really know this already. 'Even the smell of nuts can give me a severe allergic reaction. In the UK, the packets of nuts always have a label stating "may contain nuts" but these didn't.'

The receptionist looked confused. 'So in the UK, you have warning labels on packets of nuts that say "may contain nuts"?'

I could sense she wanted to burst out laughing at the absurdity of this nut-labelling revelation, but I had to hand it to her, she maintained her professionalism very well.

'Yes! Why were the nuts in my mini-bar? I could've opened them by accident and died!' I slapped a hand on the reception desk for emphasis.

She had the good grace to look horrified. 'I'm so very sorry about that, madam. We at the Plaza had no idea. I'd be very happy to get our Housekeeping Manager to come and talk to you about it straight away.'

'No!' Kalem shouted.

She flinched. 'Is there another problem as well, sir?'

'Yes. And it's a very delicate matter. I'd rather not talk to a woman about it, if you don't mind. I really need to speak to Mr. Kaya about it personally.' Kalem dropped his voice again, looking around the reception area as if it was a top military secret he was talking about.

'Well, can you give me some sort of idea please?' She smiled again.

'The condoms in the mini-bar,' he whispered to her.

She wrote *condoms* down next to the *nuts* she already had on her piece of paper. 'And what's wrong with the condoms, sir? Have they been near the nuts? Is that why you're worried?'

'No, they're too cold. I nearly...' Kalem coughed, as if he were highly embarrassed. 'Look, I really can't discuss our condoms with a woman.'

'Or our nuts,' I interjected.

'I really need to speak to Mr. Kaya himself,' Kalem said.

'Right away, sir. I would be very happy to call Mr. Kaya and ask him to speak with you.'

About bloody time.

She dialled a number and repeated our request to Mr. Kaya. She nodded a few times, still smiling, then replaced the receiver. 'Mr. Kaya will be down in fifteen minutes to speak with you. In the meantime, please have a complimentary drink at one of the bars while you wait.' More smiling. 'Please be careful though, madam, as there may be nuts on the bar. And they do contain nuts.'

'I'll make sure I look out for them. Thank you.' I smiled at her.

'Thanks very much for your help,' Kalem said.

We edged away from reception.

'I want to get a look at the Queen Cleopatra sculpture while we're here. I have to see it. It could be the only chance I ever get to actually look at it in real life,' Kalem whispered to me.

'Is it already on display? Or are they just putting it out on the opening night?'

Kalem shrugged. 'I have no idea. The article didn't say. But I have to try and get a glimpse of it if it's already here.'

'Are you really sure you want to look at it? It's cursed. You might die if you look at it.' I sighed. All this talk about nuts and statues was wearing me out. I felt a hopeless fatigue settle over me. Maybe I was just weak from hunger and needed something to eat.

'It's not cursed.' He shook his head at me.

'Hmm,' I said in a disbelieving tone.

We peered into the bar areas. No ugly statue. Good.

'How about the restaurants?' Kalem said.

Nope, we peeked in all of them. Lots of party-frocked and poshly-suited people, but no sculpture. We covered the ground floor and couldn't see it. What a shame. *Not!*

'What about the lower ground floor?' Kalem suggested. 'Maybe it's down there somewhere.'

We descended the stairs to the lower ground floor. Wow! The hotel was huge. Classy – and obviously very expensive – boutiques lined either side of a large walkway. As the boutiques came to an end, the spa and fitness centre loomed in front of us.

We didn't bother looking in there. Unless Cleopatra was finally getting an upper lip wax, it seemed an unlikely place to show it.

We had a choice of going to the casino, or taking another walkway off to the pool, beach, and the hotel's own port.

Hmm, probably not enough time to go traipsing around the pool. 'Let's look in the casino then.'

'OK.'

I felt like I'd stepped into a scene from *Oceans 11*. Lots of ching ching and bling bling going on.

We eased our way around the poker tables, roulette wheels, and various slot machines, and came across a free merchandise stand. I ignored it. Why would I want a baseball cap or T-shirt with *Plaza Casino* on it? Instead, something much more interesting caught my eye: A free buffet area. My stomach growled at me. I hadn't eaten anything since lunchtime. God, I was starving. Yes, that was definitely what I needed. Food.

I grabbed a plate and hastily piled it high with food: some warm, fresh Turkish bread topped with toasted sesame seeds and aniseed, garlicky humus, some spicy Turkish meatballs, and salad.

'What are you doing?' Kalem raised an eyebrow at me.

'I'm starving,' I said, in between shovelling food in my mouth. 'I'll be two minutes. You go and look for it while I eat this. I don't really want to clap eyes on the ugly sculpture anyway. It might give us an even bigger curse.'

Kalem disappeared on his mission while I stood at the buffet, scoffing. My eyes wandered around the room, taking in the high-rollers betting thousands of pounds on the flick of a chip. I was just studying the sombre expression of a business-suited elderly guy with a woman hanging on his arm who looked about twelve, when I stopped eating mid-bite.

It was Ferret Face. Here! In the casino. With us!

His black beady eyes darted around, as if casing the joint; getting the lie of the land, so to speak (think I'd heard those expressions in a crime movie once).

An icy chill slammed through my veins.

Where the hell was Kalem? And what if Ferret Face saw him?

I craned my neck, searching for Kalem. *Where are you? God, where the bloody hell are you? (Oops, sorry to blaspheme – very stressed, you know.)*

I slammed the plate down on the buffet table, keeping my eyes firmly locked on Ferret Face's position, and went in search of Kalem.

I darted around the tables. No Kalem. Up and down the rows and rows of chiming slot machines. No Kalem. Back to the buffet. No sodding Kalem.

By this point Ferret Face was making his way out the casino door.

I clutched my heaving chest. Hurrah!

I stood there without blinking, eyes glued to the door, until they started watering. And then...

'Agh!' I felt a tap on my shoulder and must've jumped half a mile in the air.

I swung around.

'Only me.' Kalem observed my distraught face. 'What have you done now?' He grinned.

'Ferret Face was in here,' I hissed. 'Where did you go? I was trying to make sure he didn't see you.'

'I couldn't find the statue, so I went to the toilet.' He jerked his head towards the toilets in the corner of the casino. 'Come on, we need to go and meet Mr. Kaya.'

'Yes, but what if Ferret Face is still out there?'

'OK, if I keep my head down, hopefully he won't recognize me. But just to be on the safe side, you can go in front and I'll loiter behind you. If you see him, scratch your head. Then I'll know he's there and I can hide somewhere.'

'Good plan.' I nodded and crept back to reception. Well, it wasn't a particularly good plan, but in the absence of something better it would just have to do.

'May I help you, madam?' Different receptionist, same helpful smile.

'Mr. Kaya was coming down to deal with my complaint.' I fanned at my face. All this action was giving me a hot flush.

'Oh, I think I just saw him leaving. If you're quick, you might be able to catch him.' She pointed out to the car park. 'His white Hummer limousine may still be out there.'

'Oh, no!' I yelled and swung around to see where Kalem was. I spied him hiding behind a pillar near the reception desk and, trying not to draw attention to the fact he was there, I casually strolled over to him. 'OK, you carry on waiting here behind this pillar until I know the coast is clear,' I said to the pillar and then flew out the entrance and into the car park.

My head sprang from side to side like I was watching a tennis match.

No Kaya. I spotted his limo cruising up the driveway and ran after him. Realizing I wasn't going to catch him, I finally gave up, out of breath.

'Damn!' I walked back down the driveway towards the entrance and, as there was no Ferret Face around, I caught Kalem's eye, peering around the pillar, and gestured to him that it was safe to come out.

Kalem surreptitiously sneaked out the entrance to the hotel, turning his head one way and then the other to check that the coast really was clear.

Then my jaw dropped as I saw Ferret Face appear from the balcony of one the bars on the first floor overlooking the entrance. He stared down at Kalem, and a look of recognition flashed across his ugly mug. He slammed his drink down on a table and disappeared from view sharpish.

'Run, Kalem!' I screamed.

Kalem furrowed his brow. 'Why?'

'Ferret Face is coming!' I sprang towards the Land Rover with Kalem following behind at rocket launching speed.

I slid through the door and Kalem jumped in, shoving the key in the ignition.

He turned the key. Nothing. Not even a click.

I banged on the dashboard. 'Hurry! He's probably on his way down here now. We don't have much time.'

Another turn.

Slight click.

I craned my neck around, looking back at the entrance to the hotel. Ferret Face emerged into view, running through the long lobby inside.

'He's coming!' I grabbed my camera and snapped a picture of Ferret Face, just in case we needed it for identification. 'I knew we shouldn't have hired a Land Rover!' I yelled. 'Quick!'

Ferret Face was half way across the car park when Kalem turned the key again.

The engine sprang to life.

We sped up the driveway as Ferret Face ran to a nearby black

Mercedes and climbed in.

I heard a loud banging noise in my ears from the engine, then realized it was actually my heartbeat.

Kalem took a left at the top of the driveway and turned onto the main road we'd followed earlier out of town earlier.

'Faster!' I cried. 'He's gaining on us.'

'I'm trying!' Kalem slammed his foot flat to the floor. 'Land Rovers aren't exactly known for their speed.'

'We're going to die. We're going to die. And we haven't even had sex since we've been here!' Strange, the things that come into your mind when your life is in jeopardy.

Dust scattered in the air behind us as we sped along with Ferret Face barely inches away.

We turned off onto the coast road that we'd taken earlier in the day to Deniz and Yasmin's house.

'We're never going to lose him in this.' I made a mental note to take the Land Rover back and hire a Ferrari or a Porsche.

Ferret Face took the turning too.

Kalem pushed the Land Rover to top speed. 'Look for a track that leads off this main road. The only way we're going to lose him is if we take one of the tracks that lead towards the mountains.'

My eyes darted around in front, looking for some kind of escape route that we could take. 'We're going to die. We're going to die,' I whispered.

'There!' Kalem suddenly swerved the Land Rover to the right onto a narrow dirt track lined with trees that led off the main road.

Ferret Face swerved onto it too.

We bounced up and down, over rocks and bumpy dips, the branches of bushes and trees scraping against the side of the Land Rover like nails on a blackboard.

I shivered inwardly.

In the distance, I could see the dark silhouette of the mountains, lit up by the full moon. *Agh! A full moon.* That couldn't possibly be a good sign, could it? There might be werewolves up there or some of those scary demons.

Kalem manoeuvred the Land Rover across a deep, dried up riverbed with all the expertise of an experienced off-roader.

The Mercedes slowed down, trying to get up the other side of it. His wheels caught on the sandy ground, spinning and churning up more dust.

We gained a couple of metres advantage.

The track climbed higher here and was lined with bigger rocks and boulders fallen from the mountain side.

The Land Rover creaked and groaned on the rugged terrain.

'We're going to die!' I yelled.

We turned a corner on a particularly hairy bend with a steep drop down the mountain side.

My stomach fell to my feet and bounced back up again.

Kalem steered the Land Rover past a large rock and shortly afterwards there was a loud crunching sound behind us.

I whipped my head around and saw that the Mercedes had ended up wedged on top of the rock, smoke billowing up into the night air.

As we disappeared around the corner, I heard Ferret Face revving his engine hard.

I kept my eyes on the rear window, waiting for him to appear again. It wasn't until the revving sounds faded into the distance that I allowed myself to finally breathe.

'We lost him,' Kalem said. 'I know I said I wanted to take you off-roading, but this wasn't exactly what I meant. Now we just have to work out how to get off this mountain in the dark.'

Uh-oh. What about the demons?

Chapter 8

Surprisingly, I fell into a coma-like sleep as soon as my head hit the pillow.

The previous forty-eight hours had really taken it out of me. When I woke up at 9 a.m. to a loud banging on our hotel room door, I felt like I'd been run over by a bus. I ached. My head hurt. My throat felt scratchy and dry. I guess that's what stress overload did to a person.

I heard the shower going full blast in the bathroom.

Putting on Kalem's T-shirt, I padded to the door.

'Room service,' Charlie sing-songed on the other side.

'I love you.' I grinned at him when he wheeled in a trolley stacked high with breakfast.

Ayshe and Atila kissed me as they wandered in behind.

'Morning.' Kalem appeared from the bathroom with a towel around his waist, his hair still damp from the shower, and his chest glistening with beads of water.

Yummy. If we didn't have an audience, I would've pounced on him there and then.

After Kalem and I had tucked into a hearty breakfast, it was time to get down to some serious business. The capture of a crazed jewellery thief and sniper for starters. The wedding dress – or lack of it – for seconds.

I had four days to go to the wedding, and if I didn't get my lucky dress back, I didn't really want to go down the aisle wearing a French Fancy. Four days to go, and I was thinking about curses, murderers, and queens with moustaches, instead of thinking nice happy thoughts like floaty wedding dresses, Kalem looking sexy in his wedding suit, dancing, drinking, and laughing at the wedding party. And lots of slow, sensual love making at the after-wedding party.

'Right. First things first.' I clapped my hands together. 'How are Yasmin and Deniz?' I asked Ayshe.

'Dad's acting a bit funny, actually,' Ayshe said.

'Yes, but that's normal,' I said.

'I think he's going through a mid-life crisis,' she went on. 'I'm getting a bit worried about him.'

'He's seventy. He's leaving it a bit late.' I giggled.

Atila nodded. 'He's had three packets of condoms off me already from our mini-bar. What the hell is he doing with them?'

'I haven't got a clue. They're a seventy-year old married couple! It's not like Yasmin is going to get pregnant, is it?' I shook my head.

'They'll have an injury at this rate.' Kalem wrinkled up his nose. 'They've got food poisoning. How can they even be considering doing…you know? God, it just doesn't bear thinking about.'

'I've given Dad some magazines, so hopefully he won't be quite as bored, and it might take his mind off any…' Ayshe winced, 'condom activity.'

'OK, we'll stop off and see them later,' Kalem said.

'But what about you, Helen? I feel so bad that I haven't been around to help you with anything. I want Sunday to be the happiest day of your life.' Ayshe glanced at Kalem and smiled. 'And yours too, of course. Especially as it was my fourteen-day life challenge that got you both together in the first place.'

'As long as I've got Helen it *will* be the happiest day of my life.' Kalem beamed back at me.

'What am I going to do without you when we all go back to the UK and leave you here?' Ayshe asked, sniffing back tears. 'Oh, I'm sorry. I keep doing this. I don't want to spoil your wedding preparations with depressing talk.'

'I'd rather have it spoiled by you than Ferret Face.' My face crumpled. 'Anyway, you'll have to come out and see us. Lots. And we'll come back to see you. I couldn't stand it if we hardly ever saw each other.'

'Yes, but I'm used to seeing you every day. And Atila can't just up and leave his restaurant. He's such a perfectionist – he wants to be there all the time, even though he's got a fantastic manager.'

'Yes, I *am* here,' Atila pointed out. 'I *can* hear you. You don't have to talk about me as if I'm not.'

She wiped at her eyes. 'Oh, look at me. It must be all the baby hormones flying around.'

'Actually…maybe there is a way.' Atila suddenly sat forward with an excited look on his face.

'What?' Ayshe asked. 'A way for what?'

Atila pushed his floppy fringe off his forehead and leaped up. 'Just an idea.' He gave us all a vague smile. 'Do you need me for anything? Want me to come with you when you go to the apricot festival? Wedding dress shopping? Anything like that? If not, I want to strike while the shish kebab is hot.'

'Pardon?' I frowned. Maybe the heat was getting to him, because he didn't seem to be making any sense.

'I have to organize a wedding present for you,' Atila said.

'We've already got them a wedding present. Are you OK?' Ayshe looked up at him, worried. 'Do you think it's the heat? Maybe we should turn on the air conditioning.'

'I'm perfectly fine, thanks.' Atila grinned.

'No, we don't need you.' I gave Atila a puzzled look. What was he up to?

Atila hurriedly kissed Ayshe and me and then left.

'What was all that about then?' I said.

Ayshe shrugged. 'I have absolutely no idea.'

'Right. So, second on the agenda. What are we going to do about Ferret Face?' Charlie asked. 'Are you still going to the festival to try and speak to the President? Or did you manage to finally tell the authorities yesterday?'

Kalem relayed the previous evening's events. 'So, we're no further forward. We have to try and speak to the President at the festival somehow.'

'OK, well I'll put my thinking cap on.' Charlie mimed putting a cap on. 'We need to do something to catch his attention; or cause a distraction, or something, so you can get close to him to have a chat.' He tapped his lips.

'Easier said than done.' I frowned.

'Hmm. What can we do?' Charlie carried on tapping. 'Ooh, I know! How about I distract his bodyguards by streaking?'

I giggled.

Charlie looked hurt. 'I've done it before. I did it at Wimbledon once. I had security guards and a whole TV crew chasing me. They said on the news that I was the best streaker they'd ever had.' He grinned, looking rather pleased with himself. 'And the security guards were quite fit if I remember.'

'Somehow, I don't think that would work quite as well at an apricot festival,' Kalem said.

'What about if Helen streaked?' Charlie added, trying to be

helpful.

'Maybe I'll add that to my list of possibilities.' I rolled my eyes at him. 'What else can we do?'

'Throw darts at him?' Charlie said.

I gave Charlie another eye roll.

'Mmm. Take your point. Probably no darts here. We could throw olives instead? Or apricots.' Charlie looked at me for approval.

'Also a possibility, as long as we want to get arrested,' I said.

'I've been to these festivals before, when I was a kid. They have lots of stalls selling local produce, little cafes set up, and lots of entertainment. I'm sure we'll be able to get some opportunity to speak to him.' Kalem shrugged. 'It's worth a try. What have we got to lose?'

Ayshe nodded. 'Well, it's the only thing I can think of at the moment.'

'In the meantime, we could see if Osman recognizes the photo of Ferret Face,' Kalem said. 'If he's local, Osman will know him. He knows everybody. And if he is local, maybe we could find him and try to do something to put him out of action if all else fails. That way he won't actually be able to do anything at the opening night, anyway.'

'What, like drug him?' Charlie asked.

'I don't know. We'd need to come up with some sort of plan. Look, why don't we all go and see Osman and have a think on the way. I'm sure we can come up with something between us,' Kalem said.

'OK. What about a possible replacement wedding dress? Did you find one?' I asked Charlie.

He pursed his lips. 'Er…no. I went to all the wedding shops I could find. Only French Fancies available.'

'Shit! What am I going to get married in? A bikini and flip-flops?' I ran a hand through my hair.

'You can wear my new cream strappy shoes. I brought the ones with the heart shaped diamantes on them that you liked.' Ayshe squeezed my hand and gave me an encouraging smile. 'I'm not up for wearing high heels anyway at the moment. I might topple over. No sister-in-law of mine can get married in flip-flops.'

'And I'll trawl round all the non-weddingy shops,' Charlie

said. 'I'll look in all the women's boutiques. If we can't find an actual wedding dress, I'll find the next best thing. I promise. I'm your wedding planner. I will not let you down.' He sprang to his feet. 'Come on. We can't sit around here all day chatting.'

'Merhaba,' Osman greeted us *Hello* in Turkish, wearing a white vest, rolled up trousers, and wellies, as we pulled up outside his rustic farm on the outskirts of town. 'How are you all?' he said, then turned to Charlie. 'And who is this lovely lady? I don't remember meeting you when we dropped off Helen and Kalem at the hotel.'

'This is my best man, Charlie,' Kalem said. 'You did meet him the other night.'

Osman looked slightly confused. It was an easy mistake to make, since Charlie was wearing the pink kilt, a white top with a big pink heart on the front, and a pink sweatband on his forehead. I have to say that I wasn't entirely sure that his red, leopard print flip-flops went with the outfit, but I'd seen him in a lot worse, so I supposed I had to be grateful for small mercies.

'Where are Deniz and Yasmin?' Osman asked.

'They've got food poisoning,' Ayshe said. 'They're confined to their room until they feel better.'

'Deniz has food poisoning? I remember him eating all sorts when we were children. He never got ill.' Osman smiled, reminiscing. 'One time he ate a raw snake.'

'I've eaten a few of those in my time.' Charlie nodded, although I didn't think they were quite talking about the same variety.

'We must have Turkish coffee. Mother will want to read your coffee cup,' Osman said to me as he started off up the dirt track to the simple, flat-roofed old Cypriot house with blue wooden shutters, archways, and hand-carved wooden doors.

There was a lean-to over the front door, made with what looked like off-cuts of ancient wooden beams. Hundreds of potted plants lined the small terrace underneath.

Under the shade of a tall eucalyptus tree at the rear of the house I could see large pens of goats and sheep, babbling away to each other in Shoat language.

'How is Kuzu?' I tried to spy her in one of the pens.

'She's very well. She can now find Kedi with no help.'

'Who's Kedi?' I asked.

'Our cat.'

'And what does Kedi mean in Turkish?' I asked.

'Cat,' Ayshe said.

The house was basic and sparsely furnished with old wooden chairs and tables. The armchair that I'd seen on top of the car at the airport took centre stage in front of a huge, iron wood-burning stove in the kitchen-diner. It was spotlessly clean, though, but it looked like Osman wasn't really into DIY.

Kuzu came running towards us, wagging her woolly little tail.

Charlie clapped his hands together. 'I want one! She's so cute.'

Kuzu chewed on the bottom of my dress. I bent down to stroke her, scratching behind her ear, which she seemed to particularly enjoy.

'She likes you.' Osman grinned. 'Maybe I'll give her to you as a wedding present.'

'Do you keep her in the house?' Charlie asked.

'Yes. I hand-reared her after her mother died. She follows me everywhere.' Osman petted her on the head.

Osman's mum appeared, grinning and pinching our cheeks. She set about making the coffee in a small pan on top of the burner, squawking in high-pitched and animated Turkish to us all.

I thought I could make out her saying a sentence with the words "cucumber" and "toilet" in it, but I must've been mistaken because I couldn't possibly imagine what she was talking about. Maybe Charlie would know.

She handed us all small, ornate Turkish coffee cups, which must have been reserved especially for guests. I sipped on the strong coffee, feeling the caffeine rush zap through me like a bolt of adrenaline.

Charlie downed his in one go, forgetting about the thick, pasty granules left at the bottom of the cup that weren't for drinking.

He coughed and spluttered loudly, tears streaming down his eyes.

I slapped him on the back.

Osman's mum shook her head and said something to Ayshe.

'She says there's an ancient saying that the one who swallows the seed of the coffee will turn into a donkey.' Ayshe laughed.

'Which particular part of the anatomy will turn into a donkey?' Charlie looked pretty excited at the prospect.

Kalem pulled the camera out of my bag and showed the digital picture of Ferret Face to Osman. 'Do you recognize this man?'

Osman stared at the picture. Frowned. Stared some more. Scratched his curly, long hair. 'No. He's not Turkish Cypriot,' Osman said.

'How do you know?' I asked.

'You can tell by his facial features. This is a small island, where most people are related to each other in one way or another. Practically everyone you meet will be a cousin of a cousin of a cousin.' Osman pulled up a wooden chair. It creaked under his weight. 'In the old days, people lived in small villages and didn't go outside the village to look for a wife or husband. People intermarried with cousins. It's easy to tell who is Cypriot and who isn't.' He pointed to the camera. 'This man has tiny little eyes, like a mouse, and a pointed nose and chin. He looks like a ferret. No, this man isn't Cypriot. He definitely looks foreign. Maybe Syrian or Israeli. Why do you want to know?'

I debated about whether we should tell him. I quickly decided that maybe we should just spill the beans on what was going on. Maybe Osman could help us find him. Then I decided equally as quickly not to. What would a shepherd know about dealing with a crime of this magnitude? Probably not much more than us. And if we did tell him, then he'd tell Yasmin and Deniz that we were caught up in this whole scary thing. They would freak. And what if they had a stroke? Or a heart attack? Especially as they were ill. And they were getting on a bit now, too. The shock could kill them. Even I'd been having palpitations, so what could it do to them? Maybe it was psychological, but as soon as I thought that, I could feel my heartbeat jumping around.

No, we absolutely, definitely, one-hundred-percent couldn't tell him.

I glanced at Kalem. He shook his head slightly at me, affirming what I thought.

'Er...I thought he looked like someone I used to know,' I said vaguely, hoping Osman wouldn't think that was a strange explanation.

Osman paused for a while, watchful, as if pondering my answer.

I held my breath, wondering if he was going to question us further.

Then Osman slapped Kalem on the back. 'So, it's the big day on Sunday. How are all the plans going?'

I let out my breath and smiled. I didn't know if he was suspicious or if he was just being too courteous to probe further.

'Well, we still need to find a wedding dress. Helen's case went missing, and we don't know if we'll get it back,' Kalem said.

Charlie jumped up. 'I'm on it. Let me borrow the Land Rover, and I'll go hunting.'

Kalem's mobile rang. He went outside to take the call. When he came back in, he looked pale.

'Who was that?' I asked him.

'It was the University. My new boss wants to have a chat with me immediately. And he didn't sound very happy. Charlie, can you drop me off at the University? I'll quickly pop in and see my boss, and you can drop me back here before you go shopping.'

'No problemo.' Charlie waved to Osman and his mum. 'Byeee.'

'Is that OK with you?' Kalem kissed me on the cheek.

'Yes, of course.'

Osman's mum asked Osman something as the boys left.

He turned to me. 'Yes, of course!'

'What did she say?' I asked, smiling at her.

'She says that she still has her wedding dress, and you must wear it if yours has gone missing.'

I swallowed back a lump that had suddenly appeared in my throat, and my smile evaporated into thin air.

'I'll go and get it.' Osman disappeared.

I didn't want to be ungrateful or anything, but Osman's mum looked like she was about a hundred years old. I couldn't get married in some frumpy looking wedding dress that came up to my chin. All floppy and flappy down to the ground. Probably with moth holes in it, too.

'No!' I said, a little too quickly. 'Really, it's OK. I'm sure I'll find something else.' I beamed back at her.

Ayshe translated it to her, then waited for the reply. 'She says she can't take no for an answer. It would make her really proud. She says you have to wear it.'

Oh, my God! 'Tell her I can't possibly take it. Charlie will find

93

me something else and there won't be a problem.' I was so desperate for her not to give it to me that the sentence came out like one long word.

'She'll think it's really rude if you say no. She'll get upset.' Ayshe pulled a just-take-it-we'll-think-of-something-later face.

'Here it is.' Osman came back in the room, carrying the dress folded up in tissue paper.

'Er...thank you.' I took the package, trying to sound like it was the best thing since Vera Wang's wedding collection.

I rested it on my knee, not daring to sneak a peek at it for fear my face might give me away. Maybe if I didn't look at it Osman's mum wouldn't say anything else and just forget about it.

Osman's mum smiled a gappy-toothed smile at me, then said something else.

'She wants you to open it,' Ayshe translated.

Bugger. Wishful thinking. With shaky hands I unwrapped the paper.

Actually, I was wrong. It wasn't a frumpy wedding dress. It was far worse.

All eyes were on me as I took in the brownish-white stained dress with a hint of mildew and something else that I didn't even want to think about. Sheep's poo perhaps. Even a super strength dry cleaner couldn't get that lot out. It had long sleeves, a high neck, and was about five sizes too big for me. I think it used to be made of lace and, believe it or not, maybe sheep's wool. But now it was just, well, holey was the only word I could use. I fought the urge to scratch myself.

'It's lovely,' I croaked.

Osman's mum beamed back at me.

'Good. That's all settled then,' Osman said to me. 'Would you like to help me milk the sheep? They need milking now. Mother can read your Turkish coffee cup afterwards.'

'Er...OK.' How hard could it be? And when in Rome, as they say. In fact, it would be really sweet, milking a cute little Kuzu lookalike.

'Good. Follow me.' He strolled out the back door, wellies squeaking as he went.

'I'll come too,' Ayshe said.

Ayshe, Osman's mum, and I followed Osman towards the pen.

Ooh, the smell was a lot stronger here.

Osman grabbed a well-used looking white bucket and handed it to me.

Ayshe and Osman's mum leaned over the pen, stroking the sheep.

'What am I supposed to do with this?' I asked, waving the bucket at him.

'Collect the milk, of course.' He grinned.

'Right.' I frowned and whispered to Ayshe, 'Don't they have one of those milking machines that clamp on their nipples?'

'Would you want something clamped on your nipples?' Ayshe whispered back.

Well, when you put it like that, probably not.

Osman waved his arm at the sheep. 'As you can see, we do things in the old, traditional way here still.'

'I see. And how do I milk them, exactly?' I asked.

Osman opened the large pen and herded a giant, hairy, dirty sheep into a small pen at the side. It went straight up to a trough of grains and munched away. He crouched down behind the sheep and held his hand out for the bucket.

The poor thing's swollen udders looked about to burst.

He put both chubby hands round two teats and squeezed in a rhythmic motion from top to bottom. 'OK, you just squeeze the teats like this.'

The sheep didn't look too bothered, though. It didn't even seem to notice.

Osman quickly filled a third of the bucket, then led the sheep back into the main pen. He returned with another one who trotted off to the food, taking the opportunity for a quick chowfest.

Osman smiled at me. 'Your turn.' He handed me the bucket.

I glanced behind at Ayshe and Osman's mum, who were watching me with interest. Ayshe gave me an encouraging nod.

I crouched down behind the sheep. *Whoa!* It was even smellier from this angle. And it had crusty bits round its backside. Why did I agree to this?

'That's it; put your hands round the teats,' Osman said.

I squeezed and squeezed like I'd seen Osman do, but nothing would come out. 'I can't do it.'

'Keep trying, you'll get the hang of it in a minute.'

No, still nothing. The sheep looked up from her food, turned round in my direction, and I could have sworn she gave me a dirty look.

'I'll get another one.' He led Grumpy Sheep back to the pen and returned with another.

I clasped my hands round the teats again. This time I got a drip. Just the one, mind you.

'I can't do it. You make it look so easy.' I carried on trying anyway until my hands hurt. I dreaded to think how her poor teats felt. My boobs started hurting in sympathy.

'OK, try one more.' Osman brought another one in.

This one had a really big tail hanging down, encrusted in...well, you know. I scrunched up my face and turned it sideways, holding my breath as the smell was so overpowering. I lifted up the tail with one hand, feeling for its udders with the other. *Where are they?* I bet he wouldn't let me finish until I'd found one, and the idea of milking sheep didn't seem too appealing anymore. I carried on, my hands searching by touch. I wasn't going to stick my head under there, that's for sure.

'Ah, found it!' I grabbed its warm udder, trying to find the teat. 'Huh? This sheep has only got one teat.' I turned my head back around again.

Osman and his mum howled with laughter behind me.

'That's because it's a ram!' Osman guffawed.

'Urgh! I dropped its thingy and scrambled far out of sheep thingy squeezing distance.

Ayshe had to shove her hand in her mouth to stop the laughter.

Osman doubled over, clutching his stomach. Osman's mum gave me a gappy-toothed cackle.

'Oh, look, Helen, you made the ram smile!' Ayshe giggled at me.

Yes, playing practical jokes must definitely be a Cypriot thing.

I held my dirty palms up in the air to him, giggling. 'Come here, Osman, I want to give you a big hug.'

He backed away and legged it out of the pen, back into the house. 'No, no!'

I scrubbed my hands for ten minutes at the old ceramic sink before Osman's mum and Ayshe came into the house, still chuckling. Osman's mum said something to Ayshe.

'She wants to know if you enjoyed it,' Ayshe translated for

her.

'It was...' I glanced at Osman. 'Interesting.' I dried my hands on a piece of kitchen roll.

Osman's mum beckoned me towards her.

Uh-oh. What now? This family was definitely crazy.

'She wants to read your coffee cup,' Ayshe told me. 'Which means she's going to see babies, rings, and marriage – just like Mum does.' She grinned at me.

'Well, that's a dead cert at the moment, seeing as I'm getting married and you're pregnant.' I sat down next to Osman's mum, Turkish coffee cup in hand.

Ayshe sat forward in her chair. 'OK, you have to put the saucer on top of the cup, with your thumb on top, then flip it over. That's right. Now, leave the cup upside down to drain in the saucer.'

Osman plonked himself on a rickety wooden chair. 'She's so accurate, it's amazing. People come from miles around to get their coffee cups read. She's been doing it since she was a little girl. Her grandmother taught her. She's got the gift, you know.' Osman beamed at me.

Osman's mum lifted up my coffee cup, placed the saucer to one side, and stared intently into it. She sucked her teeth.

Was that good or bad?

She slowly rotated the cup clockwise; starting at the handle and working her way back round. She smiled. Tutted. Frowned. Then looked like she'd seen a ghost.

'What? What can you see?' Butterflies flew around in the pit of my stomach.

The whole room was silent as we all waited in anticipation.

When she finally spoke, Ayshe translated.

'She can see a ring.'

I relaxed with relief. She was probably just being a drama queen, and all she would see was exactly what Ayshe had predicted.

'This means marriage.' Ayshe translated Osman's mum's rapid Turkish and gave me a sceptical look.

Surprise, surprise.

'She can see a baby.' Ayshe patted her stomach. 'She says it's a girl.' Ayshe looked at Osman's mum open-mouthed. Ayshe really was having a baby girl. 'And she can see a rat.'

'A rat? Ew. A rat sounds bad. What does a rat mean?'

Osman's mum tilted the cup to get a better look.

'It means something will be stolen,' Ayshe said.

I thought about the sculpture. Ayshe and I passed an "oh fuck" look between us.

Osman's mum brought the coffee cup closer to her face, peering inside, tutting again.

'She's looking to see if there's a dot inside it,' Ayshe said.

'What does a dot mean?' I shouted anxiously.

Was it like a black dot? Maybe it meant a sniper shot! Murder! The dreaded black dot of death.

'She says if there's a dot inside, the item will be returned.'

Look for the dot! Look for the dot!

Osman's mum tilted the cup again.

'She says she can't see clearly. There might be a dot or there might not be. But she can see a ladder.'

Hmm. A ladder could be good, couldn't it? It might mean I'd be climbing to great heights.

'But it's broken.'

Oh. My shoulders deflated. Not so good. More like falling into a pit of despair, then.

'It means you have a difficult journey ahead of you,' Ayshe translated.

Oh, for God's sake, tell me something I don't *know.*

'She can see a Turkish coffee cup,' Ayshe said.

I know that! Get to the good bits.

Ayshe said something to her, then turned to me. 'It means someone will be drinking Turkish coffee.'

Well, that wasn't exactly hard in a country where practically everyone drinks it.

'And a glass of water next to it.'

'Yes, but what does that mean? Everyone drinks water after having Turkish coffee because it's so strong,' I said.

'She's not sure. But she can see a man. He's lying down.'

Osman's mum gasped at the cup.

'Is he...sleeping?' I asked hopefully.

'She can't tell. He could be sleeping, or he could be dead.' Ayshe locked fearful eyes with me.

The palpitations started again. I did some deep breathing. In. Out. In. Out.

'And she sees a fish.'

Agh! That man lying down would be sleeping with the fishes!

'She sees a big fish. It means money, apparently. A lot of money.'

I thought about the five hundred thousand dollars in the suitcase. Well, that bit was accurate, at least.

Osman's mum drained the coffee cup residue into the saucer and turned her attention to that.

No, not more. I didn't think I could take much more. Maybe it was better not to know what was going to happen.

'She can see a cross.'

Uh-oh.

'Sometimes a cross means victory. But it could also mean a hospital sign.'

No, no, no. I definitely couldn't take any more. Ibrahim Kaya was going to be shot by a black dot and would end up in hospital, then he'd die and be swimming with the fishes.

I was about to slap my hands over my ears so I couldn't hear anymore when, thankfully, Kalem and Charlie returned.

Kalem looked pale, bordering on a greenish tinge.

'What's the matter?' I asked him.

'My job.' Kalem swallowed hard. 'They've cancelled it. They said the funding has unexpectedly been cut for their department and there's no job available anymore.' He slumped down in a chair.

Chapter 9

'They can't do that,' I said to Kalem on the drive back to the hotel.

'They just did. They told me the government has suddenly cut their funding without giving them a reason.'

My mind started running away with me. 'Who in the government?'

'He didn't say.'

Why would the funding suddenly be cut when the University had practically begged Kalem to take the job? I thought back to Erol Hussein and his interest in Kalem's job. Call me cynical, but it had to be him. Who else could it possibly be? He probably didn't want us running around town, spouting off about suitcases filled with hundred dollar notes or plots to kill Kaya and steal the Cleopatra sculpture, because he didn't want anyone to know about the money. I bet he was probably spending it as we spoke. Horrible little man.

'That was my dream job.' Kalem shook his head, more to himself than anyone else.

'Kalem, I'm so sorry,' Ayshe said from the back seat.

'What do you think happened?' Charlie asked.

'I bet it was that bloody Erol Hussein,' I said.

Although, actually, maybe he'd done me a favour. I know this is going to sound really bad, but I didn't know if I could really live here now, anyway. I thought that moving abroad to start a new life in the sun would be an exciting adventure. I'd wanted to live the dream, but so far it had been a complete nightmare instead. I ran through my mental list, counting off the reasons I had not to stay. I mean, yes, I did have a list of nice things about the country that were probably good reasons to stay – things that I couldn't experience in the UK. But the list of reasons to leave was getting worse by the day…

1) Crazy extended family.
2) Involved in assassination and art heist.
3) Cursed by Queen Cleopatra's statue.
4) Spooky demons and giants running around mountains

100

scaring the shit out of people.

5) No convenient superstores or big shopping malls.

6) French Fancy wedding dresses.

7) Erol Hussein.

8) No job for Kalem.

9) No custard creams.

I felt a kind of weight lift from my shoulders. I'd really wanted to tell Kalem that I was having some serious doubts about moving here, and that I wasn't sure if I was cut out for the simple life. I know it might sound selfish, but now I wouldn't have to pretend anymore that I really wanted to stay here for Kalem's sake. If there was no job for him, we couldn't stay anyway. At least it meant that after the wedding there was no chance of us running into Ferret Face again if we were on the next plane home. But it was awful because I did feel heart-broken for him, losing his dream job. And all probably because of some greedy, nasty little man and my clumsiness in picking up the wrong suitcase. It was all my fault.

'Do you think we should try and speak to Erol again?' I suggested, because inside I was battling with thoughts of relief that we could leave the island, versus thoughts of self-loathing that, if it hadn't been for me, everything would be just going along as we'd originally planned. Poor Kalem.

'It won't do any good,' Kalem said. 'You saw him throw the evidence in the bin. He's not likely to investigate anything if there's a chance the money will be discovered. He just wants us off the island, so we don't tell anyone he's got it.' He paused for a beat. 'No. No, we'll just have to go back to the UK, and I'll have to find another job.' He smiled, but it was half-hearted, and I could see the pain behind it.

'I'm sure the college will give you your old job back.' Charlie tried to be helpful.

Kalem glanced in the rear-view mirror. 'Thanks, Charlie. When I left, they said I could always come back. It's just that this job was so perfect for me. Whereas in the UK I was teaching sculpture and woodcarving, here I was finally getting the chance to teach about my passion – historical sculpture. Now we've got to tell Mum and Dad that we won't be living in their house as well. They always knew my dream was to live the simple life

101

here. They'll be really disappointed. And Dad will want to kill Erol Hussein.'

'Why don't we wait until after the wedding to tell them,' I said. 'It's probably not a good idea to tell Deniz now. His blood pressure is pretty high as it is, without being ill as well.'

'My lips are sealed.' Charlie clamped his lips shut.

'We've got enough to worry about at the moment. We're getting married soon, and I want to be able to relax on my wedding day. And in order to relax, we need to get the President to take notice of us tonight, and I need to find my wedding dress.' I kissed Kalem on the cheek.

Kalem took his hand off the steering wheel and gripped mine. 'Yes, you're right. My job – or lack of it – will have to take a backseat until we get this mess sorted out.'

'I found you a possible replacement sort-of wedding dress,' Charlie piped up in the back.

I knew he couldn't keep his lips sealed for long.

I swung around in the front seat. 'What's a "sort-of" wedding dress?' I dreaded to think.

Charlie pulled a face. 'It's a gorgeous dress, and it would look super-freaking stunning on you...but...there's a slight problemo.'

'What?' I asked.

'It's black.'

'Some designers are saying that black is the new white,' Ayshe said, trying to lessen the bad news.

'Black! No. Absolutely not. No way. No sodding way. I can't wear black at my wedding.' I shook my head manically.

It was a sign. I was sure of it. And it wasn't a good one.

'OK, don't panic. I'll go back out and keep looking for something else when we get back to the hotel.'

'I can't get married in Osman's mum's dress, either. It's hideous.' I rocked back and forwards in the seat. I might have a nervous breakdown at any minute. Help. Mama. Mama.

'I don't care what you get married in, as long as I get to actually marry you.' Kalem caressed my cheek as he drove.

But all I could think was that the black dot of death and the curse of Queen Cleopatra were upon us.

At 6 p.m. Kalem and I were standing with the hordes of other

President wannameets at the Apricot Festival. It was being held in the village of Esentepe, at their wedding park, which, yes, you guessed it, was where the locals held their wedding parties.

The village was charming – quaint, with an eclectic mix of Cypriots and other nationalities. The wedding park had been set up so that little stalls, selling various wares, lined either side of the entrance. Further into the park there was an amphitheatre where the entertainment would be shown. To the side of the park, little cafes and makeshift bars had been set up. The smell of smoky barbeques and slowly roasted lamb cooked in traditional clay ovens wafted through the air.

I hopped from one foot to the other, fingering the letter in my hand.

I had it all figured out. I'd written a detailed letter to the President, explaining everything that had happened so far in concise detail. All I had to do was to get close enough to hand it to him.

'So, as soon as he's cut the ribbon to the entrance, we'll both rush forward and try to hand him the letter,' I said to Kalem.

'OK.'

I craned my neck over the crowd. A black Range Rover with tinted windows pulled up.

Right. Get ready.

The crowd let out a roar as the President exited the vehicle. Four bodyguards with earpieces flanked either side of him.

He gave the crowd a huge smile and an enthusiastic wave. Then he made a speech.

I carried on hopping. I needed a nervous wee as well. Stress was so not good for your bladder.

The speech seemed to go on for ages.

Oh, get on with it!

Ten more minutes of speeching, and then someone handed him a pair of scissors. He said something else in Turkish and cut the ribbon to huge applause.

Here we go!

I jostled my way through the crowd, all elbows and argy-bargy, with Kalem close behind. I heard a couple of yelps as I accidentally stood on a few feet. 'Sorry,' I mumbled.

I was half a metre away from him when a grumpy looking bodyguard stepped in my way.

103

'Hello.' I gave him my best no-of-course-I'm-not-going-to-attack-the-President smile. 'I just need a quick word with the President.'

Kalem said something to him in Turkish.

Grumpy shook his head, holding his ground.

Kalem said something else, his hands making urgent gestures as he talked.

Grumpy glowered at him and did more head shaking.

Some of the other bodyguards pushed the crowd away from the President.

I pushed forward again. Ouch! Someone's bag jabbed in the base of my spine.

Grumpy pushed me back.

In all the kerfuffle the letter got ripped from my hand. 'Hey!'

I scrambled around in the middle of the crowd, frantically trying to get a view of the letter on the ground.

Where are you? Where? Come on, I know you're here somewhere.

I twirled around in a circle, eyes glued to the concrete.

Kalem tried to barge his way closer. He shouted to the President, trying to catch his attention, but the President just waved his hand in return.

The weight of the moving crowd pushed us back further as the President moved.

There! I bent down and grabbed the note from the concrete. When I looked up, the President had drifted another metre away from us.

Oh, this was ridiculous. There was no way I could get close enough to give him the letter. Maybe I could throw it at him and hope he'd catch it.

I quickly turned the letter into a paper airplane, aimed it at the President, and shot for dear life.

It sailed through the air, above the heads of the crowd, in a perfect arc.

I held my breath. Just another bit further. *Come on. Come on. You can do it.*

And that's when it hit Grumpy Bodyguard, slap, bang in the eye, and then fell to the floor in amongst the crowd.

Oh, shit.

Grumpy's hand flew to his eye. With his other watery eye, he

104

scrutinized the crowd for offensive weapons.

He looked at me.

I ducked.

When I got up again the President was gone – through the crowd and making his way to chat with the stall holders, bodyguards protectively positioned on either side. The crowd around the president gradually reduced as they sought out the excitement of the food stalls and the entertainment which had just started in the amphitheatre.

'Look.' I pointed to a stall at the end of the line, selling household goods. 'There's no one on it. We'll just pretend it's our stall, and I'll write out another note to give to him when he stops.'

We ran to the stall and stood behind it. I grabbed a pen out of my bag.

'Why did we have to get the worst stall?' I stared at everything with dismay. 'What can we write on?' Why hadn't I brought some spare paper with me for just such an event?

Toilet brush holders, mugs, toilet rolls, wooden spoons, potties.

What the hell could I write on?

I glanced up. The President was three stalls away.

To my right, a tall guy was heading our way, waving his fist at us.

Oops, must be the stall holder.

'Kalem, go and distract him before he comes back.'

Kalem shot off to talk to the stall holder.

I looked around the stall frantically. *What can I write on? A potty? No way. A mug? No. Toilet roll! Yes.*

I took a toilet roll out of the packet and quickly scribbled:

Ali Kaya will be assassinated! Statue will be stolen. Please help. Must do something! Not a joke!

The President appeared at the stall. Grumpy stood next to him, rubbing his red, and very watery, eye.

'Hello, Mr. President,' I said, ignoring Grumpy. He couldn't prove it was me, anyway.

If the President noticed my flushed, sweating face, he didn't let on.

He held his hand out to shake mine. 'Hello.' He politely studied the stall for a moment and went to move on.

'Wait!' I shoved the toilet roll in his hand. 'It's a lucky toilet roll for you, Mr. President.'

He looked down at the toilet roll, slightly perplexed. Then he smiled politely. 'Thank you.' He gave me a slight nod and handed the roll to his bodyguard. The bodyguard frowned at it, as if wondering what he was supposed to do with it and they wandered off.

Kalem appeared at my side as the President strolled leisurely around the rest of the festival. 'Did you give him a note?'

'Yes.'

'I had to give the stall holder two hundred lira not to come back.'

'I had to write on a toilet roll,' I groaned with all the ferociousness of a wounded zebra.

'What? You gave the President a toilet roll?'

'It was a lucky toilet roll!' I cried.

'Why is it lucky?'

'I don't know. I just made that up, so he'd take it. And there wasn't anything else to write on. Do you think he'll read it?'

Kalem looked doubtful. 'Would you?'

I carried on watching as the President made his way back to his Range Rover.

Look at the toilet roll! Look at the toilet roll!

The bodyguard, still holding the toilet roll in one hand, opened the door to the Range Rover with the other, and the President slid in the back seat.

I sent him silent *open it! open it!* signals as the Range Rover slowly rolled away.

My gaze followed the Range Rover as it went further down the hill.

Its brake lights came on. Then it stopped. Its reverse lights illuminated as it slowly came back up the hill. My stomach bounced up to my throat. This was it! He must've read the note. He was going to come back and talk to us. I clutched my chest with relief.

The Range Rover screeched to a stop, and slowly the car door opened. Then Grumpy threw the toilet roll in a roadside rubbish bin, and they pulled away again into the starry night.

All the blood in my body seemed to rush to my head, making me dizzy. I launched my arms around Kalem's neck to steady myself and burst into tears, my nerves bristling with the hopelessness of our situation and my failure to make someone listen to us. It wasn't as if I'd asked for all this to happen. I didn't exactly have a choice in the matter, and I was trying my hardest to make someone listen. It's just that my hardest didn't seem to be good enough.

He crushed me in his arms as my shoulders heaved, my nose blocked up, and Kalem ended up with a big, watery mascara patch on his shirt.

Slowly, the sobs turned to deep sighs, and I struggled to catch my breath. 'What...are...we going...to...do...now?' I wailed in between sniffs. 'I don't want to go back to the hotel. I can't face telling everyone that we failed again.'

He grabbed my hand. 'Come on. I'm taking you to the beach. We'll think of something.'

'The beach?' I wailed, slightly louder this time.

'It's getting late. We can't do anything now. We've still got three days to think of another plan before the opening night. But now we need some *us* time. And I need to cheer you up.'

We grabbed a bottle of wine and some plastic glasses from the village shop and headed to the nearby beach.

Even though it was nine o'clock at night, the sand still warmed the soles of my feet as I slipped off my flip-flops. No one else was around. Just Kalem, me, and the gently rolling waves of the sea – oh, and a couple of crabs.

I looked up at the sky. It felt like the clear, black expanse was giving us our own personal light show. Thousands of stars, sparkling up above, winking at us. I could make out the Plough and Orion's belt, and – oh! A shooting star!

I quickly made a wish. *Please let me have the perfect wedding, save the statue and Ibrahim Kaya, and live to tell the tale.* OK, those were three wishes, but I said it really quickly so maybe the star fairies would only think it was one.

Kalem placed a beach towel from the Land Rover on the cushiony sand, and we sat down.

'This is beautiful,' I said.

He unscrewed the wine and poured out a couple of glasses. Handing me one, he said, 'To us.'

'To us.' I lifted the glass to my lips and paused, gazing at him over the rim, the full moon casting a silvery glow over his face. 'What are we going to do now?' I sniffed through my blocked up nose. 'No one wants to listen to us.'

Kalem sipped his wine, staring out to the ocean. 'We need to find Ferret Face.'

'And then what? Tie him up? Shoot him? Tar and feather him?' I sloshed wine around my mouth for a moment, thinking.

'Actually, I wouldn't mind shooting him myself at this point.'

I swallowed. 'Even if we could find out where he is, and he could be anywhere, I think someone in the police must be involved in all this. Why else would he have been talking to that officer at the police station? So if we find him, what do we do then? It doesn't seem like anyone actually wants to help us.' I glugged down my wine and poured another.

I wasn't cut out for this. I was a wedding photographer, for God's sake, not a bloody spy who's trained in international crime solving. I didn't even watch *CSI*. How was I supposed to know how to save an ugly statue and catch bad guys? I might have watched *Miss Marple* and *Poirot* a few times, but, to be honest, I think I fell asleep, so I hadn't even learned any useful tips on how to solve a crime. In fact, everything I knew about crime solving could be written on a flea's big toe.

'We have to take things into our own hands.' Kalem looked up at the stars. 'If we find him, we have to stop him from turning up at the opening at all. The statue will be going back to Ibrahim's private art collection afterwards, anyway, so I doubt if Ferret Face will have the opportunity to steal it again. And if he's incapacitated somehow, and he can't turn up, then he won't be able to assassinate Kaya either.'

'OK, we could try to find him and stop him going to the opening, but he could always try and kill Ibrahim Kaya another time after that. How can we stop that? We can't get to the President to tell him, we can't tell the police if we don't know who's involved there, and we haven't been able to get hold of Ibrahim Kaya himself.' I picked up handfuls of sand, letting it sift through my fingers absent-mindedly

We both thought about that in silence for a while until Kalem's voice interrupted the noise of the surf. 'I don't know. We've still got three days to find him before the opening night. I guess we'll have to take it one step at a time.'

But it all seemed so hopeless.

'Hang on a minute!' I clutched Kalem's arm. 'I've just had a thought.'

'Oh, God, I hate it when you do that. It's dangerous.' He grinned at me.

'OK, Ferret Face had floor plans of the hotel and casino in his case. But the other night when we saw him there, he looked like he was checking out the casino. Perhaps he'd already been around the rest of the hotel too. We also saw him in the bar at the Plaza afterwards.'

'Maybe he wanted to make sure the place was laid out exactly according to the floor plans.'

'Yes, if you're going to steal a priceless statue and try to kill someone, you would have to make damned sure that your sniper view of Kaya and your escape route was exactly as you'd planned it according to the floor plans, wouldn't you?'

Kalem nodded.

'And if you wanted to surreptitiously check out the Plaza to make sure, you'd want to blend in, wouldn't you?' I asked.

Vigorous nod.

'So the best way to blend in is to actually be a guest there. The staff wouldn't bat an eyelid at a guest roaming around.'

His eyes lit up. 'Yes! So we just have to scour the Plaza and find him.'

'Yes,' I said, although I didn't exactly relish the prospect of coming face to face with Ferret Face, but what other choice did we have? 'Well you can't look for him. He'll recognize you. I'll have to do it.' I took a deep breath, trying to psych myself up for such a horrible job. 'But there's something else as well. If Ferret Face is going to assassinate Ibrahim Kaya at the opening night, then someone else must be involved in actually stealing the statue. He can't do two things at once.'

'The assassination attempt must be a distraction so his accomplice can steal the statue.'

'Who would want Kaya dead?'

Kalem shrugged. 'I don't know. I don't know enough about him. We need to try and get more evidence. Then Erol will have to take us seriously.'

'Even if we get more evidence, Erol won't want to investigate because it will mean giving up the money. It looks like the only option we've got is to try and stop Ferret Face and his accomplice ourselves.' I swirled the wine round in my glass thoughtfully, worrying about the enormity of such a task. I looked up at the stars, hoping they would miraculously give me some kind of answer. They didn't.

'Our container is arriving at your parents' house tomorrow morning. So we have to be there then. Straight afterwards we can put Operation Find Ferret Face into action. Let's try and forget about everything for a while and concentrate on what we were supposed to be doing this week: having some relaxing, pre-wedding couple time.' Kalem took my glass and set it down on the sand.

Yes, he was right, of course. We couldn't do anything else tonight, and I seriously needed some kind of distraction from it all. 'Ooh. And what did you have in mind?' I giggled.

In the moonlight I saw his eyebrow lift slowly. 'How about skinny dipping, for starters.' He took my hand and pulled me up, then quickly stripped off his cotton shorts and shirt. 'You coming?'

I didn't need asking twice. I yanked my sundress over my head and threw it on the towel, quickly followed by my knickers.

'Oh, wait!' I folded my knickers inside my dress. 'I don't want to catch crabs.'

We slipped into the warm water, hand in hand.

'It's like a bath.' I wrapped my legs round his waist and slid my fingertips over his back.

Kalem groaned in the silent air, his shoulders tensing as he held me close. 'You look even more beautiful in the moonlight.' He murmured into the curve of my neck. 'So beautiful.' His lips brushed against my neck, my ear, my collar bone, my chin, the edge of my mouth.

'Mmm.' God, did he know how to work his lips. I shivered with delight.

Slow, erotic nips against my lips turned into sensual kisses, his mouth gliding against mine, his tongue sensually teasing me.

'I love you.' I ran my hands up and down his spine, sighing in ecstasy before he silenced me with a kiss.

An explosion of pulses swept through my body like a tsunami. I gripped his buttocks, pulling him closer, licking, tasting,

110

stroking.

He plunged his hands in my hair. 'Maybe we should get out.' His voice was throaty as he suddenly drew back, cupping my face in his hands.

His eyes were intense and dark, like coal shimmering in the moonlight. He nodded towards the towel on the beach.

Well, I didn't need asking twice.

We hurriedly slipped from the sea, our bodies shiny and wet with salt. Lying down on the towel, entangled in each other's limbs, I was aware of only the heat from his body against mine as we moved to the rhythm of the tide.

Later, as we lay facing each other, his fingertips tracing a line up and down my hip, and mine gently stroking his thigh, I heard a noise a little further up the beach. It sounded like something was moving along the sand.

I turned my head to get a better look and saw the most amazing thing. Clutching Kalem's arm, I pointed in the direction of the noise.

A turtle dragged itself over the bumpy mounds of sand, etching a trail along the beach. It looked huge, probably a metre long. In the moonlight you could see a greenish tinge to its mottled shell.

'It's a green turtle,' Kalem whispered to me. 'She's come up to nest on the beach. We need to be really quiet until she starts to lay her eggs. Otherwise we'll disturb her.'

'She's gorgeous.' I stared at her, slack-jawed in amazement, knowing I was about to watch something that I'd only ever seen on TV before. How cool was this? To watch a turtle laying its eggs a short distance away. Wow.

We dressed silently as she wandered up the beach for a while, then seemed to think better of it and changed her mind, coming closer towards us again.

'They go into a trance when they lay their eggs, and we'll be able to get right up close to watch it.' Kalem grinned at me. 'I thought nothing could be as fantastic as making love on a deserted starlit beach, but this is just amazing.'

After a few more trails up and down the beach, the majestic beauty seemed to decide on the right spot and started digging. Her flippers dug slowly, flicking the sand away from her body with force, so that it flew in the air and landed way behind her.

111

She carried on for what seemed like an hour, stopping now and then for a rest. Dig, dig. Stop. Breathe. Dig, dig. She carried on until the hole was a deep bowl shape. And finally, when she seemed satisfied, she stopped, face turned up to the sky.

Kalem grabbed my hand, and we padded silently towards her. I held my breath, just in case she could hear me. She didn't seem to notice us as she started to lay large clumps of eggs into the nest, plopping into the cavity at speed.

We stared on in awe, not daring to move a muscle. It was the most spectacular thing I'd ever seen.

'When will they hatch?' I whispered.

'In about two months. They have a Turtle Project here every summer to aid conservation. Students from all over the world come and scour the beaches during the laying season so they can put protective covers over the nests once they've laid their eggs. It stops wild dogs and other creatures digging them up and ensures the maximum number of baby turtles hatch.'

When she finally finished, she had the mammoth task of refilling the nest chamber with sand. The poor thing looked exhausted. The muscles in the back of my neck started to ache as we stood for probably another hour, watching her cover up the nest.

Then she slowly lumbered back towards the sea and slipped into the moonlit water, her job done.

'That was absolutely unbelievable.' My smile felt like it stretched from ear to ear.

Kalem looked deep into my eyes. 'It was magical. You see, this is what I've been trying to tell you. This is exactly what the simple life is all about. Getting to experience nature and life in a way that we can't in the UK. God, Helen, I really want to stay here. I know my dream job has disappeared, but this is priceless. Sitting on a star-packed beach, just us; watching the stars with a bottle of wine, making love on the sand, and seeing a turtle lay her eggs. We're so lucky to be here. To be experiencing this. I don't care if I've got to take a less exciting job, we're going to stay.' He picked me up and spun me around.

Chapter 10

To say that things were not exactly going too well at this point would be a slight understatement. To be more precise, in spite of the spectacular evening on the beach, I'd had a stressed out, stomach-churning, shit-heap few days.

I wasn't exactly looking forward to having our container arrive at Yasmin and Deniz's house either. Partly because I wanted to get on with Operation Find Ferret Face. Now we had some kind of a plan to find him, I wanted to hurry up and get on with it. Also, partly because having all of our possessions arrive meant that we would definitely have to stay here. And the hard thing was that I really didn't know whether I could stay here after all that had happened so far. Never mind the fact that I would hardly ever see Ayshe again, the lack of shopping, and the crazy extended family who had a sniffer sheep as a pet, our arrival here had been tainted and cursed since the very beginning. And that, like some kind of domino effect, seemed to be spiralling my doubts about living the simple life here out of control. But Kalem so badly wanted to stay, that I couldn't tell him how I was feeling, could I? No, it wouldn't be fair to him. Yet with the container arriving, it felt like some sort of finality, and it looked like moving abroad was beginning to be the worst mistake of my life. I'd also now developed some sort of peculiar phobia about customs men, and guess who was accompanying the container to fill out all the paperwork?

I felt horribly sick and overwhelmingly depressed. This was supposed to be the most important week of my life, but all I wanted to do was curl up under the sheets and never come out again.

The only spot of good news in all of it, I supposed, was that at least all my other clothes and shoes would arrive in the container, since I was rapidly running out of things to wear.

'We'd better go and see your mum and dad.' I forked in my last mouthful of breakfast in the dining room and pushed away my plate. 'See if they're getting over the food poisoning yet.'

Kalem nodded.

Ayshe blew on a cup of steaming herbal tea. 'Not only is Dad obsessed with the condoms, he's now really into *Cosmopolitan* magazine. So be warned.'

'What's wrong with that? I *love* Cosmo.' Charlie dabbed at his lips with a napkin.

'Yes, but you're not normal.' I chuckled.

'Where's Atila gone?' I asked Ayshe.

'He's another one that's acting strange. He was having a really weird dream last night, mumbling something about place settings and illuminated menus. And he keeps getting calls at all hours from the manager of his restaurant in London. Maybe the manager can't cope without Atila there to sort things out.' She shrugged. 'I don't know, but something strange is going on. I'm sure of it.'

'Well, maybe he's just worried about leaving it,' I said. 'This is the first time he's actually left control of it to a manager, isn't it? He's bound to be a bit worried. You know what a stressy perfectionist he is in the kitchen.' I thought about how Gordon Ramsayish he gets in the kitchen, barking out sweary orders to his staff, which was a complete contrast to his normal, laid-back self.

'Yes, but he whispers down the phone like something top secret is going on. Maybe it *is* the heat, it's certainly having an effect on me.' She fanned at her flushed face with a napkin. 'Ah! Maybe he's having an affair.' She stopped fanning abruptly. 'Do you think that's it? Maybe it's not the restaurant manager phoning him at all. Maybe it's his bit on the side!'

I stood up and enveloped her in a hug. 'Of course not. That's just ridiculous. He loves you to bits. No.' I shook my head firmly. 'There is absolutely no way he's having an affair.'

She patted my arm. 'No, you're right, of course, he wouldn't be having an affair. My brain has just turned to pregnant mush, thinking all these stupid things. Just forget I said that.'

'Forgotten.' I smiled at her. 'Charlie, are you still willing to go to the Plaza and try and find Ferret Face until we get back from sorting out the container?'

'Absolutely. I always wanted to be a private dick!'

'If you find him, just keep an eye on him and ring me. This is what he looks like.' I handed him my camera with the picture of Ferret Face safely stored on it. 'OK, let's go and see Yasmin and Deniz.'

114

When we arrived at their door, there was another note addressed to the maid. Kalem snatched it up.

'Oh God, I dread to think what is says.' I rolled my eyes.

Kalem read it out loud. '"Dear Maid, please don't leave the cheese and pickle condoms anymore, they leave an unpleasant after taste. The spicy ones are a little too spicy. Are they vindaloo, by any chance? Do you have any korma to madras spiciness varieties? If so, please leave ten. If not, I will make do with ten mild ones, but only under duress."' Kalem's eyes nearly popped out. 'What the hell are they doing? They'll kill themselves.' He banged on the door.

Yasmin opened it, looking terrible. The air conditioning was set to the highest temperature possible – sun-baked desert. Deniz had the covers pulled up to his chin with his nose buried in *Cosmopolitan*.

Yasmin climbed back into bed like it was a huge effort.

'God, it's boiling in here.' I wafted a hand around in front of me to fan the air.

'I'm freezing.' Yasmin shivered, her teeth chattering.

'Me too.' Deniz peered over the magazine at us. 'Have you brought me any condoms? I've got through eight packets from the mini-bar now.'

'I don't think you're in any fit state to be thinking about condoms,' I chided. 'You need to conserve all your energy for getting well.'

'I told you – he's obsessed.' Yasmin tutted. 'He thinks the maid fancies him now.

'She does!' Deniz put the *Cosmopolitan* down.

'She's about seventeen. Why would she fancy a seventy-year-old, wrinkly little man?' Yasmin snorted at him.

Deniz ignored her. 'She wants me.' He tapped the side of his nose. 'I can tell when a woman wants me.'

'Have you seen the maid?' I asked. 'I didn't think they'd come in if you had a *Do not disturb* sign on the door.'

'Of course he hasn't seen her. He keeps writing her notes about the mini-bar, though, and leaving them outside.' Yasmin sighed.

'The maid thinks I'm virile,' Deniz said.

'Oh, no, I feel sick again,' Yasmin said.

So did I, just thinking about it.

'How are you both, then? Any better?' Kalem asked, trying to change the subject.

'Worse.' Deniz said.

Yasmin rested her palm on her forehead. 'And my back's killing me.'

I wasn't surprised if he'd put away eight packets of condoms.

'Still, at least Mr Seventy-year-old wrinkly man is keeping himself busy with magazines and not annoying me too much.'

Deniz looked at the magazine, shaking his head to himself. 'It's *fascinating* the things in here. *Fascinating*. Did you know that there was so much choice with a fu fu?'

Kalem and I all looked at each other, horrified about where this was all going to end up.

'What's a fu fu?' Yasmin said.

'You *know* – a woman's lady garden.' Deniz pointed to the magazine. 'You can have the Playboy Strip, the Landing Strip, the Moustache – that one doesn't sound very nice – the Triangle, the Brazilian, the Arrow. Wait until I get on to the next article: *The Secret Diary of a Talking Penis (Age 35)*.

Kalem stood in the centre of Deniz and Yasmin's bungalow, head tilted, wondering where to put our container full of stuff. 'I'm going to move the furniture around so we've got room for all the boxes and extra furniture when it gets here.'

'Do you want a hand?' I asked.

'No, you and Ayshe spend some time together and relax. It hasn't exactly been the ideal pre-wedding couple of days we had in mind, and there's not much else you can do until the container gets here anyway.'

'That sounds good to me.' I grabbed a couple of cushions for the sunbeds, and Ayshe and I positioned ourselves on the terrace for maximum tanning exposure.

'What a crazy couple of days,' Ayshe sighed.

'You're telling me.' I tilted my face to the sun and closed my eyes. 'Crazy *and* scary. This is more like it, though. I could get used to this. God, I hope Charlie manages to find Ferret Face.'

'And what about the wedding dress? Has Charlie found a replacement?'

'No,' I groaned and opened my eyes. 'I don't want a replacement. I want *my* one.'

'Of course!' Ayshe slapped her head. 'It's got your nan's charm sewn into it. Oh no! Helen, I forgot.'

'I know. I have to have that charm at my wedding. Apart from the fact that it will feel like some part of Nan is there with me, I've got this horrible feeling that if I don't get it back, our wedding will be doomed to bad luck from the start. Everything isn't going particularly well now, and we haven't even got married yet.'

She reached over and squeezed my hand. 'I'm sure everything will work out OK.'

But I wasn't so sure. 'And if I don't get it back, how can I get married in Osman's mum's dress? It's hideous.'

'I know, but she'll be offended if you don't wear it.'

'I'll just have to think up some excuse. I don't want to offend her, but it's the most important day of my life. I wanted it to be perfect,' I groaned.

'Have you got any dresses in the container that you could use as a wedding dress?'

I thought about my vast shopaholic wardrobe. 'OK, maybe there is *something* I could probably wear, but that isn't the point. I want *my perfect* dress.' I flapped a hand in the air. 'Anyway, I don't want to think about this for five minutes. I'm sick of thinking about gun-wielding maniacs and yucky statues. Say something to take my mind off it.'

Ayshe sank back in the cushions. 'OK. Barack Obama, David Cameron, and Nelson Mandela. Who would you marry, sleep with, or throw off a cliff?'

'Ooh, that's an easy one. I'd marry Nelson, sleep with Barack, and throw David off a cliff.' I giggled. 'Your turn. Superman, Batman, and Spiderman.'

'No! It has to be real people.'

'Who says so?' I laughed.

'Oh, OK, then. Superman's got a dodgy haircut and a bit of a Kryptonite issue, Batman looks sexy in black rubber, and Spiderman's quite agile. Hmm. I'd marry Batman, sleep with Spiderman, and throw Superman off a cliff.' Ayshe giggled. 'Right, let me think of a hard one.' She tapped her lips. 'I know. George Clooney, Brad Pitt, and Antonio Banderas.'

'That is hard. I want to marry all of them. Well, wouldn't mind sleeping with all of them either, actually.'

'No you have to choose,' she said.

'I'd marry Antonio, sleep with Brad, and throw George off the cliff.'

'How could you throw George off a cliff?' She cackled.

'You made me!'

'Container's here,' Kalem shouted from the house, interrupting our howls of laughter.

I got up. 'You and bump stay here and chill out while we get everything sorted.' I wandered into the house and looked out of the lounge window.

A huge lorry with our twenty-foot container on the back had pulled up outside. Behind it, a Customs and Excise vehicle parked. A short guy got out, followed by a taller one, who looked a bit like Julio Iglesias.

'OK, so what's the procedure?' I asked Kalem.

'We'll unload all the stuff, and the customs men might ask us to open up a few boxes and make sure the contents are the same as what is listed on the inventory we provided. Simple. As long as you don't do anything strange.'

I raised an eyebrow. 'Me? Strange?'

'Yes. Probably best if you just let me do the talking.' He wandered towards the front door.

'Fine. I just hope they don't ask to look in the box with my Rabbit in it.'

He stopped suddenly and swung around to face me. 'Didn't you pack it in your case?'

'No, was I supposed to?'

'I thought you knew they might look in some of the boxes!'

'Well, it's a good job I didn't pack it in my case, isn't it? Otherwise Ferret Face might have got it instead.' I shivered at the thought. 'Urgh! Imagine that.'

'Oh, God. What else have you got in those boxes?' Kalem gave me a worried look.

'Nothing. Apart from our personal stuff and the usual household items.'

'You're sure?'

I suddenly remembered something else. 'Oh, and twenty-eight packets of custard cream biscuits.'

'You're not supposed to bring food in a container,' he hissed.

I shrugged. 'I wasn't sure if you could get them here or not, so

I packed a few to tide me over, just in case.'

'What else is in there that shouldn't be?' Kalem's olive skin turned pasty.

'Nothing else!'

'What did you describe the Rabbit as on the inventory?'

'Pet equipment.'

He stared at me.

'Well, it's a Rabbit!'

'What about the box with the custard creams in it?'

I tilted my head to the side, thinking. 'Um…I think I put them in with the pots and pans. Come on, they're not going to be interested in opening a box with pet equipment and pots and pans in it, are they?' I dragged him outside.

Hellos all round. Then Julio asked us to inspect the seal number on the container against our inventory paperwork. Yes, it was the same one. Could we please cut the seal in front of them? Yes, did that. Then down to business.

Two burly guys with the lorry driver helped Kalem and me unload the boxes into the house as Shorty and Julio stood by the side, looking into the container for secret contraband with serious looks on their faces.

'What's that?' Julio pointed to a table top patio heater I'd recently bought.

'A patio heater,' I said, climbing off the container with it.

They looked at each other, glanced up at the scorching sun, and burst out laughing. 'In Cyprus? Ha-ha.'

I was just about to say that I could use it in winter and then thought about Kalem telling me to leave the talking to him, so I just smiled at them. I didn't want to get arrested for smuggling custard creams into the country on top of everything else. I admit that I did have a teensy habit of letting my mouth run away with me sometimes, so maybe it was for the best if I just kept schtum.

Julio peered at one of the larger boxes, checking the number on it. He ran a finger down the inventory list to check what the contents were listed as. 'Gas barbeque,' he said, glancing up at us. 'Is this a barbeque?'

'Yes,' I said, avoiding Kalem's eyes.

'No,' Kalem said at the same time.

Kalem looked at me, puzzled. 'But we haven't got a barbeque.

119

I knew I should have done the inventory myself. Let me have a look at the list, there must be some mistake.' Kalem held his hand out to Julio, so he could inspect the inventory list.

Julio ignored his hand and frowned. 'Open it.'

'Yes, well, the thing is, we have actually got a gas barbeque.' I pulled an embarrassed face at Kalem.

'Why would we need a gas barbeque when we can cook on a natural charcoal barbeque? Or better still, we could cook in the traditional Cypriot clay oven that Mum and Dad have got in the garden,' Kalem said to me, attacking the tape on the outside of the box with a utility knife.

'I bought it as a surprise for you,' I said. 'You know – for our new al fresco lifestyle. It's all bells and whistles.'

'How much was it?' Kalem asked me.

I avoided his gaze. 'Er…a few hundred pounds.'

'How many is a few?' Kalem said.

'Well…slightly more than four hundred pounds.'

Julio and Shorty stood around as Kalem opened the top of the box, revealing a supersized, top of the range gas barbeque, complete with an external wok ring looming up from the side like a giant steering wheel.

'Four hundred pounds! On a barbeque? What, does it convert into a sit on lawnmower? Or a golf buggy?' Kalem pointed to the wok ring. 'Or maybe it's a satellite dish.'

'OK, no need to get funny about it,' I huffed. 'I thought it would be a nice surprise.'

'That doesn't look like a barbeque.' Julio suddenly looked more serious and official. 'What's that?' He pointed to the wok ring as well. 'A steering wheel?'

'It does look like a golf buggy.' Shorty tried to turn the wok ring around and around, as if he was trying to steer it.

'No! It's a wok ring,' I cried.

Shorty and Julio exchanged puzzled looks.

'It could be a satellite dish,' Julio said to Shorty. 'You have to pay extra for electrical equipment.' He got a calculator out of his pocket and started working out how much import tax we'd have to pay. 'That will be two thousand lira tax for a satellite dish.'

'Two thousand lira!' I said. 'But it's not a satellite dish *or* a golf buggy. It's a barbeque!'

'Well, so far the *barbeque* will have cost us an absolute

fortune,' Kalem said the word barbeque as if it were an imposter and only pretending to be one. 'I thought we were supposed to be living the simple life.'

'I thought it would be a nice surprise,' I said, head down, staring at my feet.

'OK, if it's a barbeque, you give us a demonstration,' Julio said to me.

'Right. OK. No problem at all.' Then hopefully we could get this little misunderstanding cleared up and get on with things. 'I just need a wok.' I looked at Julio's copy of the inventory to see which box my wok was in. 'There's a box of pots and pans in here somewhere. I'll just grab one of those, and we can be cooking with gas,' I quipped, then noticed their serious faces. 'So to speak.'

Oh, no. Wait a minute. I had a mental head-slapping moment. The custard creams were in the pots and pans box. I couldn't draw attention to those. They already thought we were importing bloody satellite dishes. I didn't want to get into any more trouble.

'Hmm. Probably best if I get a wok from inside the house. Your mum and dad must have one in the kitchen. I'll be right back.' I zoomed off the back of the container like a spaceship in sight of Area 51.

By the time I'd rummaged around in all the cupboards, Julio, Shorty, and Kalem had lugged the barbeque into the garden and hooked it up to the gas bottle that was connected to the kitchen cooker.

'Da-da!' I waved a wok around. 'Here we go.'

After a demonstration that Jamie Oliver would have been proud of, they finally let us carry on with unloading the boxes, and a sweaty forty-five minutes later, we were down to a few boxes at the back of the container.

Shorty pointed to one of the boxes. 'There is a hole in that one.'

I climbed into the container to get a better look. He was right. There was a hole. And it looked like something had scratched or gnawed its way through.

Urgh! Rats. I bet we had a rat somewhere in the container when we loaded it up. Just my luck! I hoped it hadn't chewed up all my clothes or the sofa or done a plop in my knickers or –

agh! I noticed my scrawled label stuck on the box. Shit. It was the pots and pans box. Help! They were going to find the custard creams.

Shorty and Julio climbed aboard.

'Open it up,' Julio said.

Oh, no. Not good. I slowly bent down and undid the packing tape, wondering how many years I'd get for this. This was it. I was going to be arrested and hauled off to jail.

Shorty leaned over my shoulder as I opened the box.

I held my breath.

He rummaged around inside. Amongst the saucepans and frying pans, he found twenty-eight packets of empty custard cream wrappers.

He narrowed his eyes and said something to Julio in Turkish.

Kalem jumped on board. 'Everything OK?'

Shorty turned around to Kalem, waving a custard cream wrapper at him in a vaguely threatening manner. 'What's this?'

And that's when I heard a funny squeaky noise from behind the other boxes.

I ran to the opposite end of the container. 'Rat!' I pointed a shaky finger. 'Rat!'

Julio moved the other boxes out of the way. Shorty and Kalem huddled around to get a better look.

'What?' I yelled. 'Is it a rat?'

Kalem slowly bent down and picked something up from the floor. He turned around to show me what he was holding. In his arms, he had a skinny bundle of grey, fluffy fur, which looked suspiciously like our previous next door neighbour's cat.

The poor thing was obviously worn out and must have been severely dehydrated. Well, I suppose I would be as well, stuck in a container for several weeks with no water and only the custard creams to eat. It looked at me with sad, fragile-looking eyes, and made a funny squeak, like it had lost its meow.

My hand flew to my face. 'Oh, my god!' I walked towards Kalem. 'It looks like Smoky, our old neighbour's cat. He must've climbed in the container when we were loading it up.' I stroked his soft fur and thought I could just about make out a faint purr. 'We need to get him to the vet as soon as possible.'

Shorty and Julio were having some sort of hushed conversation. Now I was probably going to get arrested for cat *and* custard cream smuggling, but I didn't care. I might be able to live with that – well, OK, maybe not – but I couldn't cope with knowing that poor Smoky might die, and I would be responsible for murdering my neighbour's innocent cat.

'You take it to the vet and come back.' Julio pointed at me with a stern look on his face. 'Do you know where one is?'

I shook my head.

'My wife is a vet in Kyrenia. You go there.' Julio rattled off some directions to me.

Kalem quickly emptied one of the final boxes and placed Smoky's feather-light body inside. I carried him to the Land Rover, praying it wouldn't pack up again.

It started first time. Hurrah!

I drove like a maniac to the vet, beeping the horn, and doing a few scary overtaking manoeuvres. Luckily, the vet was in reception when I arrived and ushered me straight into the treatment room.

The vet reached into the box and examined him. 'What happened?'

'He was stuck in our container from the UK. He had twenty-eight packets of custard creams to eat, but no water in there.'

She nodded. 'He's severely dehydrated and has lost a lot of body weight. You get condensation in the metal containers. He probably would've licked the walls, but it's not enough. I need to get him on an IV drip straight away.' She grabbed a cannula from a nearby draw. 'You can leave him here. I'll call you when he's well enough to go home. Leave your details with the receptionist.'

'So you think he'll be OK?'

'I'm pretty sure after a few days on the drip he'll be a lot better.'

'Oh, thank you! Thank you!' I left the vet's after giving them my contact details and rushed back to face the music.

Maybe I wouldn't be arrested, I thought as I came up the hill to the house. Maybe I'd just be deported, which was actually quite a welcome idea at the moment. But...hang on a minute, where was everybody? I noticed the lorry and car had gone.

'Kalem?' I jumped out the Land Rover and rushed into the house.

Maybe Kalem had been arrested for aiding and abetting an

international biscuit smuggling ring, and they were holding him hostage to make sure I turned myself in.

'Hi, how was Smoky?' Kalem looked up from hauling a box into one of the bedrooms.

'The vet thinks he'll be OK. What happened to the customs men?' I lowered my voice to a whisper. 'Are they hiding in wait for me?'

He chuckled. 'They've gone. Luckily for us, that singer, Jayde, is arriving on a flight soon, and they got called back to the airport for reinforcements, in case there are any rowdy paparazzi there.'

I clutched my chest. Thank God. I'd just been saved by a superstar. I vowed to buy every single one of her records as soon as I got the chance.

'But what did they say about Smoky or the custard creams?' I flopped down in a chair. 'Oh, no. I get it. They're coming back later to arrest me, aren't they?' I squeezed my eyes shut, waiting for Kalem to give me all the horrible details. 'It's OK. You don't have to break it to me gently. Just spit it out and get it over with.'

'Julio's sister rang him when you left the vet's to say that if it hadn't been for your custard creams, the poor cat would have starved to death. Julio decided to overlook the incident because he felt sorry for Smoky. Count your lucky stars that he's an animal lover.' He kissed me on the nose and put the box on top of a mountain of others.

'Well, that's a relief.' My hand flew to my chest. 'Smoky should be OK, but how are we going to tell his owner that his cat is about two and a half thousand miles away from home? Poor thing.'

'I'll give them a ring in a minute.'

'Where's Ayshe?' I asked.

He nodded towards the terrace. 'Asleep on the sunbed.'

'How did she manage to sleep through all that palaver?' I shook my head. 'Right, now that's all sorted out, we need to get on with Operation Find Ferret Face.'

'I just spoke to Charlie on the phone. He hasn't had any luck finding him.'

'Great.' My face crumpled. 'The trouble is, he could be absolutely anywhere.'

'He's going to meet you back at our hotel for some lunch before you go back to the Plaza with him and carry on looking. Like you said before, I can't come with you because he'll recognize me from the airport, and it might tip him off, so I'll stay here and sort out some of these boxes. Do you want me to dig out some of your clothes?' He scratched his head, staring at the daunting mountain of boxes everywhere.

'Yes, please.'

'OK.' He stood in front of me and rested his arms on my shoulders, giving me a serious look. 'And if you do find him, ring me. I don't want you doing anything crazy or stupid that's going to jeopardize your safety.'

'Absolutely. And we need to synchronize watches.' I glanced at my watch.

He frowned. 'Why?'

'I don't know, but I saw it in a spy film once.' We adjusted our watches until they were both showing the same time down to the very second. I didn't know exactly what it would achieve, but it sounded proactive.

'What about Ayshe?' I peered through the patio door to check she was still asleep.

'She can stay here with me and sleep. I think the heat is affecting her pregnancy more than she's letting on. She looks wiped out.'

'I'm going to sleep for a week when this is all over.' I rolled my eyes to the sky.

The only problem was… would I still be alive?

Chapter 11

I met Charlie at the poolside bar of our hotel. No, actually, I rendezvoused with him (also saw that in spy film).

I'd asked him to wear something inconspicuous to stakeout the Plaza in search of Ferret Face, but his idea of inconspicuous was not wearing pink. Instead, he had on a lime-green pair of cut-off trousers and a canary-yellow T-shirt with the words *Sex Goddess* on the front.

'I couldn't wait for you to eat. All this running around the Plaza has given me an appetite.' He tucked into a plate piled high with moussaka and rice mixed with noodles.

I ordered an iced coffee and a hellim cheese salad when the harassed waitress came over.

'So, no luck finding Ferret Face, then?' I asked.

'No.'

My eyes wandered around the pool area. Lots of people sunbathing, leisurely swimming, and tucking into bright-coloured cocktails at the bar. It wasn't fair. That's what I should be doing as well.

'He must have an accomplice, but we don't know who he is either,' I said. 'Oh, Charlie, what are we going to do?' I slumped down in my chair.

'Well, if it was me, I'd hide and not come out until Christmas,' he said through a mouthful of rice.

'Thanks for that helpful suggestion.'

'Or get on the next plane back to the UK.'

I glanced up at him. 'That has actually crossed my mind. I'm not even sure if I want to live here after all this. It hasn't exactly been what I was expecting.'

'What? I love it here! Well...apart from the shops. Imagine never being able to nip down to a huge shopping centre to buy clothes.'

'That's exactly what I thought. Do you think that's shallow and materialistic?' I said as the waitress brought my order.

Charlie pouted at me. 'You're talking to the queen of shallow here, so I'm probably not the best person to ask, really. But,' he raised his forefinger in the air, 'that's what living in a hustling-bustling city does for you. It's constantly drummed into us that we have to spend, spend, spend to be happy. And, of course, everything is convenient, too. I mean, what would I do without internet shopping, for God's sake? Order your groceries in the morning and two hours later, hey presto – they're being delivered to your door! And what about our supermarkets or DIY shops? Having everything you could possibly need under one roof. Whoever thought of that is a genius!' He finally paused for a breath.

I shook my head. 'No internet shopping here, I'm afraid. They're lucky if they have an internet connection half the time, apparently.' I forked a piece of rocket and tomato into my mouth.

'Ew. Very Seventies.' He screwed up his face. 'I think they need my fabulous computer programming skills over here.' He grinned. 'Well, maybe if it's a slower pace of life here, you won't be able to rely on the convenience factor, like in the UK, anymore. It might take you a bit longer to get things done, but,' he shrugged, 'that's the sacrifice, I suppose, for living the dream. I mean, being here is like stepping back in time, which doesn't necessarily have to be a bad thing.'

'Well, yes, there are some fantastic things here, but I'm not sure if I'm cut out for the simple life. Don't get me wrong, I didn't want it to be a mini UK in the sun. I just thought it was going to be more...more cosmopolitan and modern. And I can't tell Kalem. He wants to find another job and stay here.'

'OK, so what did you expect when you moved to North Cyprus?'

'Well, when Kalem asked me, it was at the same time that he proposed. So of course I was excited. I had a vision in my mind of moving from the gloomy UK to sunny Europe. Kind of like a *Shirley Valentine* moment, I suppose. Of course I've done lots of research in the last six months, so I knew it was going to be unspoiled and not like the commercial holiday destinations that I've been to before. But I'm a city girl. *And* a shopaholic.' I prodded a piece of hellim. 'How am I going to get to wear my Jimmy Choos when I'm up to my ears in olive picking and mucking out chickens? And I didn't know that some of it was going to be so...so basic. I found out that they don't even have a postal service. How weird is that?'

'No postal service? Hmm.' He thought about this for a second. 'What about takeaway delivery?'

'Oh, they have that. Just not out in the sticks where we'll be living.'

He waved a dismissive hand. 'Actually that might be quite nice, not getting any junk mail. I'm fed up with getting bloody leaflets asking me if I want Viagra. I mean, honestly, do I look like I need it?' He wiggled his hips. 'How could this perfect specimen need Viagra?' He took a sip of gin and tonic and lounged back in his chair, eyeing me carefully. 'It's just different here, that's all.' He shrugged. 'And, anyway, some of it *is* cosmopolitan and modern. You've got the big, fancy hotels, haven't you? OK, some things might be a smidgen basic, and they still like to do things in the old traditional Cypriot way, but I think it's quite quaint, and it actually makes this place unique. It's just a case of taking a bit of time to get used to it, that's all.' He leaned forward and pointed his fork at me. 'OK. What's the worst that could happen if you stay?'

'We could get killed by Ferret Face.'

'Forget about that for a minute.' He waved his hand and a blob of rice fell off the fork and onto the table. 'Close your eyes.'

'What?' I chewed on a piece of hellim that made my teeth squeak and frowned at him.

'Just do it. Go on, close your eyes.'

'Charlie, you're being ridiculous, why should I close my eyes?'

He sighed. 'I want you to use your imagination for a minute. I know you've got a rather bizarre one, so humour me.'

'OK,' I huffed, putting down my fork and closing my eyes.

'Right, I want you to imagine a mini film in your head of everything you've seen since you came here. A lovely, happy, little film.'

'Charlie what's–'

'Ssh! Just do it.'

I sighed and closed my eyes.

'Are you doing it?'

'Ye-es,' I grumbled. 'But my salad's getting cold.'

'OK, now think about what Cyprus has to offer that the UK doesn't.'

I took a deep breath and thought about it. 'Well, lots of

sunshine for a start. I hate the winter in the UK. Brrr. It's got lovely, unspoiled beaches here – Oh, my God, and I forgot to tell you the other night that we even saw a turtle laying its eggs on the beach! It was amazing. And we saw a baby goat being born by the side of the road. It was so sweet.'

'That's it. That's the kind of thing I'm after. OK, what else?'

'Erm…it's got lots of culture and historic places to explore. Miles and miles of rolling countryside and mountains. It's got an unhurried, casual pace of life that is actually really appealing. It kind of makes you feel free, like you don't have to look at your watch every five minutes to make sure you're on time for the next appointment or job so you can earn more money and rush off to pay more bills.'

'So, basically, it's less stressful?'

'Yes. And it's light and bright and makes you feel kind of energized. It's got delicious fresh organic food. It's so sweet to see the sheep and goats wandering around, nibbling on the wild plants. It has views that I've never seen in the UK. And it's cheaper.'

'Hmm. So, when you put it like that, it's actually got quite a lot going for it.'

I opened my eyes then and looked at Charlie, pondering what I'd just said. It did actually sound like a fantastic opportunity to move here when I put it like that.

Charlie shot me an amused look. 'What about the bad things?'

'Well, Ayshe and you will be in the UK, and I'll hardly ever see you. Kalem's extended family are nutters. No big shops. No takeaway delivery away from town. No internet half the time. No postal service. Power cuts. My wedding dress is missing with my nan's lucky charm. Erol Hussein is out to get us. Kalem hasn't got a job now. We're cursed by the Queen Cleopatra statue. I might end up like Felicity Kendall in *The Good Life*. And all of that's without even including Ferret Face. I think that's plenty, really. Oh, why did we have to come here?' My face crumpled. You see, when I put it like that, it sounded more like a horror film. 'Everything was perfectly normal before this.'

He tapped his lips. 'Yes, I see your point, although I can't quite see you as Felicity Kendall. And I don't think Osman and his mum are nutters.'

'But they've got a sniffer sheep, he made me milk a ram, and they crack boiled eggs on any available surface. That's so not normal.'

'I'd say that just makes them quirky, but then you aren't exactly quirk-free, are you, missy?' He carried on eating.

I tilted my head. 'Well…no.'

'So, if you hadn't picked up Ferret Face's suitcase, everything would be going as you planned, and you'd probably actually enjoy being here? Apart from the shops and Ayshe and me.'

I narrowed my eyes, deep in thought for a minute. 'I think so.'

Charlie put down his fork and slapped a hand on the table. 'Well, let's go and find the bad guys and do something about it.'

I drained the last dregs of my coffee. 'Yes, you're absolutely right.' I vaulted out of my chair.

We moseyed through the front door of the Plaza like a couple of chilled-out holiday makers. A different receptionist was on the desk. The smile was the same, though: helpful and courteous. I bet they all had mouth ache when they finished their shifts. Our flip-flops clicked across the glittery marble reception area as we made our way past the loungey leather sofas to the bar at the side.

No Ferret Face.

OK, not a problem. It was early days yet and the place was huge. Huger than huge, in fact. It was like a mini town.

'Let's do the inside first, then we can go out to the pool area,' I said, sauntering past an open-plan piano bar with only a few people inside.

We took the stairs down to the lower ground floor, past the trendy boutiques. No Ferret Face doing a spot of haute couture shopping. Not surprising, really, judging by the state of the contents in his suitcase.

'Let's try the spa.' I pointed towards the doors and pushed them open.

Ooh, very nice. Subtle low lights, terracotta walls, scented candles dotted around, and the smell of…well, I wasn't sure, but it was pretty yummy, whatever it was.'

'Hello,' I said to the perfectly made up spa receptionist with super shiny black hair. How did she manage to get it like that? 'Is it OK, if we have a look around?"

'Hello, sir, madam. I'm the spa manager here.' Another very

helpful smile. 'Let me give you a tour of the facilities. We at the Plaza want you to have the maximum enjoyment experience.'

Oh, if you must, but be quick about it.

She led us past the desk, around a juice bar with lots of weird-coloured drinks that had bits of vegetables sticking out the top, and we entered a corridor. Leading off to one side were some inviting-looking sunbeds. The urge to lie down and sleep myself into oblivion was overwhelming, but we had more important things to do.

'This is the chill-out area,' she said, carrying on up the corridor, through some glass doors, and sauntering towards an empty indoor pool.

Very nice. Lots of mosaic tiles and Roman-looking murals. Past the pool to another glass door that led to a gym with the latest hi-tech equipment.

'And here is our luxurious spa,' she announced after we'd gone up yet another corridor and through some more doors.

God, you could get lost in the spa area alone.

'Is it OK to look at the changing rooms?' I enquired sweetly.

'Yes, of course. That is the men's.' She nodded to Charlie. 'Feel free to have a look.'

I mouthed to Charlie, 'Look for Ferret Face.'

'Ooh, yes, please!' Charlie seemed a bit over-enthusiastic at checking out the men's changing rooms.

'And this is the women's.'

'Yes, it's lovely.' I nodded, making a mental note to check myself in for a five-hour massage when this was all over.

Charlie emerged from the men's at the same time we came out of the women's. 'Lots of fit men in there!' Charlie's eyes had popped out on stalks.

Trust him to get sidetracked. I rolled my eyes and made an impatient *well?* gesture at him, turning my palms upward and shrugging at him.

He shook his head at me.

No Ferret Face. Damn.

'And here are the treatment rooms.' The spa manager proudly swept a hand towards five empty rooms and one closed door at the end, which had a *Do not disturb* sign on the door.

Well, as if that would stop me!

I knocked on the door.

'You can't go in there, madam. Someone is having a treatment!' she said.

'Man or woman?' I asked.

'Pardon, madam?'

'Is it a man or a woman having a treatment? I'm doing a survey on how many men have beauty treatments for *Just for Women* magazine.' I gave her a gleaming smile.

'*Just for Women* magazine! Oh, you should have said. That's wonderful. I buy it every month,' she gushed.

Was there even such a magazine? I'd just made it up.

She held her hand out to me, ready to shake. 'It's so lovely to meet someone from the magazine. If there's anything you need, anything at all, please don't hesitate to ask me.'

She tilted her head, waiting for me to ask something.

'Well, I'm definitely going to give this spa a mention.' I beamed at her.

She clapped her hands together and gave me a smile so wide I could almost see what she had for breakfast. 'Oh, that's wonderful! I loved the article you did last month: *How to Have the Best Orgasm.*'

'Great! I'm glad you liked it. I did that one.' I gave her a conspiratorial wink.

'You know – I never knew you could use a –'

'So…man or woman?' I cut her off, inclining my head to the treatment room, waiting for an answer.

'Oh, it's a woman in there, madam.'

'OK, thanks very much. You've been very helpful.'

'Are you her assistant?' she asked Charlie.

'I'm the magazine make-up artist.' Charlie flicked an imaginary stray hair off his forehead.

She clapped her hands together again. 'This is *so* exciting. How big will the piece be?'

'What piece?' What was she going on about?

'The piece in the magazine about our spa.'

'Ah! That piece. Er…I don't know. I haven't made up my mind yet.' I smiled at her.

Charlie peered at her make-up. 'Very nice use of eyeliner.'

She blushed. 'Can you give me a sneak preview of what will be in the next issue?'

I tapped my nose like it was a state secret. 'It's all very hush-

hush. Wouldn't want our rivals getting hold of it, would we?'

We left her standing there with an excited expression on her face.

Next up was the casino. Lots of gamblers who looked like they'd spent the night in there, but no Ferret Face.

We took the lift to the rooftop swimming pool. More plants, heavy-duty wooden sunbeds with lush-looking beige cushions, swim-up bar, poolside bar, lots of oiled up guests. The place was heaving, to say the least.

'Ooh, I love the shade of pink that couple has gone. What would you call that?' Charlie whispered to me. 'Pink Blush? Hot Tulip?'

'More like Scorched Raisin, I think.'

We scoured the whole area: The Perfect Couple with matching face lifts and other bits that defied the laws of gravity, the Tanned Couple who had their legs at uncomfortable looking angles to make sure they didn't miss a spot, the Loud Couple with screaming kids that looked like they could star in *The Omen* film as a Damien stand-in. And lots of varying shades of Speedos, but no Ferret Face in any of them.

We took the mirrored lift all the way back downstairs.

'Are we ever going to find him?' I stamped my foot.

Four restaurants? Nope.

Three other bars? Nope.

Maybe I was wrong. Maybe he wasn't even staying here. What did I know? I was just a wedding photographer, after all. It seemed like a good idea yesterday, but maybe it was all just a hopeless waste of time. Maybe we'd have to scour the whole of North Cyprus looking for him. The only problem was, we didn't have enough time to do that before the opening night.

'Let's check the downstairs pool area.' Charlie wandered back past reception again and outside.

I put my sunglasses on and scanned the crowd, taking in the Olympic-size kidney-shaped pool, complete with a waterfall in the middle and a Jacuzzi at the side of it. Another pool bar. Hammocks. Giant cushions that you could easily fall asleep on if you didn't have to worry about running round trying to find criminals.

Past the pool and down a flight of steps, and we found ourselves staring at a huge stage area in front of the sea. Behind the stage was the hotel's port, with several yachts that looked like they cost an arm and a leg – or maybe a whole army's worth of arms and legs. A few other smaller speedboats bobbed around in between them, lowering the tone a bit. To our right and left were a host of outdoor bars and restaurants.

'I'm hot and thirsty.' I stomped towards the stage bar and collapsed onto a cream sofa so soft that I almost got swallowed up in it, like I'd been attacked by a giant marshmallow. 'This was a ridiculous idea. We're never going to find him.'

Charlie patted my knee. 'Don't give up hope. I'll get some drinks. Back in a jiffy.' He darted off.

I flopped my head back on the chair, people-watching the crowd.

Suddenly I sat up again.

It was Ferret Face. Making his way down the steps with another man. A short, stocky, and very hairy man with really long arms who could have easily passed for a gorilla, or possibly the Missing Link between man and ape.

I watched from behind my dark glasses as they approached the bar, ordered two glasses of amber-coloured liquid, and sat on another sofa about five metres away from me. They leaned together, heads almost touching, having some sort of animated conversation.

Sit closer to me! Sit closer! Stupid people. Didn't they know I wanted to listen to them?

Charlie sat down with two glasses of freshly squeezed orange juice. Ferret Face and Co. were now directly behind him.

'He's over there,' I hissed. 'With another man. I bet it's his accomplice.' I rummaged in my bag, looking for my camera.

Charlie turned around to get a look-see.

'Don't look at them!' I pretended to take a photo of Charlie and zoomed in on Ferret Face and his friend behind him, snapping off a couple of pictures.

They sipped their drinks slowly as we looked on, then stood up to leave.

'Quick. We need to follow them.' I stuffed my camera back in my bag and grabbed Charlie's arm.

They wandered up the stairs, past the pool, through Boutiquesville, and past reception with us following close behind.

'Excuse me, madam!' The receptionist from the other night called after me. 'Ibrahim Kaya is in the building at the moment. I can ask him to come and speak with you about your nuts.'

'No time! Will come back later.' I waved at her and hotfooted it out to the car park, just in time to see Ferret Face and Missing Link heading up the drive in a black four-by-four of some kind.

We jumped in the Land Rover and pulled out onto the main road, following a few car lengths behind. What was the usual distance for tailing a car? Directly behind? One car behind? Two? What if we lost them?

I held my breath and overtook one car, just in case. Right, now they were just one car in front.

Ferret Face raced over a roundabout and headed towards town, just as the last of the dusk turned into night.

Charlie grabbed the door handle as I raced behind Ferret Face, trying to keep up with him. 'You go, girl.' Then something caught his eye. 'Hey! Another wedding dress shop!' He pointed out the window. 'Must check that out later.'

'Ouch!' I whacked my head on the roof as we bounced along over a speed hump. 'Where's he going?'

We drove through the narrow streets in the centre of Kyrenia, and Ferret Face took a sharp right turn. Then he parked up and they got out.

I drove past the four by four, eyes scanning around for a parking spot.

Charlie pointed. 'There, further up.'

We jumped out of the Land Rover without bothering to lock it and followed them on foot all the way to the harbour.

They passed some open air cafés and then turned into one next to the sea.

'Maybe they're getting another drink,' I said.

But no. They walked through the bar area and opened a wooden gateway at the end that led to the gang plank of a very expensive looking yacht, sandwiched in between a traditional Turkish gulet boat and a fishing boat.

We plonked ourselves down in the café and watched them climb aboard the yacht, which had the words *The Israelite* on it. They slid open a darkly tinted patio door and disappeared inside. A few minutes later, we saw them appear on the roof deck with an older man. As they sat down, we could barely see the tops of their heads.

'I need to get closer,' I whispered. 'I can't see or hear anything.'

'OK, I'll stay here in case they leave.'

The gulet to the right of the yacht had two couples on it, drinking wine. I heard the clink of glasses and soft laughter. The fishing boat to the left was in darkness, so I crept through the gate towards it. The good news was that it looked empty. The bad news was that it stunk of fishiness.

I pinched my nose and crept up the gangplank, keeping a beady eye on the yacht to my right. The fishing boat bobbed a little under my weight as I slipped onto the wooden deck.

From here I couldn't even see the tops of their heads anymore. I needed to get even closer. Making my way past the cabin, I eased up the deck. Now I was close enough to touch the side of the gleaming white yacht. The fishy smell was even stronger here. Yuck!

The yacht had a lifebuoy dangling from the railings on the top deck above me. If I could just grab on to it, I could pull myself up higher to be in prime listening position against the side of the yacht.

I reached up, but it was a teensy bit too high. OK, only one thing for it.

I climbed onto the railings of the fishing boat, hands against the side of the yacht, trying to keep my balance as I lifted up on my tiptoes. *Come on. Come on. Yes*!

I snared the buoy in my right hand. So far, so good. From this position I could just about make out what they were saying.

'We're going to the Sultan's Palace restaurant after this,' one of the men said.

'Make sure you try the lobster. It's the best on the island,' another one said in a gravelly voice.

'Good idea.' I recognized Ferret Face's voice. 'After that I'm going to the stage bar at the Plaza. They've got the best vintage Courvoisier there.'

Oh, who gives a shit what you're going to eat and drink. Get to the good bit!

'I want this to go like clockwork,' Gravelly Voice again.

'Don't worry, Mr. P, we've got it all covered.' The other one spoke again, and I was guessing it was Missing Link. 'I've

136

already hacked into the hotel's security system and covered my tracks. It won't show any disturbance to their security features at all. They won't have a clue that we've intercepted their security system. As soon as he fires the shot to kill Kaya, the security system is set to completely disarm the lasers on the outside of the statue case, and the glass casing below will slide down. The shot will cause a distraction. It will be a full-scale panic. People will be running away, screaming, and all the guards will rush to Kaya, who will be on the stage in front of the port.'

'Excellent. Excellent.' I heard the excitement in Gravelly Voice's words.

'Then I'll take the statue from the stage area and jump onto the speedboat, waiting at the port,' Missing Link carried on.

'But what if the guards don't leave their post at the statue?' Gravelly Voice asked.

I took a sharp intake of breath. It sounded like an explosion in my ears, but they didn't seem to hear it because they carried on talking.

'I'll shoot them as well if I have to.' Ferret Face this time. He sounded like he'd enjoy doing it too. 'My bedroom is in prime sniper position overlooking the stage area. Don't worry. Even if the shot to kill Kaya doesn't distract the guards, I will have a clear shot of anyone getting in my way.'

I gulped.

'Just make sure you kill Kaya,' Gravelly Voice said. 'He can't double-cross me and get away with it. That hotel was supposed to be mine. My plans. My idea. And soon, it will be mine with Kaya out of the way. I'm going to take over his business empire, piece by piece, just like he did when he tried to ruin me.' He followed with a throaty chuckle.

'It's a done deal, Mr. P,' Ferret Face said. 'You don't have to worry about a thing.'

'Good. It had better be. I didn't pay you half a million for nothing.' Gravelly Voice again. 'Tomorrow my biggest enemy will be out of the way, and Kaya's precious little statue will be en route to the art dealer in South Cyprus. Bye bye.' He chuckled again.

Another gulet suddenly chugged into the harbour with a rowdy bunch of tourists. Music blared away as they danced on the top deck.

Oh, shut up. I want to listen! I strained my ears, trying to make out more conversation.

The party boat turned around, repositioning itself to reverse into a spot further up the harbour, sending the water bouncing up and down, bumping against the fishing boat.

As the fishing boat dipped down on a wave, I lost my grip on the buoy and catapulted backwards off the railings, legs shooting in the air like I was a human cannonball being launched.

'Agh!' I landed backside first in a large plastic box of fish and crabs in front of the cabin.

I rolled over onto my back and tried to sit up, but the slimy wet fish seemed to keep sucking me back into a slippery abyss. One of the crabs clawed at my hair and another attacked my legs.

'Help!' My arms and legs flailed in the air, trying to grab something to hold onto so I could pull myself out. 'Ouch!' A crab nipped my bum. *God, that really hurt*!

I heard a thudding noise from the engine room below as someone ran up the stairs, and a fisherman appeared, looming over me.

'What the–?' He frowned at me and held his hand out.

I grabbed it, and he pulled me out of the box. 'Thanks!' I twisted around to look at my bum, which now had a crab hanging off, its barnacle-encrusted pincers locked firmly on. 'Oh, my God! Get it off, get it off!' I thrust my bum towards the fisherman, vaguely aware that the people in the harbour had stopped talking and were all turning to gawp at me. 'Ooh, hurry up! It hurts,' I said to the fisherman, who seemed to be taking a long time to prise the thing off me. Maybe he was enjoying it. Pervert!

Out of the corner of my eye, I saw Ferret Face, Missing Link, and Gravelly Voice leaning over the top deck of the yacht, pointing and laughing at me.

Great.

I heard a crunching sound as the fisherman pulled the crab off.

I twisted around again to make sure it had gone. Yep, no crab. I rubbed the spot where it had clung on for dear life, wondering if it had actually taken a chunk out. Did crabs eat humans? I didn't have a clue. Maybe it was a killer crab.

I shuddered.

The fisherman eyed my backside with appreciation. 'That is a dangerous red crab.'

I gulped. 'How dangerous?'

Gravelly Voice leaned on the railings of his boat, looking down at us and watching the show.

'Very,' the fisherman said. 'You've only got ten minutes to get to the nearest hospital.'

I felt a warm glow crawling up my legs. No! It had started already. The poison must be seeping through my veins. 'How far away is the nearest hospital?' I cried.

'Fifteen minutes away.' The fisherman let out a smutty chuckle. 'Want me to suck out the poison?'

Missing Link thought this was hilarious, leaning his head back and howling up to the sky.

See, I was right. In fact, he could've been a close relative of that giant hairy man who lived in the woods; what was his name? Oh, yes. Bigfoot!

'Yoo hoo!' Charlie climbed aboard to the rescue. 'Oh there you are.' He winked at me. 'I thought I'd lost you. Come along.' He linked my arm and tried to steer me off the boat.

The fisherman blocked our path. 'Hey, not so fast. What are you doing on my boat interfering with my crabs?'

I opened my mouth to say that the crab actually interfered with me, but thought better of it and clamped it shut again.

'I get it. You're from that big fishing company, aren't you? Trying to steal my catch again and force me to sell out, aren't you?' He narrowed his eyes at us. 'I've had enough of–'

'No, we're from the…Turtle Project.' I interrupted, straightening myself up and dusting off my clothes, trying for my best authoritative look. 'We've had a report of a turtle on one of these boats in the harbour, and we're just checking it out,'

He frowned.

'Have you seen one?' I asked him, covertly rubbing my bum.

Missing Link howled even louder. 'How is a turtle supposed to get on a boat?'

'I saw one earlier,' Gravelly Voice shouted down at us. 'Yes, I saw it leaving the Chinese restaurant with a bag of seaweed. It just left on a Jet Ski.' He pointed out to sea, trying to contain his amusement and failing.

Missing Link nearly wet himself. Ferret Face slapped the

railings of the yacht, tears streaming down his face. The fisherman cackled.

OK, OK, it's not that funny.

'Right, well, if you see one, please let the Turtle Project know.' I gave the fisherman a haughty look.

He stepped aside and let us pass.

Charlie wrinkled up his nose at me. 'You stink.'

'Well so would you if you'd been squished in fishiness,' I huffed as we bolted out of the harbour with a hundred pairs of eyes following us. 'Do you think that's what Osman's mum saw with the fish in the Turkish coffee cup?'

Charlie shrugged.

'God, what if everything else she said comes true?' A chill slithered through my bones.

'You don't really believe in all that, do you?'

'Of course not! Don't be ridiculous!' I didn't want to even contemplate it. I ran a hand over my matted, squelchy hair. 'Have I got crab poop in it?'

'Do crabs poop?'

'I don't know, but I can feel something in it.' I waved a hand in front of my face to try and disperse the smell. 'I need a shower. Can you drop me off at our hotel and pick up Kalem from his parents' house for me?'

'You need more than a shower. You need a decontamination chamber.'

'Do you think it was a poisonous crab?'

'No. No such thing.'

I guessed that I'd find out in about another five minutes.

Chapter 12

I grabbed a quick shower. Well, no, I thought it would be quick, but a whole bottle of papaya and lemon shower gel later, I could still smell bloody fish. You don't even want to know what I pulled out of my hair!

Another ten minutes of bubbles and spray left me pink and blotchy. Now I smelled like a slightly fruity fish, so I squirted a quarter of a bottle of perfume and half a bottle of body spray on. Great, now I was carrying enough fumes to gas a small country, but at least I couldn't smell any sea creatures anymore.

'What have you done?' Kalem almost shrieked at me as he rushed into the steamy bathroom, side-stepping the wet towels I'd flung on the floor. He went into a choking fit from the fumes. 'I thought you were going to ring me if you found him, not do something that could put you in danger.'

'There wasn't time! I had to follow him. And it's a good job I did, otherwise we wouldn't know exactly what they're planning.' I grabbed his arm and yanked him out the door. 'We have to go back to the Plaza and try to warn Ibrahim Kaya. He was there earlier, but I was a bit occupied following Missing Link and Ferret Face.' I filled him in on what I'd overheard on the yacht.

'OK. Well just leave all the talking to me this time. We don't want any confusion about nuts again. The opening ceremony is on Friday. This could be our last chance to get someone to stop this.'

'And what if we don't get to talk to Kaya?' I slid behind the wheel, wound the window down so we didn't pass out from the perfume fumes, and rammed the gearstick into first. 'Now we have more information about what's going down, we need a plan B.'

'Going down?' He threw me a questioning look.

'Yes, I heard that in a crime film once.'

Kalem thought about this for a while. 'The assassination is the distraction designed to get the guards away from the statue. If they can't shoot Kaya, there won't be any distraction, and they won't try to steal the statue because the guards will be posted in front of it.'

'So we need to concentrate on stopping Ferret Face from trying to shoot Kaya,' I said, feeling lightheaded at the enormity of the situation. I took a couple of deep breaths and nearly passed out from the fumes. 'And how do we do that?' My mind wandered around various scenarios. 'Hit him over the head and knock him out?'

'Do you know what room number he's staying in at the Plaza?'

'No. I didn't actually see him go into a room.'

'If we hit him over the head, we might have to do it in public, which wouldn't work.'

I glanced over at Kalem. 'Tie him up?'

'Again, how can we do that in public? And I would think Ferret Face might be a bit resistant to being tied up.'

'He might be kinky. We could find out what room he's in, and I could pretend to be a hooker and tie him up.'

Kalem gave me a not-in-this-lifetime look. 'Too dangerous.'

'I know! We could drug him.'

'How?'

I thought back to the conversation on the boat. 'Ferret Face is going to the bar at the Plaza after his meal tonight to drink posh cognac. If we don't get to speak to Ibrahim Kaya, we could buy some sleeping tablets and put them in his drink.'

'Are you nuts? No, let me rephrase that. I already know you're nuts. How are you going to put them in his drink?'

'I don't know yet. I'll have to improvise. Maybe I can pretend to be a barwoman and slip them in there, or…I know. I can try and chat him up. Yes! That's it! I can buy him a drink, shove in the tablets, and hey presto! Nighty night Ferret Face. Then we can tie him up and wait for help to arrive. The President would have to do something then, surely.'

'I don't like it. It could be dangerous.'

It wasn't really high on my list of fun things to do either. 'But we might not have any other choice.'

'Anyway, isn't he going to recognize you from the harbour?'

'Damn. I hadn't thought of that. Make-up. I need lots and lots of make-up. I've got some in my bag. And I'll put my hair up. It was dark on the fishing boat, and he was looking down at me from the yacht, so hopefully he won't recognize my face.' He might recognize my bum, but I didn't want to even think about that.

'He might need a lot of sleeping tablets to knock him out so we can tie him up with no trouble.'

I pulled into a late night pharmacy and gave Kalem a wicked grin. 'Well let's give him a lot then.'

We arrived at the Plaza armed with some extra-strength, fast-working sleeping tablets. The pharmacist assured us that one tablet would be enough to knock someone out for eight hours. I thought that if I gave him three, he'd be in the land of nod for at least thirty-two hours. She also advised us that some people could have a severe allergic reaction to them...

Me: Oh, yes? What sort of reaction?

Pharmacist: It can make your hair fall out, or give you hives, or long-lasting diarrhoea.

Me: Really? Interesting. Very interesting.

As we turned into the Plaza's entrance the traffic was at a standstill. Hundreds of cars lined the driveway, nose to tail. The car park was crammed with people trying to park, and at the entrance to the hotel, hundreds of paparazzi and journalists waited around. A white Hummer limo sat out the front, engine running.

'What's going on?' I asked Kalem.

'It must be Jayde arriving to stay at the hotel.'

I eventually found a space and zoomed into it before a TV crew, complete with cameras and furry microphones, beat me to it.

'Right, let's get proactive. We need to crush up three tablets, so they're all ready.' I rummaged in my handbag, looking for some implement to use. Notepad? No. Comb? No. Camera? No. What? Cigar tin!' I pulled out a slim cigar tin and emptied out the cigars. I waved the tin at Kalem. 'If you crush them on the dashboard, we can put the granules inside it.'

Kalem quickly got to work, grinding the small white tablets into powder and teasing it into the cigar tin as I piled on dark brown eye shadow, lashings of mascara, blusher, and a bright vermillion lipstick. I pulled my hair back into a long ponytail and surveyed the finished look in the visor mirror. Fab. I looked completely different from the harbour. Even I didn't recognize me.

He handed me the cigar tin. 'I'm coming with you.'

'No!' What if Ferret Face is outside with the paparazzi?'

Kalem stared at the mass of photographers and reporters. There were probably about two hundred people out there in the mayhem.

'I can't see him being out there with them. And if I stay in the middle of all those people, he won't be able to see me anyway.' He put a baseball cap on his head and pulled the peak down low over his face. 'I'm not just sitting in the car and waiting for you to come back. It could be dangerous. It's a chance I'm going to have to take.' The look on his face meant business.

I sighed. 'OK.' I slid the tin in my handbag and hung my camera around Kalem's neck as we got out of the Land Rover. There. Now he'd just blend in with the other paparazzi. Hopefully.

'Make way, *Just for Women* magazine coming through.' I jostled through the crowd out front.

'*Just for Women* magazine?' Kalem questioned me.

'Don't ask.' I shook my head and turned to a photographer on my right. 'When's Jayde arriving?'

'She's already arrived. We're just camping out to see if we can get any more pictures of her. Hey, did you say you were from *Just for Women* magazine? My wife loves that. Do you have any vacancies for more photographers there?'

'Sorry, they're all filled at the moment.'

'Look, here's my card. I'd appreciate a heads-up when there are any vacancies.' He handed me a white business card.

I took the card. 'Sure. Is Ibrahim Kaya here?' I asked him.

'Yes, he's busy giving Jayde the star treatment, making sure her rooms are OK and all that stuff.'

'How many does she want?' I frowned.

'She's got an entourage of about twenty people.'

'Is that his limo?' I jerked my head towards the Hummer at the rear of the crowd.

'Yes. I think he's leaving for some meeting with the President as soon as she's settled in,' the photographer said.

I leaned closer to Kalem, whispering in his ear, 'OK, let's put

144

plan B into action first. You wait here and blend in until you see Kaya. If he leaves before I get back, you can try to talk to him again. I'll go to the pool bar and see if Ferret Face is there.'

He clutched my arm, staring deep into my eyes. 'I'm coming with you.'

'You can't! We've already been through this. He might recognize you. You need to wait here in the crowd, where he won't be able to see you.' I clutched his arm, feeling tears stinging my eyes. 'I don't want to lose you. I can do this on my own. I promise.'

He let out an exasperated sigh. 'OK, but you have to able to get in touch with me instantly if you need help. Give me your mobile phone. We need to have a link to each other so I know exactly what's happening.'

I unzipped my handbag and passed it to him. He dialled his own mobile phone from mine. Reaching into his pocket he answered the call and selected the *mute* setting on his phone. Then he handed me my phone back. 'OK, now we have a direct phone line to each other. Keep your mobile in your hand, and I'll be able to listen to everything that's going on. That way, if you get in any trouble, I'll be able to hear it straight away and come and get you. My phone is on mute, so your phone won't pick up any noise from my end.'

I took my mobile phone back and held it in my hand. Swinging my handbag over my shoulder, I nodded. A bad stinging sensation worked its way up from the pit of my stomach to my throat. Sort of like indigestion but a hundred times worse.

Everything will be OK. Everything will be OK. I repeated it over and over again as I entered the foyer. A different receptionist from the night of the nuts was on duty. She smiled at me, and I waved back.

I ignored the stinging feeling and concentrated on putting one foot in front of the other. Right. Left. Right. Left. *Yes, that's it. Just one small step at a time. You can do this. You can do this.*

Before I knew it, I was coming down the steps in front of the stage. And here was the stage bar. Oh, my God. There was no going back now. This was my chance to take Ferret Face out of action, save the statue and Ibrahim Kaya, *and* get my wedding dress back.

I quickly scanned the area and saw Ferret Face sitting on the same sofa he'd been at earlier in the day. Another couple of sofas were full with a rowdy party, and five men and two women sat at the bar. One busy barman served the backlog of late-night drinkers, so I couldn't exactly pop behind the bar and pretend to be a barwoman without him noticing me. Second option: chat up Ferret Face. And then what? I didn't have a bloody clue, but I'd have to play it by ear.

Oh, crap.

I forced myself to walk to the bar, willing my stomach to stop spinning around at a hundred miles an hour like an out of control roller-coaster. I felt sick, as if I was coming down with a severe case of something gastric. I swallowed down the bile rising in my throat. *Come on, Helen, everything depends on you now. There, a few deep breaths, that's right, steady yourself on the bar. You will be fine. You can do this.*

'Would you like something to drink, madam?' the barman asked.

What a stupid question. I was about to try and chat up a psycho killer. Of course I wanted a bloody drink! 'Courvoisier, please.' I forced my lips to form into the semblance of a smile as I checked out Ferret Face from the corner of my eye.

OK. Shoulders back, boobs out, lips moistened. Here we go.

I grabbed my drink and sauntered towards Ferret Face, swinging my hips for good measure. Eyebrow slightly raised seductively, suggestive pout of the lips. Yes, this had to work.

He took a sip of his cognac, staring at me over the rim of his glass as I sat down on the sofa in front of him and crossed my legs, flashing a bit of thigh for luck.

'Hello.' I smiled. 'Mind if I join you?' I put my handbag on the floor, and rested one arm along the back of the sofa, stroking it with a shaky fingertip, praying it looked sexy and not like I had a furniture fetish. My other hand was in my lap, clutching onto my mobile phone for dear life.

He studied me for a moment, then calmly crossed his legs. The corner of his lips curled into a smarmy smile. 'Why not?' He tilted his head.

OK, first hurdle over with. Now what the fuck do I say?

I swallowed, but my voice came out croaky. 'You have nice ankles.' I looked at his flip-flop encased feet.

What? I cringed inwardly. *Nice ankles?* Why did I say that?

146

He glanced down at his ankles like he got told this every day. 'Yes.' He nodded towards my glass. 'Is that Courvoisier?'

'Yes.' I stopped stroking the sofa and took a sip of the burning liquid but nearly choked. Whoa! That was strong. Did people actually choose to drink this? 'It's my favourite drink.' I took a smaller sip.

Something feral flashed across Ferret Face's eyes. 'Good choice. I like a woman who appreciates the finer things in life.' He raised his eyebrow, examining me like I was the best thing since the AK-47 was invented.

'So, are you here on business or pleasure?' I asked, trying to give him a seductive smile.

'A bit of both.' His smile back was chilling.

Urgh! That meant he actually enjoyed killing people. What a sicko. My smile dropped a smidgen, but I recovered it quickly before he seemed to notice. 'Lovely!'

The barman placed a plate of mixed nuts on the table.

I took a sip of the warm liquid again for courage. 'And what line of work are you in?'

He waved a hand through the air. 'Let's not talk about me. Let's talk about you.'

I took another sip. If I downed it really quickly, he might go to the bar and get me another one, and I could pour the powder into his drink.

'How much do you charge?' he asked casually.

I almost choked on the cognac again. Now I had a stinging throat and a stinging stomach. *How dare you think I'm a hooker! I know I've overdone it with the make-up, but that's a bit hookerist, isn't it?* 'Oh, I'm quite cheap.' I twirled the end of my ponytail around in my finger, trying to look coy.

Ferret Face took a handful of nuts and nibbled on them. Now he looked even more like a ferret. Or maybe even a hamster. 'I like that answer. OK, we have time to discuss money later.'

Yuck! Do we have to?

'What's your name?' he asked.

What's my name? Well, I'm not going to give you my real one, you psycho moron. What's a hookerish name? 'Candy.' I smiled.

'Candy?' he said, looking at me as if he was waiting for me to say something else.

What? Do hookers use surnames as well? I didn't have a clue.

'Candy Cain.'

'Candy Cain?' He looked at me expectantly, licking his lips, like he was waiting for more.

What now? How many names are they supposed to have? 'Candy Cain Sugar Dimple Pie,' I elaborated.

He licked his lips again. 'That's interesting. I've got a condom in my room with your name on it.'

Ew! Must be a big condom. 'Fabulous!'

'So, how cheap are you?'

I wiggled my glass at him and gave him a coy smile. 'Buy me another cognac, and I'll tell you.' I winked.

He set his own half-empty drink on the coffee table in front of him and hurried towards the bar.

I rested the mobile phone on my lap. Then I quickly grabbed the cigar tin from my bag. I glanced over at the bar. Good. Ferret Face had his back to me.

Sweat pricked at my palms. *Don't drop it. You can do this.*

I dragged his glass closer to me and leaned over it, away from prying eyes. Opening the cigar tin, I poured in the ground up sleeping tablets and swirled the glass. The powder fizzed up like an Alka Seltzer.

Stop it! Stop fizzing! Oh, crapping hell.

I poked my finger in and twirled the liquid around at a hundred miles an hour, trying to aid defizzment.

Phew! It finally dissolved completely.

I glanced back at the bar again. He was still there, waiting for his order, but now the cognac was spinning around so fast, he would be able to notice something was wrong. I poked my finger in it again to still the cognac.

Gently, I put the glass back in its original position and sat back on the sofa, crossing my legs.

Ferret Face reappeared a few minutes later and handed me the drink. He picked up the tablet-laced cognac in one hand and leaned back on the sofa, crossing his legs, studying me.

'Thanks.' *Ha-ha. Pretty soon you will be sleeping for a long time. Hopefully with diarrhoea, hives, and no hair to boot!*

He put his drink back down on the coffee table and pushed the plate of nuts towards me. 'Nuts?' He grinned at this little double entendre.

Yes, thanks, but not yours. I scooted forward to the edge of the

148

seat and took a handful of nuts. I was just about to pop them in my mouth when I heard a loud scream coming from my left.

I turned my head, just in time to see the receptionist from the other night launch herself through the air at me in a kind of on-the-sofa rugby tackle.

Bam! The momentum pushed me back into the marshmallow sofa with the receptionist landing on top of me. Nuts flew through the air, and her leg caught the edge of the table, sending Ferret Face's drink crashing to the floor.

'Agh! What are you doing?' I tried to say, even though my face was now squashed in between the cushions of the sofa and her armpit.

Ferret Face leaped up. 'Oh, I didn't know you were into women.' And he hurried away.

'Let...me...up.' I banged on the sofa. 'Can't...breathe.'

She released her vice-like grip around me and climbed off, slightly panting, her eyes as huge as Cyprus olives. 'You're allergic to nuts! You would have died if you'd eaten them.'

No! She'd ruined it all. *No. No. No.*

I put my elbows on my knees and sank forward, rocking back and forth, ignoring the pain in my hip where she'd slammed on top of me. 'No, no, no.' Tears sprang into my eyes. I wanted to cry, but I couldn't. This was all wrong. Probably my one and only chance to drug him, and I couldn't even do that.

'Did you eat one? Are you having an allergic reaction? Shall I get a doctor?'

I carried on rocking. 'No. I'm fine, thanks.' I stopped rocking abruptly. Oh, God. Where was my mobile phone? I leaped up, searching for it. Kalem would probably be on his way down here right now and might bump into Ferret Face scuttling away.

My eyes frantically scanned the area. Floor? No. Table? No. There! Down the side cushion of the marshmallow sofa.

I grabbed it. 'Kalem? Hello? Are you there?'

'Helen!' A breathless Kalem answered. 'What the hell happened? I'm nearly there. I'll be with you in a minute.'

'No! Go back to the entrance and lose yourself in the paparazzi. I'm fine. Ferret Face has disappeared.

'Are you sure? Are you sure everything's OK?' Kalem said.

'Yes,' I insisted. 'I'll meet you there in a minute.'

The receptionist stared at me, eyebrows furrowed in

confusion. I'd almost forgotten she was there.

'Are you sure you're OK?' She gave me a puzzled look.

'I'm fine, really.' I got to my feet and stumbled back out to the foyer, leaving her pulling down her skirt and smoothing out her hair with a confused expression.

The paparazzi were still in full force when I got back outside. A line of policemen kept them away from the entrance. I stood for ten minutes, searching out Kalem in amongst everyone. Finally, I spotted him at the back and wound around the crowd to meet him.

'What happened then? I heard a big noise and then just muffled sounds. Are you sure you're OK? What happened to Ferret Face?' His words came out in a garbled rush.

Once I started shaking my head, I couldn't stop.

Kalem pulled me towards him, squashing me in his heavy-duty arms. 'What happened? Tell me!'

'I didn't manage to drug him. It didn't work.' I flopped my head on his shoulder and told him what had happened.

The paparazzi behind us got louder. Cameras flashed and TV crews rushed to the front doors.

I lifted my head and saw Ibrahim Kaya emerge in the night air, hand waving to the crowd.

I stepped out of Kalem's arms.

'Where's Jayde?' one of the photographers said to Kaya.

'She's relaxing for the evening.' He smiled and waved at them all.

A couple of policemen walked either side of him, trying to keep the paparazzi away, as Ibrahim Kaya made his way through the flashing throng and towards the limo.

The limo that we were standing next to.

The limo driver exited the driver's seat and made his way around to the back, opening the passenger door, ready in waiting.

The paparazzi swarmed around him, pushing and shoving to get a quote. 'What's she doing? Does she like her suite? Which colour M&Ms did she refuse to eat?'

The police officers pushed them back. Ibrahim Kaya was lost in the middle of the crowd as they came closer to us. Kalem got driven away from me in the crush of people, and I could no longer see him. I held my ground, leaning against the limo, so I

150

couldn't get swept away.

'What demands did she ask for? How many numbers is she singing tomorrow? Are her lips Botoxed? Has she got a nipple tweaker on hand?'

And suddenly, Ibrahim Kaya was directly in front of me, about to get in the limo. He ducked his head down and climbed in.

'Mr. Kaya, I have to talk to you urgently,' I said, as he began pulling the door shut.

'No more pictures tonight.' The door clicked shut on his last word.

One of the police officers put a hand on my shoulder and tried to pull me away. I shrugged it off.

'I need to talk to you. It's urgent. Your life is at risk.' I banged on the window. 'YOU'RE GOING TO DIE! YOU'RE GOING TO DIE!' I yelled as loud as I could to the limo as it pulled away.

I don't know if he heard me or not, but the next thing I knew, the policeman yanked my arm, dragging me into the back of a nearby police car.

'No! He's in danger. You have to tell him. Get him back here. I need to talk to him.'

He slammed the door on my cries.

I wriggled around in the seat, trying to search out Kalem in the crowd. Was he out there? I couldn't see him.

'I haven't done anything!' I tried the door handle. Locked.

And that's when I really did explode into tears.

Chapter 13

'But I haven't done anything!' I yelled as the door clanked shut on the communal cell.

I clung to the bars and rattled them, hoping they'd miraculously give way. They didn't. I pressed my forehead against the cold metal. What was I going to do now?

A wave of panic clawed at my insides, sending stabbing pains through my stomach and chest.

Where was Kalem? Did he see what happened? Yes, he must have done. He'd get me out. Wouldn't he?

I wiped my wet face with the heel of my hand and looked around. A noisy mix of women stared back at me. A couple of young ones huddled together glared at me, whispering and giggling to each other. An old woman sat on a metal bench in the corner, muttering to herself. A few others strutted around in miniskirts and halterneck tops.

I slouched down next to the old woman and leaned my head back against the cold wall, trying to make myself as inconspicuous as possible.

'Blah!' the woman said, although I wasn't sure if she was talking to me or herself.

Probably best to ignore her. Maybe if I shut my eyes, I could just pretend I wasn't here. Beam me up, Scotty.

One of the halterneck brigade sat next to me and eyed me up. 'What are you here for?' She put her face up close to mine. An overpowering smell of perfume assaulted my nostrils.

I sniffed and eased away from her. 'I don't know.'

'That's what they all say, honey. Are you a hooker?'

'No!'

She fiddled with an earring so big that it could have doubled as a lampshade. 'Hmm. You look like a hooker.'

'Blah,' the old woman said again. Was that a term of agreement?

A young policeman unlocked the doors with a loud click. 'Helen Grey,' he shouted.

I leaped up. 'That's me. Oh, thank you. You've come to let me out.'

'No letting out for you. Come with me.' He beckoned me forward.

I followed him down a corridor into an interrogation room. It had white walls, a bright strip light overhead, a single window where I could see into an office full of other police officers on the other side, and three wooden chairs. One of them was already occupied by a police captain of about fifty with a beaky nose and grey hair. He fingered through a folder on the desk in front of him, sipping a cup of Turkish coffee. The policeman I'd followed sat down next to him and folded his arms. It looked like the other chair was meant for me.

Captain Beaky put down his coffee. 'Sit,' he barked at me.

I sat, pretty sharpish.

He slid a photo across the desk. 'Is this you?'

I felt my forehead go clammy as I stared at a picture of me at the airport in the burka. It wasn't very flattering. I was lying on the floor, half on top of Ferret Face, with the drugs dog's snout pretty much buried in my crutch. Not a photo I'd like to repeat any time soon, and it certainly wouldn't be making its way into my album.

'Yes.' I ran the back of my hand across my forehead.

'Why were you wearing a burka?' Captain Beaky shouted.

'Well, it's like this–'

'Like what?' the younger one interrupted me.

'I'm just trying to tell you.' I sighed. 'My fiancé played a practical joke on me. That's all.'

'What sort of joke?' Captain Beaky didn't look enthralled by my answer.

'I'm getting married here in three days, and he said it was an ancient tradition that when a bride arrived to get married in North Cyprus, she had to wear a burka.' I bit my lower lip, knowing how ridiculous it all sounded now after the event.

Captain Beaky exchanged a disbelieving look with the younger one. 'And you believed him?'

'Well, yes. I know it sounds a bit peculiar, but I did believe it. My fiancé is a bit of a practical joker.'

Captain Beaky stared at me like he thought I must be a complete idiot. 'Are you an idiot? Or a good liar? Hmm?' Before I could answer that he slapped a hand on the desk. 'Why were you interfering with our sniffer dog? Are you a drug smuggler?'

'Of course I'm not!'

'What did you force feed the dog?' Captain Beaky asked.

'What? I didn't force feed it anything.'

'You will only make things worse if you lie to us.' He nodded gravely, ramming the point home.

I wasn't really sure how things could actually get any worse. 'I'm not lying. The dog just took my sandwiches.'

'And what was in them?' Captain Beaky growled.

'Er…bacon.'

They both gasped.

'You told the customs officer that it was cheese. So you did lie!' Captain Beaky leaned his elbows on the desk. 'Do you want to know what I think?'

Not really, no. I didn't think I wanted to hear any of this. I didn't tell him that, though. I had a sneaking suspicion that he was going to give me a vast range of thoughts on the matter anyway.

'I think you wanted to entice the sniffer dog with your bacon sandwiches so you could smuggle in drugs. And I think you were wearing a burka so you wouldn't be recognized.'

'But I didn't give the sandwiches to the dog. It just stole them. I told you,' I cried.

He tutted at me. 'It is a Muslim dog. It doesn't even eat bacon. You must have forced the poor animal.'

'Well, it seemed pretty happy to me when it ran off with them,' I said.

'The dog was very ill for days. You tried to poison it so that you wouldn't be detected carrying drugs.'

My jaw nearly fell off. I wrapped my arms tightly around me and tried to stave off a nauseous feeling in my stomach.

He slapped a hand on the desk again. 'You are a drug smuggler and an animal abuser.'

The younger policemen nodded to himself.

'It couldn't have been my sandwich that made it ill. And how does the dog know it's Muslim?'

'Don't be ridiculous. Of course it knows.' He tutted again, like I should know that. 'What about the cat?'

'I definitely didn't feed the dog a cat.'

'There was a cat in your household container, along with

custard creams. Not only are you smuggling drugs, you are also smuggling animals and contraband food items.'

'No, no, no. You've got it all wrong. OK, I admit to having a few packets of custard creams in my container, but–'

'Twenty-eight packets are not a few,' the younger one pointed out in a gruff voice, probably trying to score brownie points with his boss.

'Well, OK. Slightly more than a few. And I didn't know the cat was in there. It was our neighbour's cat from the UK.'

'Ah ha! So you stole the cat *and* smuggled it!' Captain Beaky said.

'No, no, no. You've got it all wrong. I–'

Captain Beaky turned to the younger one. 'I think we've got a prolific smuggler here.'

The younger one nodded his agreement.

'No, there's been some kind of really horribly horrible misunderstanding.' I stood up. 'Can I go now?'

'NO!' Captain Beaky shouted.

I sat down again.

'You also match the description of someone throwing weapons at the President,' Captain Beaky said.

'What?' I shrieked.

He picked up a phone on the desk. 'Bring him in,' he whispered into it.

A minute later, someone knocked on the door so loud that I jumped and nearly fell off the chair.

'Come in,' Captain Beaky said to the door.

I twisted around and saw the President's bodyguard from the festival, with a swollen, bloodshot eye, enter the room.

Uh-oh.

Captain Beaky pointed to me and said to the bodyguard, 'Is this the woman who threw a weapon at you?'

He peered at me through his good eye. 'Yes.'

'Thank you. You can go.'

The bodyguard gave me a one-eyed death glare on his way out.

'And if all that wasn't enough, you also threatened to kill Ibrahim Kaya tonight.' Captain Beaky glared at me.

I gasped. 'I didn't.' I shook my head so hard that I thought I could feel my brain rattling around.

155

He glanced down at his file and read a handwritten note. '"You're going to die. You're going to die."' He looked up at me. 'Did you say that?'

If my hair wasn't in a ponytail, I'm sure it would've actually stood on end with fright at that point. 'Er…yes, but there's a perfectly reasonable explanation.' A nervous giggle involuntarily escaped from my lips.

'Issuing death threats, interfering with drugs dogs; smuggling drugs, smuggling animals, smuggling food, animal cruelty, disguises, attacking the President's bodyguards and threatening his safety.' He ticked off the list on his fingers. 'You are a seriously deranged individual and a dangerous criminal. You will be locked up for a very, very long time.'

'Deranged,' the younger one agreed, nodding again.

'But I can explain,' I cried.

They both leaned back in their chairs and crossed their arms, giving me a this-should-be-good expression.

Captain Beaky raised a palm in the air, indicating that I should continue.

I glanced around the room, ready to tell him the whole horrible story and wondering where to begin, when I noticed movement through the window in the office beyond. It was the same policeman I'd seen before. The one who was talking to Ferret Face. The one who must be involved in all of this.

Oh, Goddy God. I couldn't tell them now, could I? I didn't have a clue who else in the station was involved in all of this. What if they tried to kill me to shut me up? I could be chopped up into little pieces and no one would ever know what had happened to me. No, better to keep quiet and not tell them anything. Silence trumped spilling my guts (in more ways than one).

I clamped my mouth closed.

'Well, what are you waiting for?' Captain Beaky sat watching me, tight-lipped.

'Er…well…um.' Thoughts whirled through my head in a high-speed chase. One after the other, tumbling around. 'Well, everyone's going to die, aren't they? Even you. I was just stating the obvious, really. It wasn't a death threat at all.' I let out another nervous laugh.

They didn't look particularly satisfied with that.

156

'That's it? That's your explanation?' Captain Beaky said.

I looked at the floor, hoping something miraculous would pop into my brain. I looked at the walls, but I still couldn't think of what to say. I looked at the desk with the file and the Turkish coffee cup.

'Well, no...I...I had a vision. Yes, that's it. I had a vision about Ibrahim Kaya, and I just wanted to tell him about it.'

He snorted. 'I suppose next you'll be telling me you're some sort of fortune teller. That you can predict the future!'

'Actually, yes. I can read Turkish coffee cups. I won the UK Turkish Coffee Cup Readers' Award last year.'

A disbelieving look passed between the two policemen.

'Have you ever heard of that?' Captain Beaky asked the younger one.

The younger one shook his head.

'Oh, it's huge. Lots of very well known coffee cup readers go to it.' I gave them my best convincing smile.

The captain turned his coffee cup upside down. 'OK, you can read mine.' He pushed it towards me and crossed his arms, waiting.

I wiped my sweaty palms on my dress. OK, I could do this. I'd just copy what I'd seen Osman's mum do. Easy peasy.

I took hold of the cup, turned it upright again and stared into it. I couldn't see anything. All it contained was sludgy, blackish brown coffee granules.

'Well?' Captain Beaky's voice took on an impatient tone.

I rotated the cup around slowly clockwise. Hang on a minute, though. I could actually see something. I brought the cup closer to my face.

'Well?' he said again, a bit more gruffly.

'These things can't be rushed, you know.' I scrutinized it carefully.

He sighed. 'Enough of this nonsense.'

I took a deep breath. 'I can see a woman with long, curly hair. I think she's wearing high heels. She's got...a really big nose, like Pinocchio. I think she's been telling a lot of lies lately. She's got a tattoo of...ooh, what is it?' I squinted. 'A flower. Yes, a tattoo of a flower on her ankle. I think...' I brought the cup closer. 'Yes, that's better. The tattoo is a rose. And she's holding hands with a tall man who's got glasses on.'

157

Captain Beaky made a high-pitched sound in the back of his throat.

I looked up. He'd gone a funny yellow colour too. Maybe he had a bit of a liver problem.

'That description sounds like your wife.' The young one elbowed him.

'I knew it! I knew she was having an affair! What else?' Captain Beaky said. 'What else can you see? What about the man?'

I got back to work. 'Well, he looks quite muscly.' I snuck a quick peek at his puny arms. 'I can see three stars on his shoulder. And–'

Captain Beaky leaped up, sending his chair clattering to the floor. And then the next minute, he'd run out of the interrogation room, and I saw him through the window, charging into the office next door, closely pursued by the younger one.

I watched on, agog, as Captain Beaky grabbed hold of the policeman I'd seen talking to Ferret Face and pushed him up against the wall, shouting at him.

Oops. What had I done now?

The younger policemen and several others tried to drag the two men apart, but Captain Beaky held his ground with a firm grasp on the other guy's shirt collar.

So, what should I do now? I eyed the open interrogation room doorway. Make a run for it? Wait for someone to come back?

The decision was taken out of my hands by the arrival of Erol Hussein. He waltzed through the doorway, dressed for a night on the town. I didn't know if this was a good or bad sign, but I suspected that it was probably the latter.

'Helen, we meet again. I thought you would have left the island by now, what with Kalem no longer having a *job*.' He snarled the last word at me.

'You bastard! I knew that was all your doing,' I fumed.

He looked at me sharply, then his face erupted in a stomach-curdling grin. 'Tut, tut, tut. I don't think you're in any position to be calling people names. Do you?' He pulled the blind down on the window, picked up the chair that Captain Beaky had vacated and sat down.

'Why didn't you want to look into the plot to assassinate Ibrahim Kaya and steal the statue?' I knew the answer to this

158

already, of course, but I actually wanted to hear him say it.

'I already told you. Because it's not going to happen. The statue will be in a secure and alarmed casing with guards all around it. I've personally overseen the security arrangements. Are you doubting my professional integrity?' He gave me a thin excuse for a smile.

"Professional" and "integrity" weren't exactly two words I'd use to describe Erol Hussein, but I kept my mouth shut on that point.

'I also don't believe anyone would want to assassinate Ibrahim Kaya,' Erol said.

'But I've found out more information now and–'

'I don't want to hear it.' His voice rose, echoing in the sparse room.

'It's because of the money, isn't it? You've kept that five hundred thousand dollars and not told anyone about it.'

He chuckled, giving me a superior smile that didn't reach his eyes. 'What money?'

So that was it. Basically, it was his admission of what I'd thought all along. He would rather keep the money than save Ibrahim Kaya's life. I didn't know who was worse, Ferret Face or him.

'I have a proposition for you, Helen. If you stop all this nonsense about the statue and Ibrahim Kaya, and both you and Kalem leave the island tonight, then I'll arrange to have all the charges against you dropped.' He tilted his head, eyes narrowed to ruthless slits, waiting for an answer. 'You are in some very serious trouble. I'm sure you recognize what a generous offer this is on my part.'

What? Leave? How could we leave? If we left, then Ibrahim Kaya could end up sleeping with the fishes. And what about my wedding? And my wedding dress. I was supposed to be having the perfect wedding on Sunday, and if I didn't get married in my dress with my nan's charm, I'd be doomed to a curse of bad luck. Our wedding might be over before it began. No, of course not. We couldn't leave yet. But then what was the alternative? I didn't particularly fancy the idea of getting locked up with crazy women and hookers – no offense to crazy women and hookers. I'd watched a TV show once about things that happen to people in prison, and it made my eyes water, not to mention other parts.

No, that wasn't an option either. I couldn't, couldn't, couldn't go to prison. Absolutely not.

'I'm waiting,' Erol said, more insistent this time.

I chewed on my bottom lip. 'Where's Kalem?'

His lips pursed in distaste. 'He's been causing a disturbance at the front desk, looking for you.'

'Have you told him about your *proposition*?'

'No, I thought you'd like to give him the good news.'

What should I do?

'I haven't got all night.' Erol stood up. 'Since you can't seem to make up your mind, I'll arrange for the charges to be filed against you.'

'No! Wait. We'll leave. We'll leave!'

'Good. I'm glad we see eye to eye on this.'

Well, we didn't. But he wasn't to know that.

I walked around the floor of our hotel room in circles like a caged animal, my heels slapping so hard against the marble that I thought my feet were getting friction burns. Kalem sat on the bed, staring at me with a clenched jaw, taking in what I'd just told him about my trip to the police station. My eyeballs darted from Kalem to Charlie to Ayshe to Atila.

'Well, there's nothing else for it,' Charlie said, pouring out three glasses of wine and handed them out to everyone except Ayshe. 'We'll all just have to go back home. I've seen those prison films about people who smuggle drugs abroad and get caught, you know. You wouldn't want to be stuck in some foreign prison. Don't they cut people's hands off and stuff?'

'Not in Cyprus, they don't,' Ayshe said.

'Well, either way, I don't exactly want to find out.' I glugged my drink and stopped pacing because my feet felt like they were actually on fire now.

'We'll just have to leave.' Worry lines appeared on Kalem's forehead. 'I can't risk you going to prison. No. There's no other choice. We've done everything we can to try and warn people about this plot. If no one wants to listen, then it's not our fault.' He rubbed his forehead. 'This is such a mess.'

I sat down next to him and squeezed his hand. I smiled, but there was no joy in it.

'This was supposed to be the start of a brand new life. And

160

now it's ruined,' Kalem said, the hurt filtering through his voice. 'We'll have to go back to the UK and get married. And then pick up our old lives again.'

'Well, look on the bright side,' Charlie said.

We all looked at him like he'd just morphed into an alien.

'What could that possibly be?' Atila ran a hand through his floppy hair.

'Well, Helen didn't really want to stay here, anyway,' Charlie blurted out, then slapped a hand over his mouth.

Kalem locked eyes with me, disappointment plastered all over his face. 'What? I don't understand. I thought you wanted the same things as me. I thought you wanted the simple life.'

Oh, shit. I didn't want to get into this now. I wasn't sure what the hell I wanted anymore. The only thing I knew for certain was that I didn't want to go to prison with the possibility of bits getting chopped off.

'Look, Kalem, I really don't know if I'm cut out for the simple life. I've been confused ever since we got here, but the most important thing at the moment is to decide what to do about this mess we're in. We can talk about whether we're going to stay here after that.' I couldn't meet his eyes, so I held my empty glass out to Charlie, who quickly refilled it. 'And I don't think we can leave. At least not until after the opening night tomorrow. We've still got to try and do something to stop Ferret Face. We can't just give up now.'

Ayshe gasped. 'But what about Erol's threats? Helen, you can't be serious about it. You both have to leave tonight.'

'Why don't we just move out of the hotel? Kalem and I could move into your parents' house tonight so it looks like we've checked out. Tomorrow we just have to try and find some way to stop Ferret Face killing Ibrahim Kaya. And then we can leave.'

'I don't like it,' Atila said.

'Me neither.' Ayshe shook her head.

'Nor me,' Kalem said. 'How are we going to stop him? Nothing we've come up with so far has worked.'

'I don't know.' I banged my glass down on the bedside table and pulled out my suitcase, flinging my few clothes in at random. 'But we'll have to think of something pretty quick.'

Chapter 14

I felt bone-numbingly tired, both physically and mentally, but I still didn't get any sleep.

It was after three a.m. by the time Kalem and I finished moving our belongings into his parents' house. And talking of Yasmin and Deniz, we still had to tell them what was going on. They would freak when they heard about it. Luckily, they were still in isolation in their bedroom feeling ill. Although it wasn't lucky for them, of course, but you know what I mean.

The sun oozed through the cream, muslin curtains. I could tell it was a bright, sparkly day outside of the bedroom. Birds chirped away. Cicadas buzzed their funny little electric pylon noise. It was a perfect day. For a murder.

I shivered at the thought as I lay in Kalem's arms on the bed, staring at the ceiling in silence.

I yawned hard, shaking my head to clear the fuzzy fog that had set in. 'Do you remember exactly what was in the itinerary Ferret Face had in the suitcase?'

Kalem inhaled slowly, thinking. 'Ibrahim Kaya is giving individual press interviews between three and five o'clock, then a press conference at five-thirty in the ballroom of the hotel before the concert starts at seven. Just before the concert on the outdoor stage, Kaya will unveil the statue to the public, which is going to be in a display case in front of the stage. Then there'll be a Champagne toast. After the concert, there's going to be a huge party for all the politicians, celebrities, and guests.'

I tapped my lips, deep in thought. 'How about we go to the press conference and pose as reporters?'

'He'll recognize you from last night, and we'll just get thrown out. And if he doesn't recognize you, Erol will be there, and he'll arrest you.'

'Ibrahim Kaya barely glanced at me last night before he got in the limo.' I gnawed on a thumbnail. 'How about we pose as staff from the hotel?'

'And do what? He's not going to listen to anything you say if you attempt to warn him. Look what happened last night. He'll just think you're some crazy stalker who's out to kill him. No, there's no point in even trying to tell him anything about the assassination plot. It would be better to just detain him somehow to stop him going to the concert in the first place.'

'We've still got some sleeping tablets.' I sat bolt upright. 'Yes, we could drug him instead of Ferret Face. If he doesn't come out to give his speech and toast before the concert, they can't shoot him and cause a distraction. And maybe it will buy us a bit more time.'

'They're still going to recognize us. And how are we going to get close enough to drug his drink?'

I stared at the ceiling, debating this conundrum. There had to be some way we could pull it off. 'Well, you can't do it. Erol will be at the opening. He'll recognize you straight away. Ayshe can't do it. She's pregnant, and I don't want anything to happen to her. For the same reason, I don't want Atila to get involved – he's going to be a daddy soon. I wouldn't want him to end up in prison because of all this. And Charlie...well, as much as I love him, I don't know if he would be able to pull it off on his own.'

'Yes, but Kaya and Erol will recognize you too.'

'But it's easier for a woman to disguise herself than a man.' I turned to him. 'And by the time we run into Erol, I'm hoping that I will have already drugged Kaya. Think about it: Ibrahim Kaya probably wouldn't recognize me again, especially if I wear some sort of disguise. He wasn't exactly paying attention to me before he got in the limo. I just need to get close enough to drug him somehow, and the only way to at least have a chance is to try and get in on the press interviews. If he's doing interviews for two hours, he'll be doing a lot of talking. And if he's doing loads of talking, he'll be thirsty and we can drug his drink.'

Kalem shook his head. 'And how are you going to disguise yourself? It's not like we're international espionage agents with stacks of different disguises. You can't exactly wear your knickers over your head and hope for the best.'

I shrugged. 'I could wear a scarf around my hair and put sunglasses on. I'll just look like an eccentric journalist for a flashy magazine. I already work for *Just for Women*, don't forget.' I gave him a grim smile. 'Can you think of some other way?'

'No.'

'Well, it looks like this is the only way then.' I gnawed on my lip now instead.

'And what about the wedding? We're going to have to cancel it and leave. Go back to the rainy UK. It's supposed to be the happiest day of our lives.' He threw a hand in the air in a hopeless gesture.

'And I'm never going to get my dress and lucky charm back.' I sighed.

'The only good thing is that we've still got each other.'

I snuggled into his shoulder. Well, I hoped we'd still have each other. As long as we were both alive by the end of the day and not left to rot in a prison somewhere. 'So, where did you put the boxes from the container with my clothes in? I need to try and find a suitable disguise.' I jumped out of bed.

'In the small bedroom.'

'Right.' I drew the curtains, suddenly energized with the thought of doing something proactive. 'Oh! Look.' I turned to Kalem and pointed out of the patio doors. 'There's a cat outside.'

A small, ginger and white cat sat on the patio, staring at me with cute green eyes, its mouth moving in a meow shape.

I slid the door open and bent down to stroke its head. 'Hello. Where did you come from?'

Meow.

It wound its way around my legs, nudging me with its head. 'Are you hungry?'

Meeooooow.

I took that as a yes.

'Don't feed the cat.' Kalem sprang naked from the bed and pulled on a pair of boxers.

'Why not? It's hungry.'

'If you feed it, we'll just get more coming around.'

I picked the cat up and kissed the top of its head. 'But you're hungry, aren't you? Yes.'

Meow, meow.

'Maybe it's a sign,' I said as the cat nuzzled into my neck.

'A sign about what?' Kalem shook his head. 'How can a cat turning up be a sign? There are hundreds of stray cats here. We can't feed them all.'

I shrugged. 'I don't know. The Queen Cleopatra statue had a cat carved onto the base. You said that cats were lucky in

164

Egyptian times. Maybe it's a good sign that we're going to save the statue. Yes, I think it's a lucky cat.'

'You're nuts.' He kissed me on the forehead.

'It's hungry. I'm going to see if there's something in the kitchen for it.' I put the cat down, and it trotted behind me.

I flung open the cupboard doors. Hmm. Not a lot. Some coffee, a bottle of water, tea bags, and a bottle of wine. Because of our unexpected arrival at the house, the contents left a lot to be desired.

I glanced down at the cat who looked up at me expectantly.

Then I had a sudden thought. 'Custard creams to the rescue!' I padded back to the bedroom and rummaged around in my bag until I found the half eaten packet I'd had with me since the airplane. 'Voila!' Back to the kitchen to find a bowl and da-da, breakfast à la biscuit.

I stroked Ginger's fur as she crunched on the gourmet dining like she was starving. Maybe it really was a sign. I hoped to God it was a good one.

We still had a few hours to kill before the press conference. On second thoughts, maybe I shouldn't use that phrase anymore. Correction: we still had a few hours to *wait* until the press conference, so we took a trip to Condomsville to check on Yasmin and Deniz.

The same kind of note in Deniz's scrawl greeted us on the floor outside their room.

'Uh-oh.' Kalem read it. '"Dear Maid, I am now conducting a survey for *Cosmopolitan* magazine about flavoured condoms. Do you have any other flavours available? I'm particularly interested in chilli, strawberry, and whisky flavours, but any other flavours will be carefully considered. I will have ten packets of chilli (medium to hot spiciness), five packets of strawberry (if no strawberry, any other fruit selection will be sufficient), and thirty packets of whisky flavour (preferably single malt). Thank you."'

'Do you think he's got Alzheimer's?' I whispered. 'I mean, I know he's not exactly normal.' I drew quotation marks in the air. 'And I know I can't exactly talk, but he's acting even more weird than he usually does. Maybe the food poisoning has affected his brain. Can you get brain poisoning from eating

165

dodgy fish? Do you think we should call someone? A neurologist or something?'

'No, I think it's just Dad being Dad.' Kalem banged on the door. 'Dad? Mum?'

'Oh, hello, Kalem.' Deniz opened the door looking flushed. He peered around us, checking the floor to see if the note was still there. 'Hmm. Maid hasn't been yet, then?'

'Are you feeling any better yet?' I asked as he followed us back inside.

'Not bad. Still a bit squitty, though.' He lay back on the magazine infested bed and crossed his legs, eyeballing me.

'I feel a bit better. Just a bit of a rumble now.' Yasmin rubbed her stomach. 'What's been going on with you all? Are you getting a bit of relaxation in before the wedding?'

Kalem and I exchanged a furtive glance.

'Yes!' It came out a bit more high-pitched than intended.

'I'm going to get a pec implant.' Deniz picked up *Cosmopolitan* and pointed to an article with a picture of a twenty-something, fit looking guy with a six-pack, firm chest, and bleached teeth. 'Look at this bloke. Look.' He shook the magazine at us. 'Look at his pecs. Fantastic!'

Yasmin tutted at him. 'For God's sake. He's about twelve. You're seventy! You can't have pecs that look like his.'

Deniz looked a bit put out by this revelation. 'Why not?'

'Will you talk some sense into him?' Yasmin shook her head at us. 'I'm fed up with hearing about these bloody magazines giving him stupid ideas.' She thought about that for a moment and rephrased it. 'Well, more stupid than normal.'

'What's wrong with a bit of male plastic surgery? Women have it all the time. Look at her.' Deniz picked up another glossy women's mag with a picture of an aging actress who looked like she'd had the whole works done several times over. 'See, if she has any more face lifts, she'll be shaving.' He let out a loud huff and changed the subject. 'I'm going to apply to be an agony aunt.' Deniz said. 'I've been reading the problem page, and I think I can give some much better advice than them.'

I seriously doubted it, but I smiled to humour him.

'Take this one, for example: "Dear Kelly,"' he peered over the magazine. 'That's the agony aunt.' He glanced back again, running his finger under the page as he read. '"I'm a thirty-

166

something mother, and I'm concerned that my five-year old child is being taught bad habits in the classroom. When the nursery teacher reads Postman Pat, I don't think it's appropriate for them to mention the black and white cat. It's very racist". For God's sake, the world's gone mad!' Deniz raised his eyes to the ceiling. 'Right, here is what my reply would be: Dear Mother, get a grip! If you're not allowed to be sexist, racist, or animalist these days, then a simple children's book like Postman Pat and His Black and White Cat will turn into Postperson Pat and Its Spectrum Species! And then we come to the children's game of hangman. Are we not allowed to say that anymore because we might upset people on death row? To hell with political correctness!'

I didn't think Deniz would be getting an agony aunt's job any time soon.

At one-thirty, after carefully applying my disguise, Charlie and I were at the hotel, ready and waiting for our plan to begin. Charlie wanted to come along as backup, although I wasn't too sure exactly what that would entail. At the moment, he had my camera around his neck to make him look more like my assistant. Kalem was waiting in the car – head down, with a baseball cap on, the peak pulled low over his face, just in case the evil Erol Hussein spotted him.

The place was already wall-to-wall bodies: reporters, guests, and hundreds of staff putting the finishing touches to the outside stage – ferrying drinks around, and setting up the seating arrangement for the concert. And somewhere amidst all of it were Ferret Face and Missing Link.

'You actually look quite nice in that getup. Very fifties film-starish,' Charlie said to me.

I glanced at myself in a boutique window as we descended down the central stairs and walked towards the spa. Actually, I did look pretty good. I had a black and gold scarf covering my hair, tied in a stylish side-knot at the back of my neck, and a huge pair of dark sunglasses. All topped off with a stylish beige lipstick called *Nearly Nude*. A complete contrast from the other evening I'd been here.

'Hello!' I breezed into the spa area, giving a huge smile to the spa manager behind the desk. 'Do you remember me?'

She furrowed her eyebrows for a minute.

Hmm, this was good. She didn't recognize me either. I lifted up my dark glasses and a spark of recognition ignited on her face.

She clapped her hands together again. 'Of course! *Just for Women* magazine! Have you come to do some more research for the article?'

I leaned my elbows on the reception desk, giving her a little conspiratorial smile. 'Well, actually, there's been a slight mix-up, I'm afraid. *Just for Women* magazine doesn't appear to be on the list for the private interviews with Ibrahim Kaya that start at three.'

She gasped. 'No? That's terrible. Right, don't worry about a thing. I'll make sure you get your interview for the magazine. We can't have a little administrative malfunction affecting our spa story, can we?' She rushed around to my side of the desk. 'Wait here. I'll go and get your pass and make sure you're number one on the interviewing list.' She waved a hand at the comfy looking gold sofas. 'Have a seat or help yourself to a drink at the juice bar while you're waiting. I won't be a moment.' And she'd gone. Out the door as fast as her little white spa flip-flops would allow.

'So far, so good,' I whispered to Charlie. 'You've got the sleeping tablets, haven't you?'

He patted the cigar tin in his pocket. 'Check. All ground up and ready to go if the opportunity arises.'

I felt in my black trouser pocket for my tin for the hundredth time and patted it as well. 'Me too. Whoever gets the opportunity first will stick it in Kaya's drink. Two should be plenty to knock him out for at least sixteen hours, but I've added an extra one just in case.'

'Check.'

'And then that should be it. We'll just hang around to make sure he doesn't show up at the concert, and then the opportunity to assassinate him and steal the statue will be over.'

'Check.'

'Stop saying that!' I hissed.

'Ch…OK. If you're not alive for me tell you later, I think you're very brave.' He patted my hand.

'Thanks. That makes me feel a lot better. *Not!*' Any bravery I did have had suddenly packed its bags and deserted me at the very mention of its name.

I heard a scurrying flippy floppy sound behind me, and the spa manager appeared, looking flustered.

'Here you are.' She handed us a couple of press tags with *Just for Women* on them. 'The interviews will be in the cocktail lounge. Mr. Kaya prefers an informal setting. If you go there just before three, you'll be first on the list.'

The cocktail bar! All the better for drugging people's drinks in.

'Thank you so much. I'll make sure your spa gets a two-page centre spread.' I gave her a grateful smile, and we hustled out the door.

'What's the time now?' Charlie asked.

'Two. We've got an hour. Let's go down to the stage and see if they've got the statue in place yet.'

We weaved our way through the crowds and down the corridor to the outside pool area. As we walked along the side of it, I had the skin-crawling feeling that somewhere, in one of the bedrooms overlooking, Ferret Face's ferrety little eyes could see us.

I shivered, even though the relentless summer sun was high in the sky. No, I couldn't let myself think about him.

We descended the steps at the end of the pool area, down to the restaurants and bars overlooking the stage. The stage bar to the right was doing a roaring trade with all the reporters, photographers, and guests, but I wasn't interested in them.

In front of the stage, an area was cordoned off. The only people inside the cordon were four hefty looking private security guards, all with handguns strapped to their sides. They were arranged in a square, and in the centre of them was a display case, draped in a deep purple velvet cover.

'Hmm. They look manly.' Charlie raised an appreciative eyebrow.

My eyes focused on the port behind the stage. Eight speedboats, five yachts, and three sailboats. One of them would be used as the getaway boat, and I was guessing it was one of the speedboats.

'We could tamper with the speedboats, do something to their engines, or something, so they can't escape afterwards,' I suggested.

'Do you know anything about boat engines?'

'No, I don't even know anything about car engines. Do you?'

'Nope. Wouldn't have a clue how to tamper with the engine. And anyway, someone would see us. The place is crawling with people.'

'So probably not an option. We'll have to go with our original plan then and...' I had a sudden brain wave, remembering something in the article from the plane about Kaya that might actually help us. I headed towards the bar. 'Come on, I need a stiff drink before we interview Kaya.'

'Coffee, or something stronger?' Charlie asked.

'Coffee with something stronger in it.' I ordered a double Irish coffee and stared at the guards, desperately hoping the whisky would stop my hands from trembling.

An efficient looking woman with an earpiece and a clipboard stood guard outside the entrance to the dimly lit cocktail bar. She perused the list and glanced up at the queue of salivating journalists. '*Just for Women* magazine, please.'

Oh, shit. This was it. It was now or never. But, oh, this was hopeless. I didn't have a clue how a journalist was supposed to act. Visions flashed into my mind of newsreaders on the BBC with ramrod straight backs and posh, plummy accents. Should I put on a posh accent and look like I had a poker up my arse, or should I be myself? Would he be able to guess I was a fake?

OK, God, I know I don't pray very often – well, only when I want something *really* badly, but this isn't really for me, so maybe you can just see it in you to do one tiny little miracle for me. Please, please, please, God, couldn't you just arrange for Ibrahim Kaya to be struck down by a sudden stomach bug. Or better still, make Ferret Face and Co. have simultaneous heart attacks or something? Please? Can you hear me? Can you work a miracle for me?

'*Just for Women* magazine? Are you here?' Miss Clipboard raised her voice again.

Damn. No miracle in sight.

'Here!' I shouted, making my way up to the entrance.

'Right. You only have a fifteen minute slot,' she said to me, then looked at Charlie. 'Are you the photographer?'

Charlie waved his camera at her. 'Yes, darling.'

Fucky fuck. Only fifteen minutes. We had to do this right. A squeezing pressure clamped itself around my skull and wouldn't let go.

She moved aside to let us through.

Ibrahim Kaya sat on a deep black sofa, arm sprawled along the back, legs crossed. He wore a dark grey suit, pale pink shirt, and a purple tie. In front of him was a hand-carved wooden table with an empty Turkish coffee cup and a full glass of water on it.

Osman's mum's coffee cup predictions sprang into my mind again. I shook my head, trying to clear the visions away.

He gave us a relaxed smile as we headed towards him before standing to greet us. 'Hello. Please sit.' He shook our hands and indicated I should sit next to him.

Charlie sat on the other side of me, fiddling with the camera. I silently prayed that he could pull this off with me.

'Lovely to meet you, Mr. Kaya. I'm Helen from *Just for Women* magazine.' I decided to go for a slightly posh accent and my best newsreader-style smile, trying to ignore the dull, throbbing ache that banged away behind my right eye. 'I must apologize for not taking off my sunglasses, but I've got a terrible eye infection at the moment, and they're a bit sensitive to the light.'

'Well, OK, fire away then.' He reached over and took a sip of water.

I wanted to grab hold of him and shake him. Tell him what was really going on and try one last time to make him listen to me. Should I tell him about the plot? Yes, of course I should. But then I had a flashback of getting arrested again. It wasn't likely he would believe anything I had to say. It hadn't exactly worked out the first time, and since I was one of the few people who knew what was really going on, getting arrested wouldn't help anything. My ramrod back slumped slightly. No, there was nothing else for it. I'd just have to go with plan B.

The terrifying image of me in a barren prison cell spurred me on and I recovered my composure, straightening my spine and keeping my gaze steady 'It must be very thirsty work organizing an opening night of this calibre.' I nodded towards his water glass.

'Absolutely. It's taken five years to bring this hotel to fruition.

A lot of hard work, but a lot of fun as well. This is the twenty-first hotel I've built, and it still gives me an enormous thrill to complete a new project.' He smiled proudly at me.

'Charlie, could you just get a photo of Mr. Kaya, please, before we start.' I turned my head away from Mr. Kaya and urged Charlie on with my eyes.

Charlie flew out of the seat like I'd just pushed an ejector button. He crouched down in front of the coffee table, pretending to get the best photographic position. He twisted to the right, then the left.

'The light's not very good in here.' He thrust the camera further towards Ibrahim Kaya and knocked over his glass of water on the coffee table with his elbow. 'Oops. I'm so sorry. Let me get you another one. Back in a jiffy.' Charlie dashed over to the bar before he could protest.

'Please accept my sincere apologies about that. He's new.' I gave him a knowing smile. 'You just can't get good staff these days. But then I expect you must know all about that.'

He waved the apology away. 'No problem at all. Yes, all my staff are very carefully vetted. We want customers to experience the ultimate in pampering at the Plaza.'

Out of the corner of my eye, I could see the back of Charlie at the bar. *Don't let me down. Don't let me down. Put the powder in the water. Go on, hurry up.*

'Well, congratulations on the hotel. It's absolutely wonderful. Is this all your creation, or do you have business partners who are also involved?' I said, fishing for more information as to why Mr. P wanted him dead.

'No, I don't have any business partners. This is all my creation.'

'Here we go.' Charlie reappeared and placed the glass of water in front of him.

Now all I had to do was get him to drink it.

'Did I mention that we're also doing a special feature at *Just for Women* magazine on water?' I gave him an encouraging smile.

'Water?' He looked slightly amused.

'Yes...you know – all these healthy lifestyle issues are really interesting to our readers. We're all supposed to drink at least five glasses of water a day. Of course our magazine wants to encourage health issues, so we're featuring a centre spread of famous and influential people drinking water. In my recent research about you, I discovered that you're a health fanatic, and I thought you might be interested in this piece. Not only will we do a feature about you and your hotel, but we can also get you in on the water feature as well.' I leaned a little closer. 'It will be *much* more exposure for the Plaza.'

'I see. So you want a photo of me drinking water?'

I nodded. 'Yes, that would be fantastic.' I turned to Charlie before he could change his mind. 'Yes, Charlie, if you could take one for me. And no spillages this time.' I sent him silent *do it, do it* signals.

Ibrahim Kaya slowly reached forward and picked up the glass of water. He brought it to his lips and posed.

'We need you to actually drink the water. It has to look authentic,' I said. 'Our readers can tell when things look too artificial.'

Charlie walked a short distance in front of the table, trying to focus the camera. At least he was out of knocking over distance now.

I held my breath as he took a tiny sip. 'Was that OK?' he asked Charlie.

'Sorry, I didn't get that. Can we do it again? And just tilt your head back a little. That's it. Perfect. And action!'

Ibrahim Kaya took another small sip. 'OK?'

Drink it! Drink it! Come on.

'Perhaps if you drink the whole glass, we could get you in mid-flow,' I suggested. 'We can have a set of three pictures. One of you holding the full glass, one when you're half way through it, and one with a big smile at the end when you've finished it.' I made a photo frame in front of his face with my hands. 'Yes, that's how I'm picturing it in my head.'

'Absolutely,' Charlie agreed.

'And who else is featured in the article?' Ibrahim Kaya enquired.

Oh. Damn. Hadn't thought of that. Someone rich, famous, and healthy. 'Well, so far, we've got Arnold Schwarzenegger, Elle MacPherson, and Spiderman. All their photos were mid-flow, and they looked perfect.'

'Spiderman?' Kaya looked puzzled.

173

Shit. Spiderman? Why did I say that? I waved a dismissive hand. 'Oh, did I say Spiderman? I meant Barack Obama.'

'Barack Obama? I'm impressed. He's in *Just for Women* magazine's water article?' Ibrahim Kaya sounded pleased.

'Oh, yes!' My head went into nodding overdrive.

'Well, if it's good enough for Barack Obama, it's good enough for me. 'Sherefe!' he said, Turkish for *cheers*, and he downed the whole glass of water as Charlie snapped a stream of pictures.

'Fabulous. That's a wrap!' Charlie giggled.

'Wonderful. So, back to the hotel.' I heaved a silent sigh of relief. 'You said you didn't have any business partners, but I heard a rumour that someone else was involved in this hotel.'

'You're talking about Jacob Podsheister?'

I didn't know who the hell I was talking about. I was just fishing for information. But his surname began with a P. Could he be the same Mr. P from the boat?

Ibrahim Kaya turned to me and something like hatred flashed across his eyes. 'Jacob's father was a very successful hotelier in Israel before he came to North Cyprus to start a chain of hotels here. He was a very honourable business man. His word was his bond. So when I came up with the idea for the Plaza, I was happy to go into partnership with Jacob's father. He had the same professional and hard working ethics as me, and with two of the most successful businessmen working together, I envisioned the Plaza as being doubly successful.' He crossed his legs and relaxed into the sofa. 'But sadly, Jacob's father died a year into the planning stages of this hotel, and Jacob inherited a chain of hotels from him. In the beginning, when I was putting this project together, things were still going well for Jacob Podsheister, and I hoped we could have the same mutually beneficial partnership that I would have had with his father. But in the last few years since his father died, Jacob's love of fast cars, fast women, and his addiction to gambling, drink, and drugs have all steadily become worse. They've had a severe effect on his business decisions, which have suffered as a result. Jacob has run his hotels into the ground to pay for his addictions, and he's now on the verge of bankruptcy. I can't have somebody like that involved any of my hotels, so I terminated the partnership agreement.'

'No, quite right.' I agreed. 'But do you think he carries some

174

sort of a grudge against you for cancelling the partnership? I also read that there had been some accusations that you were involved in underhand business dealings. Do you think these accusations were made by Jacob?'

'As far as I am concerned, Jacob has no one to blame but himself. It's true that there have been other rumours that I'm involved in some kind of mafia underworld.' He smiled. 'But of course this is all nonsense put out by my rivals in order to try and sully my good reputation. Perhaps Jacob is just bitter because I bought a few of his floundering hotels to add to my own chain. Now, no more talk of Podsheister.' Although his tone was polite, it was clear he didn't want me to carry on this line of questioning.

Miss Clipboard suddenly appeared in front of us and looked at her watch. 'You have one minute left.' She flashed some perfect teeth and disappeared as quickly as she'd arrived.

'Tell me a little about the sculpture of Queen Cleopatra. Is it really cursed?' I adjusted myself in the chair, waiting, thinking that I already knew the answer to that.

He chuckled. 'No, it's been in my family for hundreds of years. We haven't been cursed yet.'

I swallowed hard. There's always a first time for everything.

'And you think it's got enough security? You don't think someone would try to steal it?'

'Of course not! The President's Secretary, Erol Hussein, has overseen the security arrangements for the sculpture. He's a security expert and has assured me that nothing can possibly go wrong. Now, I believe your time is up. I have a very busy schedule before the concert.' He gave me a courteous smile.

I stood. 'Well, many thanks for your time.'

He stood as well and held his hand out for me to shake.

I don't know why, but I ignored his outstretched hand and hugged him instead. He gave me a polite pat on the back and delicately extricated himself out of it.

Charlie and I left just as the next journalist appeared.

'I want to give Kalem a status update,' I said, weaving through the crowds and into the car park.

'A status update?'

'Yes, I heard that in a crime film once.' I knocked on the door of the Land Rover.

Kalem sat up from his slouched position, looking around to make sure the coast was clear of psychopathic politicians and killers. He unlocked the door, and Charlie and I slid in the back seats.

'We did it!' Charlie sang.

'Hopefully it will only take half an hour or so to work. We'll go back in and keep an eye on him to make sure he's nodding off.' I put a hand on Kalem's shoulder. 'Have you seen Erol anywhere?'

Kalem swung around and slid his hand through mine. 'No. I've been keeping a low profile, keeping my fingers crossed this is going to work.'

'I'm keeping everything crossed,' I said. 'Right, back to work. Let's make sure Ibrahim Kaya goes bye-byes.'

Chapter 15

3.30 p.m.

Me: 'He looks tired, doesn't he? Oh, hang on, he's yawning.'
Charlie: 'No, he's not. He's going to sneeze.'
Me: 'Shit. Why is he still awake and doing interviews?'
Charlie: 'Maybe in another five minutes he'll be asleep.'

4.00 p.m.

Me: 'Look, he's still awake. How can he still be a-bloody-wake?'
Charlie: 'Yes, but he definitely looks tired now.'
Me: 'Wait…is he going to yawn? Hang on…yes!'
Charlie: 'That was a yawn. And his eyes look red too.'
Me: 'Maybe another five minutes.'

4.30 p.m.

Me: 'Are you sure you gave him three tablets?'
Charlie: 'Positive!'
Me: 'He should be out for the count now. What's going on?'
Charlie: Oh, he's rubbing his eye again.'
Me: 'There's another yawn.'
Charlie: 'That must be at least a seven on the yawnometer scale.'

5.00 p.m.

Me: 'No! He's getting up. Why isn't he asleep?'
Charlie: 'Maybe we should have given him four tablets instead.'
Me: 'Three should have been enough to knock out a small elephant.'
Charlie: 'Look, he's walking towards us. But he looks wobbly, doesn't he?'

Me: 'Definitely a bit unsteady on his feet.'

Charlie: Looks like he's concentrating on walking.'

Me: 'And another yawn. That's a good sign.'

Charlie: 'Shit. He's going to the ballroom for the press conference.'

5.05 p.m.

Me: 'He's slurring his words. That's good.'

Charlie: 'Yes, but only a little bit.'

Me: You'd probably only notice if you were listening for it.'

Charlie: 'Good job he's sitting down.'

Me: 'Look! Did you see how he picked up that water?'

Charlie: 'He's definitely got a wobbly hand.'

5.15 p.m.

Charlie: 'He's finished the press conference.'

Me: 'He's got an hour and forty-five minutes until the concert.'

Charlie: 'Fall asleep! Fall asleep!'

Me: 'He looks like he's about to.'

Charlie: 'Ooh, he's getting up. Did you see him sway then?'

Me: 'A wibbly wobbly sway.'

Charlie: 'Where's he going now?'

Me: 'Hopefully for a lie down.'

Charlie: 'What do we do?'

Me: 'We wait. I want to make sure he doesn't come back out again. I'm going to get Kalem. I haven't seen Erol Hussein around here anywhere. Maybe he's too busy counting his money and won't show up at all.'

Charlie: 'Slimeball.'

Me: 'Fuckface Fucker!'

Chapter 16

By ten to seven you could almost feel the electric vibes in the atmosphere.

Crowds of glitter-swathed women and dinner-jacketed men packed into the restaurants and bars overlooking the stage area so it was standing-room-only left. Harassed-looking waiters and waitresses filled drinks orders; laughter and conversation noise reverberated through my bones. The port behind the stage was packed with more boats containing guests who were busy getting into the pre-party atmosphere. Lurking out there amongst the camouflage of the party-goers were some very bad people. We stood at the bar area to the side of the stage, keeping an eye on things, debating whether or not Kaya would return to unveil the statue and kick off the concert.

'This is surreal. The statue is under that velvet cover. I've always wanted to see it, and I can't believe I'm actually this close.' Kalem shuffled from one foot to the other. 'I just wish I could hold it. Even for a couple of seconds.'

No! Don't hold it. It seemed to have cursed us, and we hadn't even touched it yet. What the hell could it do to us if we did touch it? It didn't bear thinking about.

I counted the armed security guards positioned around the display case just in front of the stage. Four. One for each corner of the case.

'It doesn't look like it could be that big. What's all the fuss about?' Charlie stood on tiptoes to get a better view.

'It's only a bust size, but it's made of pure gold. Anyway, it's the only one of its kind, and that's what makes it so exciting,' Kalem said.

'Pure gold boobs? Well, they did go in for some weird stuff in the old days.' Charlie pulled a surprised face.

'No, a bust of her head and shoulders. Not *her* bust.' Kalem shook his head.

'What do you think they're going to do with it if they steal it?' Charlie asked.

Kalem shrugged. 'The plan is for it to go to a jeweller across the border in South Cyprus. They'll either melt it down and sell the gold, or sell it to another private collector. It's a really sought-after piece, worth around five million pounds.'

I was only half listening. I was too busy scanning the crowd and the hotel bedrooms beyond that overlooked the stage. Unfortunately, the sun was in the wrong position. It shone on the darkly tinted patio doors of the rooms so that you couldn't see a thing. Ferret Face could be behind any one of them. And where was Missing Link? I couldn't see him either, but then it was hard to see anyone properly in the tightly packed area.

'I've got palpitations.' I patted my chest, trying to take some deep breaths. It felt like I'd had a pacemaker fitted with dodgy batteries. 'I can't see anyone, but they could be anywhere in this lot.'

Kalem looked at his watch for the squillionth time. 'Five minutes to seven.'

'You look pale,' I said to him.

'Not as pale as you,' he said.

'I feel sick. I feel like I'm going to do a projectile vomit.' I clutched my stomach.

'I can't stand the wait. I think I'm going to do more than vomit.' Charlie crossed one leg over the other, squashing his sock and bobbing up and down like he desperately needed a wee.

A roar suddenly erupted from the crowd. Everyone in the place stood, clapping away and smiling. God, if only they knew.

I stood on tiptoes but, being short, I couldn't see much over the heads of the crowd. 'What's happening?'

'Kaya has just appeared in the middle of the stage.' Kalem tried to peer over the top of a really tall man who'd just pushed in front of us. It could've been a hairy butch woman, though, in really high heels. It was quite hard to tell in amongst all these people.

'How did he suddenly appear? Is it a magic show as well?' Charlie frowned.

'He's been lifted up from below the stage on a stage lift. He looks a bit wobbly,' Kalem said.

I clutched his arm. 'I can't see a bloody thing. How wobbly? On a wobble Richter scale?'

'I don't know. Maybe an eight.' Charlie stretched up to try and get a better look.

'Lift me on top of the bar. I want to see,' I cried.

Kalem picked me up and sat me on the bar.

I heard a few gasps amongst the crowd as Ibrahim Kaya tried to negotiate his way to a podium at the front of the stage with tottery little steps. He squinted at the ground, like it was going in and out of focus. He took a step forward, then a small step back, as if he'd forgotten how to walk. He looked up at the stage lights, confused, then back to his feet again.

I gasped the loudest, though. Why wasn't Ibrahim Kaya tucked up in bed, fast asleep, exactly where he should be when he'd just been dosed up with enough sleeping tablets to put him out for the count? I wanted to squeeze my eyes shut and pretend I was somewhere else. Instead, I just stared at him with morbid curiosity. Watching and waiting. We'd done everything we could and failed. Now it was just a downward spiral of the inevitable happening. And I didn't know if I could live with myself.

He reached the podium, clutching onto it for support. It looked like his legs were about to give way any second. And his eyelids were well and truly droopy now. He opened his mouth to speak and his lids finally succumbed to heaviness and closed.

More gasps.

His eyelids fluttered open again, and he tried to smile at the crowd, but it looked more like he had a severe case of wind.

Then he seemed to summon up the last of his willpower and spoke.

'Tha...kyou for...coming to the grand...openang of the new Plaza hotel.'

'He's slurring. He must be about to conk out any minute,' Charlie said.

Someone behind us muttered, 'Is he drunk?'

'I hope...ooo...enjoy the 'otel and facilities...as much as I enjoyed...' Ibrahim suddenly shook his head to himself, loosening his tie. 'I apologize...I seem to be feeling a...ittle light headed. Must be all the ex...citement.' His hands clutched the podium harder. He took a deep breath, forced his eyes wide open and carried on. 'As much as I...joyed building it. The Plaaaaza is my twenty-first ho...tel and is...' He paused, as if trying to kick-start his brain into gear.

'I can't look.' Charlie pressed his hands over his face.

'This is awful,' I managed through dry lips.

'Wah was I saying?' Ibrahim tried to straighten his shoulders, but they slumped. He narrowed his eyes at the crowd. He looked like he was trying to bring them in focus. 'Hotel is econd to…none. In min…Jayde will peeform.' Kaya lost his balance and toppled sideways slightly.

Louder gasps.

He quickly recovered, grabbing onto the podium for support. 'Now…now…' His eyelids drooped again. Then he seemed to get a second wind and looked up towards the crowd. 'Now…' 'Now…momant is you that been waiting for,' he slurred. 'Queen Cleo…'

And that's when several things happened at once in some kind of freaky slow motion.

Ibrahim Kaya waved a hand towards the display cabinet, his eyes sunk back into his skull, finally succumbing to sleep, and he toppled sideways.

A shot rang out from one of the hotel bedrooms.

The bullet hit Kaya and he fell to the floor, blood rapidly seeping through his chest and shoulder area and onto his pink shirt.

People screamed, eyes wide, mouths frozen open in horror.

The guards dived towards Kaya.

Wide-scale panic broke out. The crowd ran in all directions, yelling and shouting.

The display case slid down.

Kalem sprinted towards it.

Missing Link appeared at the display case, his hands grabbing the statue.

Charlie passed out and hit the deck.

A few people in the crowd fell, trying to get away. Others scrambled on top of them towards the steps to the pool area and safety beyond.

I clawed my way through the sea of people up the steps. I had to try and find Ferret Face somehow and follow him.

More screams.

My flip-flops fell off as I scrambled through the hysteric crowd. My feet slipped on the wet surface of spilled drinks.

I made it out to the car park, frantically trying to get a view through the mass of panicked guests who were crying and screaming.

Someone yanked my arm from behind, jerking me back roughly.

'Agh!' I swung around.

Erol Hussein clutched my arm in a vice-like grip and shouted, 'Arrest this woman!'

A policeman appeared at his side and wrestled me, kicking and screaming, into a police car.

Chapter 17

Police Station, take two.

Here I was again. Same communal holding cell; same halternecked hooker; minus crazy old woman.

I lay on the uncomfortable metal bench flanking the back wall of the cell, knees bent, hands over my face, wishing for a magic carpet to whisk me away to my previous life before we moved here. The bench dug into my spine, but at least the pain meant that I was still alive, and I hadn't been shot by Ferret Face. The bad thing was that I was facing the possibility of a life in prison, probably minus a few chopped-off body parts. I'd never have my perfect wedding in my perfect wedding dress with my nan's lucky charm. I'd never get married at all, in fact. I'd be left to rot in some stinky cell and turn into the crazy woman, saying "blah" every five minutes.

And where was Kalem? The last I'd seen was him running towards the statue that Missing Link had already grabbed hold of. And then what? What was happening in the chaos out there? Was Kalem alive? Injured? Did he manage to save the statue? What had happened to Ibrahim Kaya? Was he dead? The bullet looked like it had hit him in the heart. No one could survive that, surely. Had Ferret Face escaped? Maybe Charlie hadn't fainted. Maybe he'd been shot, too, by a stray bullet.

My lips trembled, and I couldn't hold back the tears anymore. They dripped down my cheeks from behind my hands, soaking my neck and arms.

'You been hooking again?' Halterneck Hooker said to me.

'Go away!' I yelled.

'Ooh, only asking. No need to get so touchy. What you in here for again, then?' She pulled a packet of tissues from her pocket and handed them to me.

I swung my legs down and sat up, wiping clumsily at my eyes. I took the tissues and yanked one out. 'I was at the Plaza. Someone shot the owner.'

She whistled. 'Oh, so that's what happened tonight. I saw lots of policemen running out of here about an hour ago. They said some psychopathic woman had carried out her threats to kill the

184

owner.'

I think my hair actually stood on end at that point. 'What?' Blood pumped to my head in a fuzzy rush. They couldn't be...no. They couldn't have meant me.

'That's what they said. Apparently, she's a real danger to society.' She nodded at me and her gigantic beaded earrings jangled. 'Good job we're in here.' She elbowed me. 'Although, it's funny you mention the Plaza. I've been servicing a guy this week who's been staying there too. Seen him every night–'

'Yes, but what else did they say about the shooting?' My breaths came in short gasps. Maybe I was hyperventilating. 'Have you got a paper bag?'

She chuckled. 'Where?' She held out her arms, indicating she didn't have anything but the clothes she was wearing. And they were pretty few and far between. 'Hidden in my knickers?' She rubbed my back. 'Take a few deep breaths. That's it.'

'So, what else did they say? Quick! Tell me!' I said, trying urgently to steer her back to the subject, instead of talking about her client, who I couldn't care less about.

'Oh, something about some woman who shot Ibrahim Kaya, and then her boyfriend stole his statue. Something like that.'

Oh, my God. I uncrumpled the tissue that I'd been squeezing in my hand, wiped my eyes, and gave her my full attention.

She stood up and stretched. 'I need to get out of here. I was hoping my Plaza guy might hook up with me again tonight. He's a big spender, you know. Got lots of money. I think those Israelis have, though.' She gave me a knowing look. 'Brings his own drink with him, as well, whenever I see him. He likes some weird, expensive cognac shit.'

'Yes, but did they say if Ibrahim was alive? What happened to the statue? And what about...' I trailed off, my brain suddenly registering what she'd just said. 'Huh?' I frowned at her.

'What, honey?' She gave me a puzzled look.

'Say that again. What did you just say about your Plaza guy who drinks expensive cognac?' I stopped breathing, waiting for her to answer. Was she...could she be talking about Ferret Face? I gripped her arm, my wide eyes staring into hers. Of course! She had to be talking about him. Didn't Ibrahim Kaya say that Jacob Podsheister was Israeli? The name sounded Israeli. And what about the yacht in the harbour? That was called *The*

Israelite and it was owned by a Mr P. That must be the connection between him and Ferret Face. Maybe they knew each other from Israel. And Ferret Face drank Courvoisier. It had to be him that she was talking about. A fiery heat of anticipation and excitement swept over me. Maybe she had some information that could help the police find him. 'What does he look like?'

She narrowed her eyes suspiciously. 'Why, are you trying to steal my customers?'

'I'm not a hooker!'

'Yes, OK. And I'm the Queen of England!'

'What does he look like?' I said, more urgently this time.

She shrugged. 'He's got blondish-brown hair and beard, piggy brown eyes, skinny. He looks a bit like an animal.'

'Like a ferret?' I sat upright, waiting for her answer.

She tilted her head, lips puckered, deep in thought. 'Yeah. A lot like a ferret, now you come to mention it.'

It had to be him. 'How did you meet him? How long have you known him for?'

'I haven't known him long. He said he was trying to pick up a hooker at his hotel, but she preferred women customers.' She shrugged. 'Still, that's her loss. He gave me a huge tip.' She grinned at me.

'Do you know what his plans were? Was he going back to Israel or into South Cyprus? Was he going to contact you tonight?'

She gave me a leisurely shrug. 'I don't know, honey. It's not like I wanted to marry him or anything.' She let out a throaty chuckle. 'My job isn't to ask questions. I just show them a good time.'

A policeman arrived in front of the bars and pointed to Halterneck Hooker. 'You're out of here.'

She stood up. 'Well, it's been real nice chatting to you.' She strutted towards the door. 'Watch out for that crazy woman.'

I shot off the bench. 'No!' I grabbed hold of her arm. 'Wait! Don't go! I need to know more about the guy.'

The policeman glared at Halterneck Hooker. 'Lena, out now, otherwise I'll keep you in here all night. And don't let me see you again this week.'

Lena pulled her arm away. 'Sorry, gotta go.' She left me standing there, staring through the bars in disbelief.

I banged my fist on the metal bars. No, no, no! *Ouch that hurt.* I rubbed my hand.

Maybe Ferret Face was going to see Lena now. Or maybe he was hiding out somewhere else. Or maybe he'd already left on the same boat that Missing Link had stashed at the hotel's port.

'I want my phone call!' I yelled down the now empty corridor.

I didn't know if I was actually allowed one, but I'd seen it hundreds of times in films. They always got to make one call, didn't they? Or did they? Oh, my brain wouldn't work. Maybe I'd dreamed it. Or maybe it was just wishful thinking.

I rattled the bars. 'I want my phone call!'

Captain Beaky from the other night appeared in the corridor to see what all the racket was about. 'Oh, it's you again. Hang on a minute.'

Uh-oh.

He disappeared from view.

Great. He was just going to ignore me! I carried on staring up the corridor, ready to keep yelling if he didn't return. I didn't care. I'd yell all bloody night if I had to. They'd soon get fed up with me then and give me a phone call.

Captain Beaky reappeared with a pair of flip-flops in his hand. He leaned in towards the bars. 'Look, thanks for the other night. If it wasn't for you, I wouldn't know for sure about my wife.' He unlocked the doors with an echoing click. 'Put these on.' He handed me the flip-flops.

I stared down at my now dirty-black feet. In all the commotion, I'd completely forgotten that my flip-flops had fallen off. I slipped them on.

'I'll take you to the phone.' He escorted me down the corridor and around the corner to the phone, standing guard so I didn't make a run for it.

'Oh, thank you. Thank you! It wasn't me. I didn't kill anyone.' My eyes pleaded with him.

'Just make your call.'

I stared at the phone and my mind suddenly went blank. I was stuck in a foreign prison, not knowing what the hell was going on out there. Clueless as to what had happened to Kalem and whether he was alive or injured. Who should I call? The A-Team? Batman? That guy who escaped from Alcatraz for some jail-breaking tips? Did I need an international dialling code to get through to them?

I picked up the receiver and jabbed at the digits, dialling Ayshe's mobile number.

Please pick up. Pleeeeeeease.

'Hello?' Ayshe's soft voice answered.

'Ayshe! It's me. Is Kalem with you?'

'Helen! Thank God. What happened? Kalem hasn't come back to the hotel. Neither has Charlie. Where are you?'

'At the police station,' my voice cracked. 'You've got to do something.'

'I heard on the news that Ibrahim Kaya was shot. They said someone got away with the statue, but the details coming in are a bit sketchy. Some people are saying that he's been killed.'

'Ferret Face shot him,' I wailed. 'And I don't know what happened to Kalem.'

'I'll be right down there. I'll round up Mum and Dad. They've made a complete recovery. They were asking where you all were.'

'Please get down here as soon as you can.' I sniffed back the tears.

'We're on our way. Don't panic.'

Don't panic? I didn't think that was likely given the circumstances.

I hung up and felt a presence behind me that made goosebumps spring to attention on my skin.

'You can take her back to the cell now and let her stew. I'll be back to talk to her in the morning,' Erol Hussein said.

PANIC!

Chapter 18

I stewed all right.

It was like being stranded in the desert for days on end with no water. My brain started thinking bizarre random things with no rational explanation. Maybe it was the stress, or the shock, or the lack of sleep. Or maybe I did actually fall asleep at some point during the early hours on the uncomfortable metal bench, and I'd really been dreaming. One minute I was thinking – or dreaming – about barbequing Smoky. Charlie wanted him well done, and I wanted him medium rare. We had a big fight over what condiments to serve with him, and Smoky turned into a ferret. Then I was flying through the air in my wedding dress – think I was actually a ghost – but I was a hundred years old and the only word I could say was *nuts*. After that, Kalem appeared, but he was covered in seaweed and had webbed hands and feet like the Man from Atlantis. He carried the Queen Cleopatra sculpture in one of his webby little hands and a packet of custard creams in the other.

What did it all mean?

'Breakfast!' the younger policeman from the other night shoved a tray under the cell door, waking me out of my trance-like state.

My first thought was where the hell were Ayshe and everyone else? She'd said last night that she was going to bring them all down here to help me. So where were they all? Surely they couldn't have just abandoned me and left me to rot in here. But then the police thought I was a murderer, didn't they? That's what Lena had overheard them say. Maybe they didn't allow suspected murderers to have visitors. Oh, my God. What was I going to do?

My eyes flitted around the cell like a mad woman, searching for some sort of possible escape route, but I couldn't see anything that would help me. I eyed the traditional Turkish breakfast on the floor with a depressed lack of interest. Olives, hellim cheese, cucumber, tomatoes, bread, and carob syrup. My stomach yelled at me in hunger, but I couldn't face the thought of food.

I stood up and stretched, kneading the knots in my shoulder. It was a good job Kalem had taught me Yoga. At least I could do that in a cramped cell. I might end up a hundred year old nutcase inside prison, but at least I'd be a supple one.

I grabbed a bottle of water from the tray and glugged it down. I stopped mid-glug as I saw Erol Hussein coming down the corridor towards the cell doors.

'Not hungry?' He eyed the untouched breakfast. 'You should eat. Keep up your strength. You'll need it where you're going. I gave you the chance to leave and look what happened.'

I opened my mouth to speak, then looked past him at a commotion further down the corridor.

The family cavalry had arrived. Yasmin, Deniz, Ayshe, Atila, Osman, and Charlie stormed down the corridor towards us, all led by another policeman who had a fancy looking circle on his epaulettes. I didn't know who the hell he was, but by the way he acted, I suspected he was pretty high-up. Erol seemed to recognize him, though, judging by how his jaw plummeted open.

'Dad!' Erol said to the policeman. 'What are you doing here?'

'I want to know what the hell has been going on,' Erol's dad spat, all red in the face.

'I can explain!' I yelled.

Erol's dad frowned at me, then turned his attention to Erol. 'I've been hearing some very disturbing things.' He unlocked the door to the cell. 'You can come with us, Helen.'

Deniz patted my shoulder. 'We tried to see you last night and get this all sorted out, Helen, but I'm sure you know that there were certain *obstacles* in the way.' He glared at Erol.

'I'm just glad you're all here,' I managed to squeak as we all traipsed into a big office on the top floor of the station.

'Did you want Turkish coffee?' Erol's dad asked me.

'No, thanks.' Not after last time.

Erol's dad ordered chairs to be brought for everyone, and we all sat.

I looked at Deniz and gave him a questioning look. He put a finger to his lips and gave me a reassuring smile. Yasmin looked like she hadn't slept. Her curly grey-black hair was spiralling in all directions, and her eyes were red. Ayshe fidgeted with her wedding ring. Attila looked the same as he did on the nerve-wracking opening night of his restaurant. Osman waited

190

patiently for something to happen. Charlie rubbed at a bruise over his right eye. And Erol looked worried.

'What's going on?' I looked from one to the other. 'Where's Kalem? Is he OK? Oh, my God. He's dead, isn't he? That's why he's not with you. Noooooooooooo. Tomorrow was supposed to be our wedding day! And I'm never going to see him again.'

Yasmin grabbed my hand and squeezed it for dear life. 'We don't know yet. No one's seen him since last night.'

The policeman spoke then. 'I am Ali Hussein, the chief of police here, and it seems there has been some kind of misunderstanding about you.' He glared at Erol. 'Now, we need to get some more information immediately so we can look for Kalem.' Ali gave me a kind smile and turned his attention to Erol with a gruff no-nonsense voice. 'That means I need to start at the beginning.'

Wait a minute. This had to be some kind of sick joke. Erol's dad hated Deniz, didn't he? So why was he trying to help? Maybe it was a trap.

'No.' My whole body shuddered. 'This isn't happening. This isn't happening.' And then I couldn't stop the tears falling as I thought about Kalem, possibly lying injured somewhere, or worse...d...d...no, I couldn't even say the D word.

'We'll find him, Helen,' Deniz said. 'You just need to tell them everything as quickly as possible, so they can look for him.'

Ayshe squeezed my other hand, her dark, oval eyes pleading with me not to think about it, but talk.

'Did he have a mobile phone on him?' Ali asked me. 'If he still has it, we can try and trace his location by GPS.'

'Yes! He did!' I rattled off the number.

He wrote the number down and handed it to another officer who had just come in. 'Trace this signal immediately.'

'No one wanted to know anything. That was the problem!' I snarled at Erol. 'We told you this would happen, and you didn't want to do anything. You'd rather keep the money than save a life. And now look what's happened! You make me sick.' If Ayshe and Yasmin weren't gripping my hands at that point, I would've punched him in the face.

'What money?' Ali glared at his son.

'I'll tell you.' And through the tears and sniffles, I told him what had happened from the very beginning.

I told him about how we'd come to North Cyprus to get married and start a wonderful new life, living the dream in the Mediterranean sun. I explained about the mix-up with the suitcase and how we'd given the money, the plans, the photo, and itinerary to Erol to investigate. I told him how Erol didn't believe anyone would try to assassinate Ibrahim Kaya or steal the statue, and how I believed his motive for not investigating was to keep the money. I also snuck in there how I suspected that Erol had arranged for the funding to be pulled on Kalem's job, so we'd have to leave the island to keep us quiet. This produced some serious glaring at Erol from his dad.

I told Ali how we'd gone to the police station to try and report all of this, but we'd seen Ferret Face talking with some high-up policeman and suspected he was involved. I explained how we'd even tried to talk to the President at the festival, and how we'd tried to warn Ibrahim Kaya, eventually resulting in me being arrested.

I went on about how Erol had made a bargain with me that if Kalem and I left the island, he would drop the charges. And how he'd assured Ibrahim Kaya that there was no problem, and that I was just some crazy woman who had threatened to kill him.

More glaring from Ali to Erol. 'And you call yourself a security expert?' he spat at Erol.

I let him know about how we'd followed Ferret Face and discovered a connection with an Israeli yacht and someone called Mr. P. I repeated the conversation, word for word, that Ferret Face and Missing Link had with Mr. P on the yacht, and I gave him my suspicions that it all pointed to a man called Jacob Podsheister, who blamed Kaya for his downfall and wanted him dead. Then I explained how I'd tried to drug Ferret Face to stop him going ahead with the assassination, but it hadn't worked, so the only option was to drug Ibrahim Kaya, but that hadn't worked either, and he'd still been shot.

Tears cascaded down my cheeks. 'And now Ibrahim Kaya is dead!' I flopped forward in the chair.

'Helen, Ibrahim Kaya is not dead,' Ali said.

'Huh?' I wailed. Had I misheard him? Did he just say that he *wasn't* dead?

'No, he's not dead. Although it is still touch and go. Because

192

you gave him the sleeping tablets, he was already falling over by the time the sniper shot him. The bullet caught him in the shoulder instead of the heart. A second later and he would have been dead instantly, I'm sure. But he lost a lot of blood. We will have to wait and see what the doctors say,' Ali said.

Yasmin handed me a glass of water. 'Here, drink this.'

I ignored the water and turned to Charlie. 'What happened to you? Did you see Kalem? The last time I saw him, he'd been running towards the statue, and Missing Link already had hold of it.'

'I don't know. I think I must have passed out. When I came to, pretty much everyone had gone, and there was no sign of Kalem anywhere. The only thing left of him was this.' He handed me the baseball cap that Kalem had been wearing the day before.

I clutched the cap to my chest as I mentally went through the conversation from the yacht in my head over and over again. 'There was supposed to be a boat waiting in the hotel's port. According to the conversation on the yacht, Missing Link was going to steal the statue and get on this boat.'

Ali picked up the phone, yelling into it. When he replaced the receiver, he said to us, 'I've instructed the coastguard and helicopters to carry out a search for this boat. It could be anywhere by now, though. It's been twelve hours.' He glared at Erol. 'If only I'd known about this sooner, it could have been prevented, or we could have been out hours ago, searching for Kalem.'

And then I suddenly remembered the photos I'd taken of Ferret Face and Missing Link. 'You might be able to recognize the men involved from Interpol or something. I took some pictures of them. Charlie, where's my camera? You had it around your neck yesterday.'

'Ah. There's a slight problem there. When I came to after fainting, I had a black eye, and your camera must've fallen off in all the pushing and shoving.' He looked sheepishly at me. 'It was gone when I woke up.'

'Oh, no!' I gnawed on my bottom lip. I didn't even care that my thousand-pound camera had disappeared. All I cared about was finding Kalem. And my camera had the evidence on it that could've helped to identify the people involved. Now it was lost.

'I'm so sorry, Helen,' Charlie said.

'We're still interviewing and trying to get hold of witnesses who were at the hotel. So far, none of them can add anything useful. Most of the people were panicking to get away in all the mayhem. So no one seems to have seen Kalem since he tried to protect the statue.' Ali glanced down at the desk, tapping his forefingers together, deep in concentration.

I racked my brain, trying to think. So much was tumbling around in there, I had trouble trying to string together rational thoughts. There was something else that I knew, something that might help, but I didn't know what. *Think, Helen, think!*

'Well, at least we have some information to go on,' Ali said. 'I need you to identify the policeman who was talking to this assassin.'

'Well, the last time I saw him, he was about to be punched by the captain who interviewed me the other night.'

'Punched?' Ali frowned.

I nodded. 'Yes, it's a long story. But the captain will know who he is.'

Ali lifted the phone on the desk and shouted something in Turkish. Then he turned to me again. 'We will bring him here for you to identify. I've also ordered a search team to go to Jacob Podsheister's yacht. They will arrest him and bring him here.'

I slapped a hand to my forehead. 'Yes! The captain has got a photo of Ferret Face. The CCTV cameras at the airport captured the drugs dog when it jumped on me, and in the same photo you can clearly see his face.'

Ali smiled. 'Good, good. Is there anything else you can think of?'

What was it? What? Something about…Lena. 'Lena, the woman who was in the cell with me. I think she knows Ferret Face. I think he was her customer. She might know something about his whereabouts.'

Erol's dad lifted the phone again and shouted something else. As he slammed it down, Captain Beaky appeared at the door with the same policeman I'd seen talking to Ferret Face in the station.

'Is this the man?' Ali said to me.

'Yes. No doubt about it.' I nodded.

'You are a disgrace, Superintendant,' Ali bellowed at him.

'You have a position of authority and you've abused it! Take him into custody!'

And the superintendant was hauled off, shouting obscenities, out the door.

Ali rose. 'I think we have enough to go on. If you'll excuse me, we need to get on with the search.' He glared at Erol again. 'I'll deal with you later. And don't think because you are my son, that you will escape charges. You have no honour!'

Erol slunk down in his chair, trying to make himself invisible.

'But...what am I supposed to do?' I cried. 'I can't just wait here while you're out looking for Kalem. I have to do something.' I looked down at the baseball cap, clutched in my hand, and put it on my head – somehow it made me feel closer to Kalem.

'I agree.' Deniz nodded. 'This is my son we're talking about. I want to come too. And the more pairs of eyes out there, searching, the better.'

Yasmin clutched her chest. 'I want to help.'

'Me, too. I can't just sit here and do nothing,' Ayshe said.

'Well, I feel partly responsible. If I hadn't fainted, I would've seen what happened to him. So count me in,' Charlie said.

'You might need me to help,' Osman said to Ali in a tone that I couldn't quite work out.

'And me.' Atila glanced at me. 'I think we should all go and search.'

'Hang on a minute.' I narrowed my eyes at Atila. 'What do you know about all of this? You've been acting really strange since we got here. Going off on secret missions and not telling anyone where you've been. Acting all cagey and suspicious. What have you been up to?' I pointed an accusing finger at him. 'Are you involved in all of this?'

Atila sat back like I'd slapped him. 'Of course not!'

'Well, what have you been doing then?' I shouted.

Ayshe wrapped her arms protectively around her stomach. 'Yes? What have you been doing? You *have* been acting strange.'

'It was supposed to be a surprise. A wedding present for you.' Atila looked between Ayshe and me, horrified.

'I've had all the surprises I can take. Tell me!' My voice jumped a few hundred decibels.

Oh, no. This was horrendous. Part of me didn't want to hear it. I didn't want to even contemplate that he could be involved in this somehow. But greed did funny things to people, didn't it? And what other reason could there be for all his sneaking around?

'Well, since my recipe books have taken off, I've been thinking about expanding my restaurant business. I don't need to be at the one in London full-time anymore. It's successful, and I've got an excellent chef and manager now to take over the reins. And I saw an amazing place in Kyrenia the other day that would make a perfect restaurant. I felt like I needed a new challenge, and this would be perfect, wouldn't it?' He slipped his hand through Ayshe's. 'I mean, I knew how sad you were about going back to the UK after the wedding and being so far away from Helen. I thought this would be the perfect solution. You could be here all the time with each other.' His forehead creased with worry. 'Have I done the wrong thing?'

Ayshe's tense shoulders slumped with relief. 'Oh, thank God for that. You had me worried there for a minute. I even thought you were having an affair.'

'An affair? Never.' He smiled at her.

'I'm sorry. I'm so sorry.' I shook my head manically, more to myself than anyone else. 'I don't know what I was thinking. Of course you couldn't be involved in anything like this.'

Atila enveloped me in a warm hug. 'No problem at all. You can't be thinking straight at the moment. It's understandable. Now, the question is, what can we all do to help find Kalem?'

Ali leaped to his feet. 'It is not protocol, of course, to have you involved in a police investigation. But we may not have much time, and Helen, you might remember something useful on the way. So under the circumstances, I will allow you all to come with me. Let's find Kalem.'

Chapter 19

We all bundled into the small interview room where they were holding the superintendant.

Captain Beaky stood behind the superintendant who was sitting in the same chair I'd been in two days before. The superintendant didn't look too happy, but Captain Beaky had a smug smile on his face.

'Right. I want to know who these criminals are, and what your involvement is.' Ali roughly pulled out a chair opposite the superintendant and plonked himself down.

'You've got the wrong person.' The superintendant folded his arms in a defiant stance. 'Are you going to take the word of this crazy woman over me?' He nodded his head in my direction.

Captain Beaky kicked the bottom of his chair out from under him, and the superintendant fell on the floor.

Captain Beaky grinned. The superintendant almost had smoke coming out of his ears as he picked himself up, dusted off his trousers, and sat down again.

Ali slapped a hand on the desk. 'Enough! We are searching for someone. It could be a life or death situation, and I'm not wasting any more time. Tell me everything you know. NOW.'

The superintendant screwed up his lips, as if debating what to say. 'OK, I admit I talked to this man. But I didn't know who he was.' He shrugged. 'He just came into the station and asked me for directions.' He let out a small, unconvincing laugh.

Ali gave an exasperated shake of his head. 'You will have to do better than that.'

The superintendant shrugged again. 'That's all I know. He came into the station saying he was lost, and I just gave him directions, that's all.'

'Directions to where?' Ali asked, even though it was clear from his tone that he didn't believe a word.

'To see my wife, probably,' Captain Beaky muttered under his breath.

The superintendant turned and gave him a killer look.

'TO WHERE?' Ali repeated, losing his patience.

I was losing mine too. In a minute, *I'd* kick his bloody chair out from under him as well. Or poke his eyes out. Or...well, something to make him talk.

'Just to the harbour.' The superintendant grinned.

'This is getting us nowhere.' Ali stood up. 'Take him to the cell,' he said to Captain Beaky.

'With pleasure.' He pulled the superintendant to his feet and practically dragged him out.

The short policeman from the other night rushed in and handed Ali a computer printout. 'We've identified the sniper from the photo at the airport. He's an Israeli citizen who is wanted in connection with several major jewellery thefts and murders in the last few years. I've updated all ports, airports, and also the border crossing with South Cyprus with the photo. He hasn't been through passport control anywhere yet, but if he's seen they'll detain him.'

Ali perused the printout. 'Good. Any other updates?'

'A search team is busy going through Jacob Podsheister's yacht. They haven't found anything incriminating yet. There's no sign of the statue or Kalem. He's denying any involvement, of course, but we've arrested him. He'll be here in a minute. We're still trying to trace the exact location of Kalem's mobile phone, and Lena has arrived, so I'll bring her in.' The policeman's stubby little legs dashed off again.

'But it all happened hours ago.' I slumped to the floor, flopping my head onto my knees. 'The criminals could have already left the country by now. They could have taken their boat to any neighbouring country. South Cyprus, Syria, Israel, Greece, Turkey.' This was getting us nowhere.

Yasmin knelt down, hugging me into her warm body. She gently stroked my hair, making shushing sounds. 'They'll find him. They have to.'

But I wasn't so hopeful.

Lena strutted into the interview room. 'Hey? Are we having a party in here?'

I jumped to my feet, clutching her shoulders and imploring her with my eyes. 'Lena, you have to tell them everything you know about that customer you were telling me about.'

She tossed her hair back and glanced suspiciously at everyone gathered in the room. 'I'm not admitting to anything. I don't want to get charged with soliciting.'

'I can arrange to have your previous charges dropped if you help us,' Ali said. 'You have my word that you won't be charged with anything, as long as you tell us all you know about this man. He is a dangerous criminal and he is involved in some very serious offences. We need to find out where he could be.' He showed her the photo of Ferret Face and me at the airport. 'Is this your customer?'

She licked her lips, pondering this for a minute. 'You're sure you won't charge me?'

'YES,' I shouted before anyone else could say anything.

She nodded at the picture. 'That's him.'

'What do you know about him?' Ali asked.

'I know that he was staying at that fancy hotel, the Plaza. I thought he might phone me last night to hook up, because I've seen him the last few nights, but I haven't heard anything from him.'

'Where did you meet him?' I asked.

She shrugged. 'I used to meet him at Jacob Podsheister's fancy boat. Jacob was always arranging parties with lots of ladies, if you know what I mean.' She winked at me.

'Well, that proves a connection between them. That proves Podsheister organized this whole thing, doesn't it?' My breaths came in short, sharp waves, feeling relief at some sort of breakthrough.

'It only proves they knew each other. It doesn't prove Podsheister hired him,' Ali said. 'But it's a start.'

'How did he contact you?' Ali asked Lena.

'Podsheister used to ring me up and arrange it.'

'And when was the last time you heard from him?' Ali asked.

She tapped her lip with her finger. 'Thursday night. I hooked up with him after I got out of here.'

Ali wrote something in a small notebook. 'Did he say where he was going after he left the island?'

Lena shook her head.

'Did you overhear anything or see anything suspicious at these parties?' Ali asked.

Lena furrowed her brow. 'Like what?'

'Well, did your client, or any of the others on board, say anything that could help with the attempted murder of Ibrahim Kaya and the theft of his gold statue. Think, Lena. Did they

199

mention anything? Anything at all that seemed suspicious?' The urgency was evident in Ali's voice.

Concentration clouded Lena's face as she thought about this.

I held my breath, praying that she'd be able to come up with some information that could help us.

Finally, she shook her head. 'No, I can't think of anything.'

I exhaled a heavy sigh.

'Well, thank you. If you hear from him again, let me know as soon as possible.' Ali handed her a card. 'Any time.'

She raised an eyebrow. 'Any time?'

He coughed. 'Er…any time in connection with this case.'

Deniz threw his hands in the air. 'Another dead end. We're running out of time. He could be injured somewhere.'

'Now what?' I said.

'Now we talk to Podsheister.' Ali picked up the phone on the desk, barking out more orders.

Captain Beaky reappeared a few minutes later with Podsheister.

'Sit!' Ali said so loud it left a ringing in my ear.

Podsheister surveyed the room with shifty eyes and sat.

'You'd better start talking. Now!' Ali poked him in the chest. 'We need to know the whereabouts of your hit man and thief, and what happened to Kalem Mustafa.'

Podsheister looked up with a sneer. 'What are you talking about? You're crazy. I'm a law-abiding businessman.'

Ali moved closer to him, his face an inch away from Podsheister. When he spoke, his voice was as cold and sharp as a steel machete. 'Don't worry. The evidence is just a matter of time. We know that you hired two men to kill Ibrahim Kaya and steal his statue. We know that you hired Lena to entertain these men on your yacht. You will not get away with this, so it would be wise of you to tell us where your men are hiding.'

'The only thing I'll tell you is the name of my lawyer. I want to speak to him now. And you won't find anything on my yacht. I'll be out of here in no time.' Podsheister grinned at us all.

'I wouldn't bet on it,' Ali said to Podsheister.

The short policeman ran up to Ali and whispered something to him. Ali's expression changed from stern to excited.

'What now? What's happened?' I ran a wobbly hand across my forehead, trying to ignore the creepy sneer that seemed to be locked permanently on Podsheister's face.

'Lock Podsheister up in the cells,' Ali said to the policemen. Then he gently placed a hand on my shoulder. 'OK, everyone else follow me.' Ali led the way out of the interview room and stopped in the corridor to brief us. 'They have traced Kalem's mobile phone GPS location to a beach further up the coast. Unfortunately, he hasn't made any calls or texts from it since the day before yesterday, though, and there must be a reason why he hasn't tried to contact anyone yet.' His tone implied that we shouldn't get our hopes up.

But I didn't care. It was a lead, and the only one we had. 'Come on.' I ran towards the front entrance. 'What are you waiting for?'

Ten minutes later, the police Land Rover turned off the coast road and onto a bumpy track. I could see a police helicopter, hovering above the small horseshoe shaped beach in front of me. I hoped they could see something because it looked completely deserted to me.

We bounced down the track, heads and elbows banging against the windows, and screeched to a stop. Three more Land Rovers arrived behind us.

I jumped out the door before Ali had even turned off the engine. Scanning the sandy beach, I looked one way, then the other. Nothing. No one was here. So where was his phone?

'Any sign of him?' Deniz climbed out.

'Is he here?' Yasmin took Deniz's hand to steady herself as she got out.

'Where is he?' Ayshe gasped.

'Yes, where?' Charlie said.

'I can't see him.' Atila shaded his eyes from the sun to get a better look.

Ali spoke briefly into a radio, then looked at us all. 'The helicopter hasn't spotted him. There is no thermal image coming from this area.'

'Yes, but what does that mean?' I grabbed his arm.

'It means that there is no body heat coming from this area,' he added with a pained look.

Which meant that no one was alive on this beach.

Ali patted my arm. 'OK, now we search the beach.'

The beach cut into soft sandstone cliffs at either end, where years of sea water had eroded them into unusual bumpy shapes like you'd see on the surface of another planet. Maybe there was a chance he'd got washed onto the rocks, and we just couldn't see him yet.

Twenty other officers spread out across the beach, looking for Kalem's mobile phone or any clues that could trace him.

We all followed together, hoping for a shout from one of them to say they'd found something.

All eyes scanned the beach. And when we got to one end, some of the officers clambered up onto the smooth rocks. A few shallow caves, like gaping mouths, were hollowed out under the rocks, but Kalem was nowhere to be found.

Back up the beach we all went again, scouring the area once more.

'Here!' One of the policemen slipped on a pair of rubber gloves and picked up a mobile phone that was wedged in the sand.

I ran towards it, staring at it with dread. 'It's Kalem's. He must be here somewhere. He *must* be.'

The rocks at the other end of the beach were bigger with more caves, and the stubby-legged policeman explored them methodically.

I shivered, wrapping my arms around me.

His back disappeared into one of the shallow caves.

I held my breath, craning my neck, but it was impossible to see into the cave from where we were standing above.

'Is he there?' Deniz said.

'Is it my son?' Yasmin wailed.

'Oh, my God.' Ayshe's hands flew to her mouth.

'No. It can't be him.' Charlie shook his head in denial.

Stubby Legs reappeared, shaking his head.

My hands flapped around uselessly. 'Where is he then?'

Osman wandered away from us, walking up the beach, gently stroking his beard as he examined the sand.

'What?' I said. 'What are you looking at?'

We all gathered around as he crouched down. 'There was a boat here. A small dinghy type of boat, not a hard-bottomed one. It was pulled onto the shore. You can see the tracks.' He pointed to the sand. 'My guess is they came here straight from the

Plaza.'

I stared at the beach until it swam out of focus, but all I could make out were some small indentations in the sand. It didn't look very much like a boat track to me, but then what did I know?

He tilted his head and, after a few minutes of careful thought, stood up with his back towards the indentations, head down, dark eyes concentrating on the ground. He walked in a straight line from the beach to the shingle area where we'd hastily parked the Land Rovers. He crouched down again by the shingle, pointing to four small indentations in the pattern of the stones. 'Look here. There was a heavy vehicle waiting – some sort of four-wheel drive. They got into the vehicle and drove away from the beach.

'Can you tell how many people there were?' I asked.

He walked from the beach to the shingle area and back again, studying the ground intently. 'There were four people. But one of them was injured.'

I swallowed hard. My throat felt dry and constricted. 'How can you tell?'

Osman pointed to some marks in the sand and the shingle. 'If you look carefully you can see three sets of footprints and one set of drag marks in between two of them. Someone was being dragged between two people.' He crouched down by the shingle, pointing to some small reddish-brown flecks on a few of the stones. 'Look, you see this? It's blood.' He glanced up at me.

I let out a strangled cry. 'Oh, God.'

Yasmin threw her head back and wailed at the sky.

Ayshe's face drained of colour.

'But which way did they go in the vehicle?' Ali asked.

We all turned to look up the bumpy track that we'd travelled on down to the beach from the main road. Further behind the track was a small viaduct that ran underneath the main road. I could see a dried-up river bed in it. It was big enough to get a vehicle through. And beyond the viaduct it looked like there were fields. Beyond ·the fields were the Kyrenia Mountain Range.

'If they went on the main road, we have very little chance of tracking them. But if they went under the viaduct, we have a good chance of finding the vehicle,' Osman said. 'Of course, with the terrain in the mountains, it's very possible that they stashed the vehicle somewhere and carried on by foot. My bet is that they are hiding out up there until the heat blows over, waiting for the search to be called off.'

I turned to him, frowning. 'How do you know all this?'

'Osman was in the Special Forces here for fifteen years. He's the best tracker the Army had,' Deniz said.

'What? I thought you were a shepherd?' I said.

'I am now. I've retired.'

I launched my arms around Osman's neck. 'Oh, thank you! You have to find Kalem for me.'

'If anyone can find him now, it's Osman.' Deniz nodded gravely.

'We have no time to waste. Come on.' Osman quickened his pace towards the viaduct, carefully checking out the ground and the tyre tracks. 'We're in luck. They went underneath it. Understandable, really. They wouldn't want to be seen on the main road.'

'I'm going to arrange for some search dogs to help you track him,' Ali said. 'If they did leave the vehicle at any point and go on foot, we'll need some dogs to search for them. ' He was just about to radio his instructions.

'No. I have a sniffer sheep,' Osman said.

'A what?' Ali looked confused.

'Yes, a sniffer sheep. I trained it myself. It's had a crash course in detecting people. Even if I can't find Kalem, I bet you anything that Kuzu will.'

Ali snorted at the suggestion. 'No, we can use the sniffer dog from the airport.'

'But he can only find sandwiches!' Osman shook his head. 'No. We don't have much time. I can only work with Kuzu. She is now fully trained, and I trust her judgment completely. I can't work with sniffer dogs that I haven't handled before and who can only find sandwiches.'

I didn't even have the strength to argue that Osman must be even more crazy than I'd first thought, and it was the most ridiculous suggestion I'd ever heard in my life. All I wanted was to find Kalem. And if it meant using a sniffer sheep, then that's what we would do.

Chapter 20

'If they went towards the mountains they could be anywhere. There are many caves in the mountain range that they can easily hide in.' Osman's voice suddenly oozed authority, like he was now running the show. 'I will go ahead on my own, and the police must stay on the beach. If Kalem is still alive we don't want to risk them seeing the police and panicking.'

Ali shook his head. 'No, I can't allow that.'

'Think about it,' Osman said to Ali. 'If they see the police, there will be an instant confrontation and shootout, and Kalem could be killed. If they see a shepherd in the mountains with his sheep, they won't think anything of it. We can observe them, get close to them, and they won't suspect anything.'

'I think that's a good idea,' Atila said.

'I vote we go for that,' Deniz said. 'I trust Osman completely.'

Yasmin and Charlie nodded vigorously.

'Me too,' Ayshe said.

'I want to come as well. I have to come.' I clutched Osman's arm. 'He's my fiancé. I have to come.'

Osman looked down at me. He gave me a strained smile, as if acknowledging the pain that must have been radiating through my eyes. 'That may be a good idea. If we find these men, Helen will be able to identify them,' Osman said to Ali. 'There could be hikers in the mountains, and I don't want to mistake one of them for the criminals.'

'OK. How do you want to do this?' Ali asked.

'First, I need to get Kuzu and my sheep.'

'What, all of them?' Charlie said.

'Of course. This has to look real. I will bring my sheep here and some of my mother's old sheep herding clothes for Helen, so she looks the part. Then we track them.'

Nods of agreement all round.

As Osman left, we all paced the ground, lost in our own thoughts. I prayed to the sheep gods that Kuzu and Osman would be able to find Kalem. Alive.

It felt like the longest moment of my life. I know everyone always says that when bad things happen, but it really is true.

Time seemed to have lost its momentum. Like it was stuck. I kept checking my watch and only a minute had actually passed since the last time I'd nervously looked. Osman seemed to be taking forever. And when he finally reappeared with his truck full of sheep, only an hour had actually gone by.

Osman jumped down from the truck and released the back section of the white pickup, pulling it down so it became a ramp to the ground. The sheep bleated and baaed away, instantly nibbling the sparse grass and sage plants.

Osman handed me a headscarf, some Turkish baggy trousers, nipped in at the ankles with elastic, and a shawl. 'Put these on. You will look like a country shepherdess.'

I pulled on the trousers.

'Do you have anything that belongs to Kalem that Kuzu can use as a guide?' Osman asked me.

I shook my head frantically. In all the excitement of the night before, I hadn't had anything on me when I'd been running after Ferret Face before I'd been arrested. 'No,' I wailed.

'Yes, you have, Helen.' Charlie pointed to Kalem's baseball cap on my head.

My hand flew up to touch it. I pulled it off my head and thrust it towards Osman. 'Will this do?'

'Yes. It will do very nicely.' Osman nodded.

I tied the headscarf around my head and clutched Kalem's baseball cap in my hand.

Osman grabbed a walking stick about two metres long from the cab section of his truck. 'Are you ready?' he said to me.

I took a deep breath. 'I'm ready.'

Ali grabbed the police radio from Stubby Legs and handed it to Osman. 'Keep me informed. But if you see them, I don't want you to do anything. Your job will be to find them and keep them in your sights. Then report back to us, and we'll do the rest.' He reached out and squeezed Osman's shoulder. 'Good luck.'

Osman turned the volume down on the radio and tucked it into his baggy trousers. He bent down and whispered something in Turkish to Kuzu. 'Let Kuzu smell the hat,' he said to me.

I handed him Kalem's baseball cap. Kuzu sniffed it, her little nostrils flaring repeatedly.

Osman handed the cap back to me. 'OK. Let's go.'

We walked through the viaduct with Osman keeping a firm

eye on the tracks. Kuzu obediently stayed by Osman's side, sniffing at the ground, wagging her woolly little tail. The rest of the sheep meandered behind us, nibbling away in their own little sheepy world, oblivious to our task. I clutched the baseball cap in my hand, hanging onto it for dear life. There was no way I was going to let it slip from my grasp if it meant the possibility of finding Kalem.

On the other side of the viaduct were fields of olive and carob trees. A wide, dusty track curved through it, heading towards the pine tree covered mountains beyond. Deep tyre tracks in the now dried mud indicated years of vehicles using this pathway.

'How can you tell which vehicle is theirs?' I whispered, keeping my voice quiet so no one else could hear us.

'Simple. They are using BFGoodrich All Terrain Tyres. I can tell by the markings in the dirt.' He pointed his stick in the direction of the mountains. 'They definitely went this way.' His voice was so quiet that I had to strain to hear him.

'I'm sorry,' I whispered.

'Sorry for what?'

I sighed. 'I'm sorry to get you involved in all of this.'

'Kalem is family. There is nothing more important than that. You don't have to apologize for getting me involved. In fact, I wish you'd told me in the beginning. I could have helped you.'

'And I'm sorry for thinking that you were crazy when I first met you.' I gave him a sheepish smile.

'That's OK.' He smiled and his moustache wiggled.

'Now I think you're the bestest ever.'

'What is that saying? You shouldn't judge a sheep by its fur?'

'You shouldn't judge a book by its cover.'

'Ah, yes.' He paused for a beat. 'You city people are strange.' He shook his head to himself. 'You have to always think too much and rush too fast and make things too complicated. Really, life is simple.'

'What do you mean?'

'Well, you're born. You breathe. You eat. You sleep. You die. Anything in between is a bonus. Simple.'

'That's the reason we moved here. Kalem wanted the simple life. Back to nature, getting back to basics, he's always loved that kind of stuff. We were supposed to be living the dream of moving to the unspoiled sunny Med and enjoying a new life.'

'And what about you? Do you want that life?'

'All I know now is that I'd give up everything I own as long as I can get Kalem back. Even if it means living in a mud hut without two pennies to rub together.'

'So you see, when it comes down to the important choices, life really is simple, isn't it?

He left me thinking about that as we walked on in silence through the vast fields, up a gentle slope, and to the foot of the mountain range. Sweat dripped between my shoulder blades and off my forehead under the scarf. I wiped it out of my eyes and focused on the mountains above, praying that Kalem was still alive.

The dusty track narrowed considerably here, becoming a bumpy trail of mountain rubble, pine needles, and fallen dead logs.

Kuzu sniffed the ground and looked up at Osman, her black nose twitching. Osman bent down, staring at the path for a while. 'They went this way.' He climbed onward.

We walked for over two hours until we found ourselves in the dense forest. Osman stopped a few times, crouching down to the ground and examining it to be sure we were still going in the right direction. Kuzu had no such reservations as she led us onwards to a sound of contented baaing from the other sheep behind.

Osman and Kuzu stopped abruptly.

'What? What's the matter?'

'The vehicle left the track here.' His eyes darted around, searching for something I couldn't see.

Kuzu smelled something, baaing like crazy, leading us to an area densely packed with fir trees.

'Kuzu is on to something.' Osman followed her.

Through the trees, the ground suddenly dipped down into a bowl shape. There, at the bottom of the dip, covered with branches of fir and pine trees, was a black Mitsubishi pickup truck.

'They have covered this up quickly, but they didn't do a good job.' Osman approached the truck with me close behind. He pulled the branches out of the way and peered in the windows.

Inside was a yellow dinghy, slashed and deflated.

Osman pulled the door open and looked inside. I stood behind him, staring at a small patch of blood on the back seat.

'Oh, no! There's more blood. It must be Kalem's.' I dug my nails into the palms of my hands in frustration. 'Do you think he's...?' No, I still couldn't say the word.

Osman wrapped an arm around me, squeezing me towards him. 'No, there's not enough blood for that.'

I sniffed back the tears threatening to pour out.

'Let Kuzu smell the cap again,' Osman said.

I bent down next to Kuzu and let her go through her sniffing exercise again.

'Come on. Let's carry on.' Osman gave my shoulder a final squeeze. 'We have no time to waste.'

Kuzu led us past the truck and onward, and as we climbed up a particularly steep part of track, something in the distance caught Osman's eye. He stopped, putting a hand up to indicate I should do the same. Back straight, ears straining, he focused on the top of what Kalem had told me was Five Finger Mountain. Five jagged peaks jutted up to the Mediterranean sun, casting shadows on the slopes below.

'What can you see?' I whispered.

He pointed to a small, dark indent in the grey rock and bushes. If you weren't looking for it, you would probably have never noticed it.

I strained my eyes, feeling the tension in my shoulders pulsating at the bottom of my neck.

'It's a cave. I can see something moving. Helen, if we find someone up there, I need to know if they are the same men you know. If you recognize them as the people involved, then cough once to confirm it.'

'Cough once. Got it. How long will it take us to get there?'

'About twenty minutes. With the rough terrain, maybe half an hour.'

Oh, God. Another half hour? Another half hour to find out if Kalem was alive. *Come on, Helen, don't lose it now. He will be there. He'll be OK. He just has to be.*

We approached the cave from the side. Osman's sheep were spread out in front of us now, munching on the undergrowth. Just a couple of shepherds and their sheep. The perfect cover.

Kuzu sniffed around with heightened excitement. Osman

studied the ground, nodding to himself. I was about to crap myself.

We were thirty metres away.

Then twenty.

Then ten.

At eight metres I could clearly see the entrance to the cave. Missing Link and another skinny guy sat cross-legged in the dark outline, looking at us with watchful eyes. Maybe Skinny Guy was the driver of the getaway boat. I couldn't see Ferret Face anywhere.

What did that mean? Had he taken Kalem somewhere else?

I kept my head down, pulling the scarf further over my face and looking at the ground, in case they recognized me. Bringing my fist up to my mouth, I coughed behind it.

Osman waved his walking stick at the men in a greeting as Kuzu ran into the cave, sniffing the ground. Osman whistled for her to come back to him, which she obediently did. He handed her a treat from his pocket and patted her on the head. It must've been a secret signal between them, because as soon as he did that, she realized her job was done and trotted off to join her curly friends.

'Merhaba,' Osman said to them, *Hello* in Turkish.

Missing Link clambered to his feet. Skinny Guy carried on sitting, watchful.

'Hello.' Missing Link gave us an uncertain wave.

The muscles in my shoulders coiled into a thousand knots. My heartbeat thumped so hard I was sure they would be able to hear it.

Osman stopped in front of them. 'Nice day for walking.' He gave them a friendly and unthreatening smile. 'You walk much up here?'

I bowed my head further towards the floor, so they wouldn't be able to get a good look at me. The only problem was that it meant I wasn't able to get a good look in the dark cave beyond them. We were three metres away from them. Was Kalem in there?

'Yes. It's good for hiking.' Missing Link visibly relaxed at the sight of an old shepherd and his wife. 'Nice views up here.'

Osman casually leaned on his walking stick. 'I've been walking these mountains with my sheep since I was a young boy. You can't get a better view than this.' He grinned at them. 'I don't suppose you've seen any goats around here, have you? I've lost some.'

'No. No goats.' Skinny Guy stood, dusting off his jeans.

I inched my face upwards slightly, trying to get a better view in the cave. In the darkness, I could make out another shape, sitting at the back, knees bent, hand outstretched to the side, behind a rock. Could it be Kalem? I narrowed my eyes slightly, trying to get a better focus. No. It was a bald man, clean-shaven. Where was Ferret Face? Hang on, though. There was something familiar about the bald man. A pointy nose and chin, beady eyes – yes, I was sure that it was Ferret Face. He'd just shaved his hair and beard off. But where was Kalem? It seemed like Kuzu had smelled him inside the cave, otherwise why would she have gone sniffing towards it? The only question was – was he alive?

All the moisture drained from my mouth, and my tongue felt swollen so much that I was having trouble swallowing.

Osman tutted with disappointment. 'Damn Goats. You can never tell where they will end up. How about a dog? A black and white one. Have you seen it? He was herding the goats, and he ran off.'

Shards of pain stabbed inside my chest.

They had guns and they weren't afraid to use them. How could we get past them and inside the cave? We couldn't exactly storm the cave, swinging a few sheep around by their tails as a distraction, and hope for the best. We were going to be slaughtered.

Osman looked calm and relaxed. He pushed his weight off the walking stick, so he was holding it at his side, elbows tucked in.

'Haven't seen a dog either,' Missing Link said. 'Maybe it's on the other side of the mountain.'

I heard a quiet moaning noise from somewhere in the cave, and Ferret Face, distracted by the sound, turned his head to the side, looking at something I couldn't see from where I was standing.

And before Ferret Face could turn his head back to us, Osman had the stick in both hands, swinging it through the air with lightning speed, catching Missing Link on the temple with a loud crack. Then he swung the stick through the air towards Skinny Guy's nuts. It all happened so fast, the stick was a blur before

211

my eyes.

Missing Link's eyes rolled back in his head. He collapsed to the ground, unconscious.

Skinny Guy dropped to his knees, moaning in pain and clutching his nuts.

Ferret Face, at the back of the cave, grabbed a gun from behind the rock and tried to lift his hand up and point it at us. But before he had the chance, Osman had reached into the waistband of his trousers, pulled out a knife and had thrown it at Ferret Face.

The knife sliced through the air and into his throat.

His eyes popped open. His gun clattered to the floor. His head slumped backwards against the cave wall. I heard gurgling sounds, like he was struggling for breath.

Osman struck Skinny Guy on the head with the stick.

Skinny Guy collapsed, face first, onto the ground, out for the count.

I heard more moaning from further inside the cave. Kalem! It must be Kalem. I ran towards the back of the cave. There was a smaller, darker cave leading off to the side of it. I could just about make Kalem out in the dim light.

As I was darting past Ferret Face, his arm reached out and grabbed my right leg, gripping it hard. His eyes were wide and manic, louder gurgling sounds coming from where the knife was lodged in his throat.

I tugged my leg away. He gripped it tighter.

'Agh!' I screamed and grabbed Ferret Face's gun from the floor near my left foot. 'Agh!' I slammed the butt of the gun against the top of his head with all the force I could muster.

The gun discharged, sending a shot ricocheting off the cave wall at the side and into the blackness beyond.

'Mmm!' Kalem yelled a muffled sound.

Ferret Face's head slumped onto his chest and then lay still, eyes wide open and lifeless.

I dropped the gun. It clattered to the floor.

I sprinted towards Kalem, who was lying on the floor with his head propped against the back of the smaller cave, hands and ankles tied up with rope, his mouth gagged with a rag.

'You're alive!' I threw myself on top of him, vaguely aware of the tears streaming down my face.

I untied the gag and smothered him in kisses. His eyebrows, his nose, his lips, his forehead.

'You're alive! You're alive!' I drew back, clutching his face in my hands.

'Are you OK?' I stared in horror at the bloody cut over his left eye that had turned a blackish blue shade, a swollen, cut lip, and a big, bloody bump on the top of his head.

'Now I know why I love you.' He smiled up at me. 'Only you could shoot me in the foot.'

'Agh! I shot you in the foot?' I fell off him and fumbled to undo his laces.

I heaved off his boots and examined his feet, expecting blood and gory feet parts.

'Huh? I didn't shoot you. There's no blood.'

Kalem struggled to sit up.

Then I inspected the heel of his right Timberland boot. A bullet hole had gone all the way through it and out the other side, narrowly missing the bottom of his foot.

I cried. And then I laughed. And then I cried with laughter. I think I must've been a bit hysterical at that point, because I suddenly couldn't stop shaking, and an icy chill smothered me. 'Oh, my God! I just killed Ferret Face!' A churning, nauseous feeling erupted in my stomach at the very idea of it. OK, so it was an instinctive thing. He'd been grabbing hold of me at the time, and I'd been trying desperately to get away. It was a flight or fight response. It was also a matter of life or death, so I didn't exactly feel guilty about it. More sort of skin-crawly uncomfortable with myself and in deep shock. It was the shock of everything, to be honest. The shock of all that we'd been through in the last six days. And the worst shock of all had been the possibility of losing Kalem.

Kalem lifted his arms, tied at the wrists, and slid them over my head, holding me tight in his protective embrace and kissing my hair.

'You didn't kill him, Helen.' Osman gave me a kind smile. 'He was dying anyway. No one could've survived that knife wound.'

'Yes, you just did what you had to. It was either him or you. I'm glad it was you,' Kalem whispered into my hair.

I took some deep breaths, willing the shaking to stop, vaguely aware of Osman's voice talking on the radio.

'This will be something to tell the children one day,' Kalem said, trying to lighten the situation.

When my shaking had finally subsided into small tremors, I looked up at Osman, who had the gun trained on the unconscious Missing Link and Skinny Guy with a steady arm. 'Police are on their way. Helen, use this knife to untie Kalem.' He pulled out another knife from his waistband and held it out to me.

'I'd rather you did it, Osman. She's just shot me. There's no telling what she might do to me with a knife.' Kalem grinned at me.

'Thank you, Osman.' I took the knife and attacked the ropes with shaky hands. 'What did Ali say on the radio?'

'He wasn't happy that I took matters into my own hands.' Osman shrugged. 'But I had to seize the opportunity and take them by surprise. Anything could've happened if I hadn't.'

'I love you, Osman.' I beamed back at him.

Osman blushed right down to the tips of his moustache.

'I don't know how to thank you, Osman.' Kalem smiled at him.

'You just marry this crazy woman tomorrow. That will be enough to make me happy.'

Kalem rubbed at his wrists and stood up. He walked over to where Ferret face lay and crouched down at the rock where Ferret Face originally been hiding his hand from our view. Slowly, Kalem reached behind the rock. I stood next to him as he picked up the Queen Cleopatra sculpture, staring at it in wonder. 'Wow! I can't believe I'm actually holding it in my hands.' He moved it around, studying it from different angles. 'It's fantastic.'

The sunlight streaming into the cave seemed to hit the gold sculpture at an angle, illuminating the whole cave and giving it an ethereal glow.

'Amazing, isn't it?' Kalem had an awe-struck grin on his face. 'Do you want to hold it?' he said to me.

Er...no. Not in this lifetime. She was the reason we'd got into this mess in the first place. 'Not a chance!'

Chapter 21

One trip to the emergency room and four stitches later, Kalem's face looked bruised and puffy, but a lot better than it had in the cave. Not ideal for the wedding piccies, really, but considering the freakishly surreal experience we'd been through, it was the least of my worries. Tonight was a family celebration. We were alive. I had Kalem back. We'd saved the statue. And hopefully Ibrahim Kaya would still be alive to tell the tale. I felt pretty damn good.

As the fiery Mediterranean sun set over the sea, and the Champagne flowed, we all drank a toast on the terrace of Deniz and Yasmin's house.

'Wow! What a week.' Deniz clinked glasses with us all. 'No whisky for five days. It has to be a record.' A wicked gleam twinkled in his eye.

Yasmin rolled her eyes at him. 'You idiotic little man. Helen and Kalem could've been killed, and you're talking about whisky! Be serious for a change.' She slapped him on the back of his head.

Deniz grabbed Kalem in a bear hug. 'I'm proud of you, Son.' Then he grabbed me. 'You too. I couldn't wish for a better daughter-in-law. Even if you are a clumsy nightmare.'

Yasmin slapped him again.

Bless him, he meant well, even if it didn't always come out quite right.

'OK, OK.' Deniz held up his hands in mock surrender. 'Why didn't you tell us what was going on? We could've helped.'

'You were ill, and we didn't want to give you a heart attack,' I said.

'Plenty of life left in this old man yet.' He winked at Yasmin. 'Eh?'

Yasmin blushed.

'What about me?' Charlie raised his hand in the air, waving it around. 'I could've been killed too.'

'Come here. I'll give you a hug too, you big girl's blouse.' Deniz gave Charlie a bear hug, crushing him.

'Ooh.' Charlie broke free. 'So, tell us all. What happened after the police got the bad guys?'

'Well, the police superintendant finally admitted to being involved,' Kalem said. 'Jacob Podsheister caved in during an interview, giving them details of how he masterminded the whole thing. Apparently, he blamed Ibrahim Kaya for his business downfall and wanted him dead. He thought with Kaya out of the way, he'd be able to take over Kaya's hotels and get back his old lifestyle.'

'Well, that's fantastic news then,' Atila chimed in.

'Ferret Face was apparently wanted in about five different countries in connection with other crimes,' Kalem went on.

'And Missing Link is wanted from the London Zoo where he escaped from the gorilla enclosure,' I said.

Charlie's eyebrows shot up. 'Really?'

I chuckled. 'No.'

'And what about the other man with them?' Atila asked. 'That skinny one.'

'He was the one driving the getaway boat,' Kalem said. 'When I saw Missing Link stealing the statue, I didn't think about anything. I just ran after him. He grabbed it, ran to the port jetty behind the stage, and jumped onto their waiting speedboat that Ferret Face had moored there before the opening night. I ran down the jetty after him and managed to jump in as the boat was leaving. We had a bit of a tussle, and next thing I knew I was out for the count. I assume he hit me over the head a few times with the barrel of his gun.' He felt the back of his head, rubbing at the bump.

'Ooh, you're so brave,' Charlie said. 'Then what?'

'I must've been unconscious for a while, because when I woke up, my hands and arms had been tied up, and they were hauling me into a dingy that Ferret Face had brought to the beach on the roof of a truck. They sank the speedboat off shore so it would look like they'd fled the country on it. When we landed on the beach in the dinghy, I was semi-conscious, and they dragged me into their waiting truck. I guess my mobile phone must've fallen out of my pocket then.'

'You're so lucky to be alive. They could've just killed you there and then,' Ayshe said.

'Yes, but they wanted the money from Ferret Face's suitcase,' Kalem said. 'They were keeping me alive until they'd got it back. Ferret Face recognized me from the airport and knew we had their suitcase. They wanted me to go and get it with them after it had got dark tonight. I didn't tell them, of course, that I didn't have it anymore. I just went along with it to buy some time. Plus, if they'd just killed me on the beach, everyone would know they'd landed there and were holed up somewhere in the area.'

'How is Ibrahim Kaya?' Yasmin sipped her champagne.

'Apparently he's OK and should be out of the hospital tomorrow.' Kalem smiled. 'Luckily, the bullet didn't do too much damage because he was already falling over when the Ferret Face shot him. If he hadn't, he would've been shot in the heart instead. He'll be in pain for a while, but he's very much alive. The statue is in one piece and has been returned to his private vault. And it's all thanks to my future wife.' Kalem raised his glass to me.

'And you.' I reached up and kissed him.

'What about your wedding dress?' Ayshe said. 'Has Ali found it yet?'

I grinned. 'Yes. It was still in my suitcase that Ferret Face abandoned in his room at the Plaza. They need to keep the suitcase for a few days for forensic evidence, but Ali's agreed to let me have the wedding dress. He should be bringing it here soon, actually.'

'So no more curses and bad luck.' Ayshe smiled. 'You'll have the lucky charm on your wedding dress, and you can have the perfect wedding day you planned.'

I rolled my eyes. 'God, I hope so.'

'But what I don't understand is why Ali helped us. Why did he get involved in all of this?' Charlie asked. 'I thought he didn't like you, Deniz.'

A secretive look passed between Yasmin, Deniz, and Osman.

Deniz's face suddenly took on a serious expression. 'Because Kalem is really his son.'

'What?' Atila, Charlie, Ayshe, and I shrieked in unison.

Kalem was taking a sip of Champagne at the time and splurted it out, looking horrified.

Yasmin slapped Deniz again.

'No, only joking.' Deniz chuckled.

Kalem let out a breath of relief.

'*I'll* explain, shall I?' Yasmin shook her head at him. 'Deniz and Ali did their national service together in the army here when they were young. We all grew up together in Kyrenia, so we were all close friends. But Ali was in love with me,' she blushed and fanned her face. 'He wanted to marry me, but I only had eyes for your father.' She glanced at Deniz, her eyes shining at him in the moonlight. 'God only knows why,' she chuckled. 'Anyway, when Ali found out that Deniz and I were getting married, he was extremely jealous and didn't want anything to do with Deniz anymore. He wouldn't even talk to Deniz. Shortly after that, Deniz and I left Cyprus to move to the UK.'

'Ooh, what happened then?' Charlie asked.

'Well, Ali got married rather quickly after we left,' Yasmin said.

'It was a rebound thing,' Deniz said.

'He moved to the UK with his new wife, and then later they had Erol. But the marriage didn't work out.' Yasmin gave a solemn smile.

'Yes, I remember at school that Erol said his dad lived in North Cyprus, and that he always went out there for holidays to stay with him,' I said.

Yasmin nodded. 'Ali split up with his wife and returned here to start a career in the police service, but Erol and his mother stayed in the UK.'

'And we never saw Ali again until yesterday, when we went to him for help,' Deniz said.

'Yes, but why did Ali help us, then?' I asked. 'I mean, it seems like he hated you both, because that hatred has rubbed off on Erol as well. Erol hated Kalem – he couldn't stand him at school, and he had it in for us here. I'm convinced he would've thrown me in jail, and he got the university to pull the plug on Kalem's job.'

'He's a nasty piece of work, that Erol,' Osman said. 'Greed got the better of him. He'd rather see you in jail and keep the half a million pounds for himself. That was his plan.'

'Ooh, come on, tell us the rest of the story. Why did Erol's dad help us then if he hated Deniz?' Charlie topped up all our glasses as he spoke.

'Ali didn't hate Deniz, not really,' Yasmin said. 'He was just upset and jealous that I'd fallen in love with Deniz instead of

218

him. I suppose he was hurting. And Deniz actually saved his life when they were in the army together, so he owed him a huge favour. And whatever else Ali is, he is very honourable.'

Osman nodded.

'I think that Erol probably blamed me for the break-up of his parents' marriage somehow.' Yasmin took a sip of champagne. 'If Ali was still in love with me, it could've been the reason why their marriage didn't work out. Erol was only a little boy when Ali returned to North Cyprus; he was probably looking for someone to blame, so it was easier to blame me. Then, of course, the blame transferred onto Kalem at school. I think that's why Erol had some kind of grudge against Kalem.'

'Families!' Atila shook his head.

'And you, Osman!' I put an arm around him. 'You are a dark horse.'

Osman blushed.

'I can't believe what a good shot you are! The way you threw that knife straight into Ferret Face's neck.' I shook my head at him in amazement.

Osman pursed his lips, looking disappointed with himself. 'I know. I must be getting old and out of practice. I was aiming for his heart.'

'I didn't know you were in the army,' Kalem said to Osman. 'I remember when we used to come here on holidays when I was little, you were always working away. From the stories that Dad told about you, I just thought you were a shepherd.' He shook his head. 'How wrong I was.'

'Osman was in the Special Operations Commando Unit of the Turkish Army for a long time.' Deniz gave Osman a bear hug. 'Doing all that secret-squirrel-undercover-super-army-soldier stuff, eh?' He grinned at Osman.

'When I retired from the army, I wanted the simple life, so I decided to become shepherd.' Osman shrugged, as if it was the most natural thing in the world.

'We need some whisky to celebrate.' Deniz stumbled inside to the kitchen and poured glasses of whisky all round. He brought them out on a tray, swaying slightly. 'Here.'

'I think you've had enough,' Yasmin said to him. 'It's the big day tomorrow. I want you in a fit state for it. I take it all the wedding plans are now finalized?' she asked Charlie.

219

'Don't worry about a thing. Helen will get the perfect wedding after all. Trust me, I'm a wedding planner. Actually, I might take this up as a new business venture.'

'Yes! You could be the wedding planner, and I'll be the wedding photographer. Fab idea! Then you won't have to go back to the UK either.' I hugged him.

Charlie tilted his head, pondering this. 'Ooh, I *like* that idea.'

'So, you and Atila are going to live here as well?' Yasmin asked Ayshe. 'It's amazing, isn't it? You're ill for a few days, confined to bed, and look how much happens!'

Ayshe glanced up at Atila, who had a wistful look on his face.

'Yes. You absolutely have to do it,' I agreed. 'I'll miss you too much if you go back.'

'Atila has signed the contract for the venue. He's going to open a restaurant here as soon as the renovations are done.' Ayshe flung her arms around me. 'So you'll never get rid of me now!'

'Are you going to serve those chocolate orgasm thingies? They are divine!' Charlie said.

'Maybe we'll have to move out here too if all the family is going to be here.' Yasmin looked questioningly at Deniz.

'And what about you, Helen? You've definitely decided you want to live here now?' Charlie asked.

I glanced down at my shoes, aware that everyone was looking at me, waiting to hear what I'd say. I thought about the lists I'd made when I first got here, going through them one by one in my head. I didn't have to worry about Kalem's extended family being crazy anymore. They weren't crazy, just different to me. They were kind and sweet and slightly quirky – but then I was Miss Quirkarama – and they cared about the most important thing in life. They cared about family. And Osman had saved Kalem's life, so it was my turn to owe him. Maybe I could return the favour one day.

We weren't involved in any more major crimes. At least I seriously hoped we weren't. Ali had assured me that the custard cream and Smoky smuggling would be overlooked now. The statue had been returned to its rightful owner, so I didn't think Queen Cleopatra would be cursing me anymore, unless she held a grudge because I called her ugly. I was sure that Ali would deal with Erol, so we didn't have to worry about him interfering in our lives now. In fact, Erol was the one facing the prospect of a life behind bars this time, not me. Kalem would find a new job here. I was also sure of that. And Ayshe would be living here as well, so I wouldn't be missing her and Atila like crazy.

The only downside was the lack of shops – I was a bit of a shopaholic, after all – but after everything that had happened, I didn't even care about that anymore. I could live without materialistic things like convenient supermarkets and custard creams. They were bad for you anyway (the custard creams not the supermarkets). I thought about what Osman had said about life really being simple. The only important thing was that Kalem and I were together – oh, and we were alive, which was also pretty important. If this whole experience had taught me anything, it was that I really would give up everything and live in a mud hut if it meant we were together. So, bollocks to the shops (sorry shops! One day I will return to you).

I thought about all the good things being here had to offer. The sunshine and how energized it made you feel. The beaches where turtles lay their eggs and start a new life on the shores on North Cyprus. If they could do it, so could I. I thought about the history and how the castle had inspired the Disney Castle. I loved the picturesque countryside and open spaces with shoats roaming around willy-nilly, and the relaxed way of life with no rat race. No more rush, rush, rush. It was a mix of old and new here – the modern hotels and the traditional Cypriot way of life, the ancient buildings, rustic villages, and the up and coming tourist spots, which, when I thought about it, really made a refreshing change. It would take a long time for North Cyprus to catch up with the rest of the world in terms of convenience, but was that really such a bad thing? And more importantly, I thought about the simple life that Kalem had always wanted, where our kids could grow up in a safe environment, where we could get back to basics and nature. A place where we could grow and change and appreciate a more natural environment at a slower pace. Now the reasons to stay far outweighed the reasons not to. I'd be mad to go back to the UK.

I looked up at them all, then fixed my eyes on Kalem. 'We're staying.' I beamed.

Kalem launched his arms around me and spun me round.

'So now all that's cleared up, do you want to know what I've been doing with the condoms?' Deniz slurred and raised an eyebrow à la James Bond.

'I do.' Charlie giggled.

'I don't think that's necessary, Dad.' Ayshe pulled a face.

Kalem tried to ignore him, suddenly finding the ground absolutely fascinating.

Deniz swaggered back inside and retrieved an open hold-all bag. He deposited it on the patio and unzipped it. 'Look in here.'

Ayshe clamped her eyes shut, but curiosity got the better of the rest of us, and we peered inside. It was full to the brim of miniature spirits from the hotel mini-bar.

Deniz looked pretty pleased with himself.

'What's that got to do with condoms? Have I missed something?' Charlie seemed a bit disappointed.

'He's been winding the poor maid up.' Yasmin shook her head. 'He wanted her to think he was a super-stud, or something, so he kept taking out all the condoms from the mini-bar and hiding them in his bag. Every day the poor girl had to fill up the bar with more condoms.'

'She wanted me.' Deniz grinned. 'I know when a woman wants me.'

'Tonight he's taken all the spirits out of the mini-bar and shoved all fifty-six packets of condoms back in.' She gave Deniz an exasperated shake of her head. The poor maid will think she's going mad like you.'

'I love these miniatures. You can drink them anywhere!' Deniz chuckled.

'Thank God for that.' A hand flew to my chest. 'I thought you were going to kill each other with the amount of condoms you were using. Death by condom.' I leaned closer to Deniz. 'And I thought you were getting Alzheimer's.'

'Ha! He got that years ago, the crazy little man.' Yasmin ruffled his hair affectionately.

'So, no more talk of pec implants?' I asked.

Deniz rubbed his chest. 'No, I'm perfect as I am. I'm definitely going to buy a subscription to *Cosmopolitan*, though. Wouldn't want to miss out on a thing after reading that! Did you know that when a woman–'

Someone knocked at the door, thankfully interrupting him.

Deniz stumbled through the house to answer it.

'Look at him! Don't anyone give him any more whisky.' Yasmin rolled her eyes to the sky, tutting at him as he swung the door open in a dramatic fashion and nearly fell backwards.

'Ah, Ali, we were just talking about you.' Deniz pulled him inside and led the way to the terrace.

Ali nodded courteously to everyone and presented me with my wedding dress in a garment bag. 'I think this is yours. I took the liberty of having it cleaned and pressed for you. I hope everything is OK with it.'

I squealed with delight, taking it and pressing it to me. Woo hoo! I'd finally got it back. I felt along the stitching to make sure the lucky charm was still in place. Yes, it was still there. Hurrah. No more bad luck. Nothing could possibly spoil my perfect wedding now.

'Super-freaking fabulous!' Charlie clasped his hands. 'That's the final detail on my wedding list checked off.'

I hugged Ali. 'Thanks so much.'

He looked embarrassed and patted me on the back. 'No, it is me who should thank you.' He took a little bow. 'Now, if you'll excuse me, I'll leave you to your celebrations. As you can imagine, I have much work to be getting on with.'

Chapter 22

Kalem and I slept at his parents' house that night, safely intertwined in each other's arms. Maybe it was traditionally bad luck for the groom to see the bride on the day of the wedding, but I figured that nothing else could possibly go wrong. And I didn't want to let him go for a second after all that had happened.

Ginger cat was ready and waiting outside the patio door when I got up. And she wasn't alone.

'Oh!' I squeaked, staring at six kittens in varying shades of ginger and white. Shit, Kalem was going to freak!

'What's the matter?' He slid his arms around my waist from behind, resting his head on my shoulder to see what had caught my eye. 'What did I tell you? Now we'll be feeding seven cats.'

'But they're so cute! And it must've been a good sign, Ginger turning up like that yesterday, because we managed to save Ibrahim.' I slid open the door and cooed at the kittens. They jumped in fright as I knelt down on the ground, but then quickly succumbed to a stroke on the head. 'Maybe Ginger really is a lucky, magic cat.'

Ginger purred in reply.

'So now we've got seven cats to feed.' Kalem shook his head at me.

'You were the one who wanted to get back to nature,' I pointed out with a grin, traipsing into the kitchen with twenty-eight paws pattering on the tiles behind me. 'And speaking of cats, did you phone Smoky's owner?'

'Yes, with all that was happening, I forgot to tell you. I've been trying to get hold of him but there's been no answer. I left a couple of messages on his answer phone.'

I knelt down and played with the kittens. 'Well, I thought it would be a little while at least before we had another mouth to feed, but it looks like we've now got a readymade family of seven.'

At ten o'clock, Charlie picked Kalem up to get ready at the hotel with the boys and dropped off Ayshe and Yasmin.

Yasmin brought a feast of food with her – enough for ten people. Warm freshly baked bread stuffed with black olives and cheese; green olives with lemon and garlic; hummus, jam, boiled eggs – courtesy of Osman's mum – cold meats, hellim cheese made from Osman's sheep's milk, and pastries with various fillings. We filled our plates and sat on the terrace, chattering away with excitement about the day ahead.

I couldn't believe, after all that had happened, that it was finally my wedding day. I know I didn't exactly have the kind of build up to the wedding that I'd planned all those months ago. But it was finally here. My perfect wedding was really going to happen after all the recent doubts.

'OK, I need a shower, and then you can both help me get ready.' I pushed my plate away, stuffed.

'Oh, I'm so excited.' Yasmin cleared away the plates. 'Why don't you let me read your Turkish coffee cup?'

'NO!' Ayshe and I yelled together.

'No more coffee cups. Ever.' I hugged her and dashed up the corridor before she could suggest it again. I'd had enough of Turkish coffee cup readings to last me a lifetime.

I stepped in the bathroom with a tube of hair removal cream and liberally applied it to my legs and armpits. Guaranteed to remove all hairs in five minutes whilst moisturizing your skin, apparently. Mmm, smelled nice and flowery. OK, five minutes to wait until I was suitably defuzzed, so I leaned over the bath, grabbed the shower attachment, and lathered up my hair with shampoo. Three minutes later, my hair was caked in moisturizer, and I climbed in the bath, pulled across the shower screen, and turned on the water to blast everything off.

Nothing happened.

'Huh?' I tried the tap again as the conditioner dripped down my forehead.

Nothing. No water. 'What's going on? It was working a minute ago.'

I tried again. Tap on. Nothing. Tap off. Wait. Tap on. Nothing.

'No!'

'There's been a power cut,' Yasmin yelled from the bottom of the corridor. 'The water pump doesn't work when there's a power cut.'

'How long will it be off for?' I wiped away some of the

225

conditioner that had now wormed its way into my eyes and was stinging like hell.

'I don't know. It could be hours.'

'But I need to wash this stuff off now!'

'You'll have to jump in the swimming pool.' Yasmin's voice echoed out to me. 'That's the only way to get it off in a hurry. It might not come back on for ages.'

I tried the tap again, frantically turning it on and off until it fell off in my hand.

Shit!

So there I was, lathered and creamed to within an inch of my life – so to speak – with a tap in my hand, and it looked like I had no choice but to jump in the pool and rinse it all off.

'Great.' I screwed the tap back on through half open, slitty eyes and, not wanting to mess up any towels, I stomped naked down the corridor like someone who'd been to a foam party for three days straight.

By the time I'd got through the patio doors, my eyes felt they were on fire, and I had to keep them clamped shut. I took slow steps in the direction of where the pool was and stepped carefully in. Dunking myself underwater, I scrubbed at my hair and body to get the bloody stuff off. And when I finally resurfaced, I could open my eyes again.

'Aggggggggggggggh!' I screamed, clapping eyes on the Julio Iglesias customs guy at the other end of the garden, staring at me with his mouth wide open.

'Aggggggggggggggh!' he screamed back.

I covered up my bits and bobs under the water. How embarrassing! And what was he doing here, anyway? Not only had he seen me naked, but he was probably about to arrest me for offences under the Custard Cream Act. Oh, no. Please, no.

Yasmin and Ayshe rushed outside with a towel. Julio turned his back to me, so I could get out of the pool.

'Who are you?' Yasmin demanded.

I wrapped the towel tightly around me and took another from Ayshe to wrap up my dripping hair.

'I'm from the customs office.' He waved his hands in the air in surrender mode.

'Are you here to arrest me?' I cried at his back.

'No. I'm making a delivery!'

226

'A delivery?' What the hell was he talking about? Was he just lulling me into a false sense of security, so he could cart me off on my wedding day?

'What sort of delivery?' Ayshe asked suspiciously.

'The cat. He's in a cage in the car.'

'What cat?' Yasmin looked at me, confused.

'Er...we accidentally had our neighbour's cat, Smoky, in our container.'

Yasmin's hands flew to her face. 'Oh! Animal smuggling is a serious offence,' she whispered in my ear.

OK, OK, as if I don't know that already. Don't remind him!

'My wife says he's OK to come home now. So I'm bringing him back to you, that's all. We managed to speak to his owner, and he doesn't want Smoky to be put in quarantine if he's sent back to England. He wants you to keep him here.' He cautiously turned around, checking the coast was clear of nudey bits.

Oh, crap! This seemed to be turning into *The Good Life* after all. Still, poor little Smoky. He'd been through a horrible ordeal. It was the least I could do to pamper him with some tinned salmon and a cosy home. Now we had a ready made family of eight.

Oh, my God! I thought I was going to faint. When Ayshe, Yasmin, and I arrived at Bellapais Abbey in our ribboned horse drawn carriage, I couldn't believe how amazing it looked.

The gardens in front of the abbey were decked out in white silk covered chairs for the ceremony, complete with bows and flowers on the back. The theme had continued in the restaurant beyond, styled in matching architecture, where our celebration meal would take place. Charlie was true to his word. No pink in sight.

Kalem, hovering at the front of the row of chairs, turned and caught my eye. He looked fabulicious in a black suit and white shirt with a cream and yellow frangipani flower tucked into the button hole. *Ooh, just wait until later, Kalem, I'll show you what to do with the tutti fruiti body paint.*

He winked. I grinned.

Deniz sat behind Kalem, sipping from a mini-bar bottle of Jack Daniels. He spied Yasmin and quickly screwed it up and stuffed it in his suit pocket. Sitting next to him was Osman.

Kuzu, with a silver lead and a silver bow on her collar, had her own chair in between him and Osman's mum, who was wearing her own wedding dress, which had actually scrubbed up quite well. Still, it looked better on her than it would on me. Charlie animatedly showed the registrar how to put the tape in the tape deck and press the *play* button, ready for *Love Me Tender* to croon out as I walked up the aisle.

Ayshe, Yasmin, and I hovered at the entrance to the gardens, waiting for Charlie to appear and issue wedding plannerish instructions.

'Yoo hoo!' He waved a hand and hurried over to us. He planted a kiss on both cheeks, then stood back to examine me. 'Super-freaking stunning!'

Charlie hadn't followed the no-pink rule himself. Pink skin-tight trousers, satin pink shirt that I could only describe as *shocking*, pink scarf draped around his neck, and pink leather shoes – I dreaded to think where he got those from. Still, at least his hair wasn't pink as well, like it was at Ayshe's wedding.

'Have you got the rings?' I asked.

He patted his shocking pocket. 'Check. Any other questions?'

'Nope.'

'Right.' He clasped his hands together. 'The registrar is ready and waiting. The tape of *Love Me Tender* by Elvis is all set to go. I've turned it up a bit because I think the sound may get lost in the acoustics of all these arches and corridors in the abbey. When you hear it, just walk through the archway to us and up the aisle. It's all up to you now. Let your perfect wedding begin. You ready?'

Hell, yeah! 'Oh, yes. I'm so ready.'

Charlie beckoned Deniz forward to come up and take my arm, as he was giving me away.

'You look wonderful!' Deniz smiled at me. 'Exactly like a French Fancy!'

If anyone else had said that, I would've been insulted. But Deniz thought that was a compliment, so I just gave him a kiss on the cheek and smiled back.

Yasmin took her seat at the front next to Osman. Ayshe squeezed my hand and took up position as my maid of honour behind me. Charlie scuttled off and stood next to Kalem for best man duties.

228

Charlie nodded at me for approval.

I nodded back.

Deniz linked my arm.

'And cue music.' Charlie pointed to the registrar who hit the play button on the tape deck.

Like a bat out of hell I'll be gone when the morning comes. When the night is over like a bat of hell I'll be gone, gone, gone.

Yasmin fell off her chair at the sound of Meatloaf rocking out full blast from the speakers – ouch! Osman's mum jumped half a foot in the air. Osman shielded Kuzu's ears. Charlie flustered around, trying to find the *off* button. The registrar looked at everyone, bewildered, wondering if this was supposed to happen. And Kalem turned around to me with an amused smile.

Ayshe and I threw our heads back and roared with laughter. I'd come this far – a tiny mix-up with the wedding music wasn't going to spoil anything now.

'Sorry! Don't panic, slight technical hitch.' Charlie pulled out the tape, turned it around so it was playing the other side, and slotted it back in. 'OK, this is the right track.'

Love me tender, love me do...

This was it. This was finally it.

I glided under the scented arches on Deniz's arm with my best friend behind me and my nan smiling down at me. My green eyes were glued to Kalem's brown ones.

Deniz positioned me next to Kalem and crushed me in a hug. Then he plonked himself down beside to Yasmin.

'It gives me great pleasure to be here today to join Kalem and Helen in marriage,' the registrar began. 'Love is one of the most important things in life, and we shouldn't ever forget that.' He glanced briefly at Charlie, who nodded to him. 'I've been told that Helen and Kalem nearly didn't make it to this day. They are lucky to be here, and it is thanks to their bravery and determination that they are. I want to wish them a long and happy life together. Now, Kalem, you have some vows to read?'

Kalem nodded and turned to face me. He took my hands in his, the heat from his fingertips permeating my whole being. He gazed deep into my eyes. 'Helen, you are the only one who makes me whole. Because of you, I laugh, I smile, and I dare to dream again. You are breathtaking like a magical sunset. You are amazing like the night stars. You are spectacular like life itself. I vow to be true and faithful for as long as we both live,' he paused for a beat. 'Helen, I choose you. I need you. I love you.'

I gripped his hands tighter to stop my knees buckling at the weight of his words radiating love.

'Now, Helen, if you will read your vows.' The registrar turned to me.

Ayshe handed me the vows I'd rewritten late last night after thinking about our whole experience since we'd arrived here.

I took the piece of paper in one hand and held Kalem's hand with the other, gazing into his eyes. Slowly, I read…

'Kalem, you are my sunlight, my water, and my air. Wherever you go, I will always be with you. Whatever possessions in the world I have, nothing can compare to your love. You are what makes my life perfect and whole. You are, quite simply, my life. I promise to treasure you, love you, and be faithful to you as long as we both live.'

Kalem squeezed my hand, blinking his damp eyes.

'And now, Kalem, Helen, it gives me great pleasure to pronounce you man and wife.' The registrar smiled at us. 'You may kiss the bride.'

Kalem slid his arms around my waist and pressed his lips to mine.

Much later, after the confetti had settled, I stared up at the stars as Kalem twirled me around to the sound of our first dance. The fragrant air mixed with the wine and excitement had made me lightheaded. The music stopped abruptly, but we were so lost in our own world that it took a moment to register.

Kalem stopped twirling me, and I came to a heady standstill.

I looked in the direction that everyone was now staring in.

A posse walked towards us, their expressions unreadable in the dark night. Ali, Ibrahim Kaya, two policemen, the President, and the red-eyed bodyguard walked towards us.

Yasmin's glass froze mid-air.

Deniz downed his whisky in one glug.

Ayshe and Atila stared at them with worried looks.

Charlie gulped.

What now?

Deniz rose from his chair. 'Hang on a minute? What's going

on here? This is a wedding celebration.'

They stopped in front of Kalem and me. The red-eyed bodyguard gave us a squinty glare.

The President was first to speak. 'Firstly, I want to congratulate you on your wedding. I extend you a warm welcome to North Cyprus. I'd like to thank you from the bottom of my heart for all you have done to save my good friend, Ibrahim Kaya. And I also want to applaud your efforts for trying to bring the heinous crime to our attention in the first place.' He shook our hands.

My mouth hung open in shock.

'I don't know how I can ever repay you for saving my life, but I'd like to give you a small appreciation of gratitude.' A pale Ibrahim Kaya, wearing a shoulder sling, smiled and handed us a hotel room key. 'This is a key to the penthouse suite of the Plaza. I would like you to be my guest at the hotel for a two-week honeymoon, all-inclusive. And if there is ever anything else that I can do, please don't hesitate to ask.' He shook our hands using his good arm.

'I have some excellent news for you.' The President looked at Kalem. 'I've had a discussion with the Principal at the Cyprus University of Architecture and Ancient Art, and there seems to have been a misunderstanding concerning the cancellation of your new post there. The Principal will be delighted and honoured to welcome you to their team as previously arranged.'

Kalem's lips curled into a huge grin. 'Wow! Thanks very much.' He shook the President's hand with enthusiasm, pumping it hard.

I glanced up at Kalem and smiled proudly. His dream job was going to be a reality again. *Woo-hoo!*

The President whispered something to one of the policemen. He nodded and scurried off.

'I also have a wedding gift for you,' the President said, smiling.

The policemen returned, carrying two suitcases. He set them down in front of us.

The President nodded to the cases. 'Helen, I'm returning your missing suitcases. I hope everything is intact.'

Two suitcases? What was he talking about? I recognized my suitcase, but the other one? I'd never seen it before in my life.

231

I groaned inside. Not another mix-up. I didn't want anyone else's bloody suitcase. In fact, I doubted if I ever wanted to see a suitcase again for the rest of my life. I think I'd developed some sort of suitcase phobia now as well.

'But I only had one suitcase,' I said, puzzled.

The President paused for a beat, then he smiled at us. 'Now you have two. Enjoy your happy life together in North Cyprus.' He winked at us so quickly I couldn't be sure if I'd actually imagined it or not, and they all departed, leaving us standing there open-mouthed.

Kalem and I stared at the rogue suitcase, not knowing what to say.

'Whose case is that?' Charlie bounded over.

'Open it,' Ayshe said.

'I'm not opening it. Look what happened last time,' I said.

'Well, someone's got to open it,' Yasmin said.

I sighed. 'OK, I'll open it, but don't say I didn't warn you.' I carefully unzipped it and flipped open the lid. 'Oh. My. God.' I closed the lid and zipped it up pretty damn quick.

'Is that what I think it is?' Ayshe said as everyone stared on in surprise.

I nodded, momentarily lost for words, which didn't usually happen.

'It's full of dollars!' Kalem stared at the case, mouth gaping, eyes huge. 'I'm getting a sense of déjà vu here, Helen.' He couldn't take his eyes off the case.

I recovered my voice enough to speak. 'It must be the money that was in Ferret Face's suitcase when we handed it in to Erol. It looks like exactly the same amount that was in there.' An excited giggle slipped out.

'How much whisky could you buy with that?' Deniz said.

I grabbed Kalem's hand and gazed up at him with a huge grin locked firmly in place. 'I think I'm going to enjoy the simple life after all.'

The End

Made in the USA
Lexington, KY
20 January 2013